COLLECTABLES

Somebody rang a bell, and all the buzzing in the room stopped. They turned to the "front." A barefoot woman with thick glasses and long gray-streaked hair came out and stood before the crowd. "Welcome to Bliss Academy!"

They all said, "Hoo-hah!"

"This is a place where one can feel at home, at peace, and truly feel your connection to the universe!"

"Hoo-hah!"

"For you are a child of the universe. The universe is there for you to play in. The universe loves you. And tonight play in it we shall!"

"Hoo-hah!"

"I would now like to bring out the Academy's supervisor, Dr. Embert Tranquility! Dr. Tranquility ..." Applause.

A little bald, wizened man came shuffling out in slippers with a colostomy bag strapped to his side.

Thank you, Eleonore," he said ... "When I first formed Bliss Academy," he continued, "the goal was to find a place where spiritual pursuits would take precedence, and that we could commune with each other, with nature, with people from outer space, and with the universe itself in total peace and harmony."

"Hoo-hah!"

-Excerpt from Bliss Academy, pages 73-82

COLLECTABLES

A Collection of Tales

By

RON HARRYSSON SUNHAUKE (SCHAEFER)

iUniverse, Inc.
Bloomington

SOLAR WIND PRESS
Milwaukee

Collectables
A Collection of Tales

iUniverse books may be ordered through booksellers or by contacting:

iUniverse
1663 Liberty Drive
Bloomington, IN 47403
www.iuniverse.com
1-800-Authors (1-800-288-4677)

ISBN: 978-1-4620-5035-2 (sc)
ISBN: 978-1-4620-5037-6 (hc)
ISBN: 978-1-4620-5036-9 (ebk)

Printed in the United States of America

iUniverse rev. date: 10/04/2011

SOLAR WIND PRESS
Milwaukee

TABLE OF CONTENTS

Dedicated to:

My family who keeps putting up with this.

FOREWORD

It has been decades since I wrote my first book of short stories (STUDIO SKETCHES), and I was pretty convinced I would never do another. After all, short stories don't pay, and collections of short stories, by a single author or a group of authors, really, really don't pay. I got tired of working for nothing and moved onto bigger formats: my main field being as a script-writer, either in writing screenplays or stage plays, with a hand or two at novellas, novels, poetry, even songs. But I found I couldn't make money at any of that, so I had to develop my own company (SOLAR WIND MULTIMEDIA) which included a press that printed my stuff.

Among the things we did when we started up is to develop our own magazine (online, of course) that has taken various incarnations over the years. The most recent (THIRD COAST ARTISTS) included a section of fiction, and as new writers kept promising new material for the publication but failed to submit or make the cut, I found myself filling in where they were stumbling or bailing out.

After awhile it became something of a habit to write a new short story for another issue, sometimes even writing one without regard to publishing it in my own magazine. And while I was working on those larger, grander visions for screen or stage or print, I found that when I got started in the morning, I would jot down a few notes that would turn into a short story before the "real" writing began. Before I knew it I had acquired a couple of dozen stories and had enough material to fill a book with such 'throw-aways'. The results are what you see here. They may have been tune-ups, mental exercises of a sort, but they made their own book.

Coincidentally, I was writing a separate book (BORN OF SACRED FIRE) that also happened to contain a lot of short stories (after I started it with a novella that I could not publish anywhere). That book idea was inspired by a contest I created for the magazine, and somewhere along the way I thought I'd try my hand at the contest rules myself without submitting anything. While those stories were all based around a common theme (and therefore, in my mind, not 'really' a storybook anthology) this one was not. This is just a collection of tales as they came to me, more or less assembled in chronological order (let's not get too fussy on what that term means). And they are quite a variety. As "Kill Or Be Killed" is as serious as any of these stories get, a number of them are more often tongue-in-cheek. On top of which, "Killer Kunts," and the "Sex With . . ." stories belong to that category of ideas that are just "too dumb not to do."

I stopped at number 40. I had to make a cut-off point somewhere. I may say outwardly that I'm never going to do another book of stories again (I certainly have no plans for it); yet, I wouldn't be surprised if I start the next day's writing with a few notes that blossom into yet another tale. And then I'd have to find some place to put that bunch—possibly in still another collection of shorts to be published down the road. C'est la vie.

MARVIN'S ZIT

First of all, Marvin was a tall, gangly, ugly kid who whined a lot, and who nobody liked. So that was one strike against him. Second, and the other very important factor, is that he had a lot of acne—which made him just slightly more repulsive. Then one day he showed up in class with a large zit on his cheek that was vying for attention from the rest of his pizza-encrusted face. It was gross and disgusting. And we loved it. Why? It was something that terrible adolescents such as ourselves could mock.

Sure we made fun of it—we were horrible brats; but hey, what else is there to do when you're growing up in a small town? It was Bobby Pojee and me who made the most of the situation. We especially used to ridicule Marvin a lot. This just gave us extra ammunition. But that's really not the story here. The story is what happened to the zit. That sucker grew and grew until you could swear it was some kind of tumor. Something from outer space that was planted on Marvin's face.

"Hey, Marvin! You growing a second nose? . . . You gonna build it into a birdhouse? . . . What's that thing on your face, an airport landing light?" Those were just some of the witticisms teenage boys come up with when they're dealing with a geek with a bad face problem. Perhaps we weren't original, but, after all, it was an extremely noticeable ailment. And we started to take bets on just exactly when it would pop.

But it didn't pop. It just kept getting bigger and bigger. And Marvin's face swelled up with it. Not only was he embarrassed by the humiliating protuberance on his face, but he was also in a certain amount of physical pain. No doubt such an extension on his face had to leave him feeling sore and tender in that area; and right around that headlight was a great deal of scarlet flesh illuminating red and purple veins.

Days went by, still he came to school with it. It surprised us that he even came to school at all. The weekend came and went. The next week returned with it still there. His mother finally took him into the doctor. The doctor said there wasn't much he could do. He was afraid that lancing it would give Marvin a worse scar than if it popped by itself.

And so Marvin continued to suffer while we had a good time at his expense.

Bobby Pojee (and me following his lead) even went out and drew all sorts of pictures of Marvin and his enormous zit, placing them everywhere we could find. The week after—it snowed, and we all went out and made snowmen with big zits on their faces.

Then the truly unusual began to happen. The head of the zit began to buckle and form odd shapes, then turn purple—and people thought they could see different pictures in it.

"Hey, Marvin's got two faces: his regular ugly one, and the better looking one he's growing out of it!" That was Bobby Pojee, of course; and more of Bobby Pojee's idea of humor. I didn't think that one up. I didn't think I was clever enough. And I laughed and laughed and laughed.

By now Marvin's face was so hideous that he stopped coming to school. So we went to his house and played jokes on him. We put up scarecrows on his lawn with big zits on their faces. His mother didn't appreciate that, and neither did Marvin.

The very next day Marvin took ill and this time he was home for a really good reason. Whether it was because we were making fun of him, or because the zit made him ill, he stayed home in bed. And that day, both of our mothers scolded us (both me and Bobby Pojee) for having picked on him. Yeah, Marvin was ugly; yeah, he was a goon; but after all, he was actually sort of—I don't know—all right. And it probably was wrong of us to pick on him, especially for something he couldn't help. So then we started feeling guilty. And, if it was any consolation, we actually hoped he would get better. Then, when he came back to school, we could pick on him all over again for something else.

So, say one of us kids should decide to go over to Marvin's house? Would that do? It eventually ended up to be both me and Bobby Pojee (partly by force). We showed up with some gum and some baseball cards as a peace offering. We knew Marvin was a real nut on baseball cards.

Marvin's mother let us into the house, looking at us somewhat skeptically. After all, we did put scarecrows on her front lawn. Marvin looked at us kind of funny too. That softened after we showed him the baseball cards. His mother was busy putting all these stained bedsheets into a big basket and taking them down to the laundry. Marvin, himself, had a big bandage over his face.

"Guess what, fellas?" Marvin said, "The zit! It finally popped!" Bobby and me looked at each other and wrinkled our noses. Marvin said, "You wanna see?!" Marvin did not suffer all of the social graces he should have, and peeled off his bandage.

"*EEEYYYEEEUUUWWW!!!!!*" we said. That baby was pumping out gallons of slime like you've never seen before. It was something that I certainly never will forget.

His mother ran in and scolded him, "Don't take that off, Marvin! You know what the doctor said!" And she sponged a couple of pounds of gooey melted lard off his face. And STINK??!! Me and Bobby Pojee ran off. And that was the last time we visited Marvin.

We saw Marvin back at school a few days later after his zit had started to heal and he was feeling much better. He not only felt more confident because the zit was gone, but now he actually had something to talk about with the other kids. And talk about it he did. Endlessly. He made everybody sick, forcing them to run to the lavatories to barf their breakfasts. But then, that was Marvin.

Looking back on it, I think he deserved all the mean tricks we played on him. Even at high school graduation, he was still telling kids about it. For all I know, he's been telling people about his zit ever since.

There was one additional incident: Prom. Marvin showed up (dateless—who'd have guessed?) at Prom with another big whopper on his face. It even had a face on it. Turns out it was stage makeup. Marvin wanted to reclaim his fame by having everyone gawk at it in horror. Then he could tell his famous zit story all over again. We grabbed a hold of him and dumped him in the high school swimming pool. It made the evening for us.

But as the saying goes: that was then, this is now. Marvin's the head of some electronics corporation and has a lot of stock in pharmaceutical companies that supply acne medicine. The zit's scar pretty much disappeared—so he was free to improvise on its importance. And, though never handsome, he at least stopped being so ugly.

Me? I work in a garage these days, and bum around on fixed up old jalopies. I'm not married like Marvin is. And I don't have kids or a home like Marvin has.

As for Bobby Pojee? He's in prison somewhere—I forget for what reason. We lost contact with him a long time ago.

It's funny how things work out.

EGBERT'S CHEESE

Mr. Egbert was an old man in our neighborhood who used to make his own cheese. We all knew about him because the smell carried throughout the entire county.

"Nothin' beats cheese like the real thing!" he used to say, as if that was some profound statement uttered by the Dalai Lama. People called the police and complained, but the police answered there was nothing illegal and nothing they could do about a man who makes cheese in his own basement. Kids used to come over to his house for free samples and to watch him mix his goo through the basement windows.

Mrs. Egbert died some years back and we always thought that was the reason why he converted to cheese. After all, we thought, when you don't have a wife anymore, what else is there to do but make cheese? And he did it with real abandon. All kinds. All sizes all shapes. He even made cheese sculpture. I don't know how he did it all, but then I avoided his basement. I avoided the entire block on which he lived. My mother used to avoid it too. She always made sure she found a different way to drive home whenever Egbert was out and about cooking up his evil brew. Winter was easier to take because the smell didn't permeate the air. He kept it bottled up inside his house, which made it uncommonly potent if you were to stop by his house and step inside or sniff a steaming vent.

"Lord knows how he can stand it!" my mother used to say.

I delivered newspapers and ended up with a route that went right past Egbert's cheese house. Throwing the paper in the door was no problem during the rest of the week. It was that painful time once every Friday when I was forced to come by and collect the fee that bothered me. Then he would open up that door as answer to my knock and out would spew that noxious odor.

"Here you are, sonny-boy, and keep the change!" he would always say to me. Even his money stank. And I would come home with a smelly pocketful of change—all because of Egbert. He would also give me some of his cheese from time to time and once I even tried it. It was so richly fermented that I broke into diarrhea on the spot, and had to run home without finishing my paper route in order to change my pants.

My mother just screamed and hollered, "When is the world going to get rid of that awful man!" Her wish came true a week later. Mother felt extremely guilty about it and even went to church—which was unusual for her because neither she nor anyone else in my family (all the way down the line as far back as my relatives go) were church going people.

But anyway . . . the following week Egbert died. He had been dead for days, but nobody knew. He didn't get that many visitors (obviously), but next door, Mrs. Wilkins hadn't seen him around—it was spring, you know, and time for Egbert to be out and about cleaning out his cheese utensils.

No Egbert.

All right, so what's going on? Mrs. Wilkins was brave enough to try to enter the door when no knock seemed loud enough. She found him in his basement hanging over one of his vats—face in the stew. Doctors said it may have been a heart-attack . . . at least that may have started it. There was no doubt in anyone's mind Egbert had been cheesed to death.

"A shocking, horrible way to die!" my mother stated, penitently. Actually, I thought that might have been the way Egbert preferred to die. Maybe it was suicide.

But that's neither here nor there.

They had to auction off all his cheese equipment. They sold it off dirt cheap—mostly to people from other counties. The cheese itself was sent to connoisseurs in Boston who seemed to prize it quite highly. We were just happy to rid ourselves of the infamous cheese house.

It took awhile to sell the place. All the wallpaper had curled and when it was pulled off it smelled like cheese. The wood smelled cheesy too. They had an estate sale too for all the other non-cheese items. People shied away from it. All the furniture—well you can guess what was holding the sale back. Anytime you opened up a drawer—*phew!*

Then one day before the sale was over, some guy in a suit and briefcase showed up and asked around to find out if Egbert had left any recipes. It turns out a chain of restaurants on Long Island in New York got a whiff (to use a phrase) of that awful stuff of Egbert's, and without him being around anymore, wanted to buy and sell the recipe outright. But it would seem Egbert's secrets died with him as his formula was apparently all in his head.

That poor old man is probably making cheese up in Heaven someplace. I'm not going to be too happy to get there if I have to confront Mr. Egbert again. I wonder if they have paper routes up there. Maybe I can get myself another job.

KILL OR BE KILLED

Moving in through the brush. Parting it like so much hair in a giant wig. Bugs buzz and sting left and right. I wait. I have no fear because I don't know what to be afraid of. Everything around here is ominous. Everything around here is deadly. There is so much death in the air. So much life. It confuses the two. Hard to keep track of what is to be feared, what is to be embraced.

I go on, creepy-quietly, looking for any sign of an advance. Any sign of the enemy. I am desperate to do right. Not that it would please me, or anyone, but that it would preserve me. I snakey-snake through the jungle brush. My rifle clutched tightly in my hands. My helmet is like a frying pan cooking my scalp. I am drenched wet. It is a combination of last minute's rain and sweat.

Birds make squawky noises over my shoulder and fly up. Enough to startle me—but I am not. I've been here too many times before. I can smell the earth, smell the mold, smell my skin, smell my breath. I am waiting. Waiting for the chance. The chance to die. The chance to spare myself that instant—that sudden death.

I step forward. Step forward again. Crack. Nothing but a twig. But its sound thunders in my ears. Surely I must have awakened everything in the jungle with just that one step.

I crouch, I wait, not to give myself away. I see spiders run from me. I see beetles ignoring me. I see mosquitoes looking for blood—and I swat. I try to ignore them all I can. You never know who's going to kill you while you're swatting a mosquito. But sometimes they bite so hard it's like they have teeth.

I wait, I watch, I listen. I step forward, step forward again. Perhaps I will discover a great tiger in these branches. And that would make me do what? Run? Shoot? Play dead? Is the tiger to be feared or to be ignored while watching for the more dangerous human?

I am unconcerned. I am only awaiting my own death—in whatever form it takes.

It is beginning to darken. Shadows growing thicker on the jungle floor. It will now be twice as hard to see what's coming to kill you. It will guarantee instant death. While it remains daylight out in the meadow, dusk gathers under the foliage. I wait, I watch, I listen. It is only the hum of mosquitoes that betrays anything.

Crack. Another broken branch. This time not made by me. Is it a warning? I step forward, step forward again.

I see only eyes—peering beneath great green leaves. Something whistles passed my head, and I hear the report of a gun. I aim quickly and fire in the direction from which it came. There is a disturbance in the foliage. It is the enemy. Alien. Different from me. Subhuman. Something to be killed. That too is what he thinks of me.

He is too close. We both fire again. And both miss. Too much jungle in the way. He springs forth just like the tiger I pictured. I spring forth in response. It is all too quick to reload, to think, to aim, to fire. We both scream a warrior's charge. Bayonets clash. The eyes of two different races meet. Hatred and zeal cover each one.

Gunstocks connect, shoving begins. Tripping over tangled lines. A blade's edge gouges my cheek. A gun-butt finds a jaw and crushes it. The enemy spits blood, stumbles backward, falls on his back. I lunge forward, he, stumbling on his feet. Point the gun downward. Thrust the bayonet into his torso. Jab the blade up into his ribcage. Tearing flesh and uniform as I go.

I grit my teeth, scream in anger, "Die! Die! Die!" The alien face changes from war-glory to shock and then panic. I watch redness spill out all over him and onto the jungle floor. Blood drains from his face. He displays a sickly pallor. He grips my gun in a desperate attempt to remove it. I force it through as much as I can until the blade comes through the other side and impales itself into the earth. The gun barrel clogs with blood, and I know I will need to clean it out before I can ever use it again.

The alien face weakens quickly. Shows resignation. Withers. Dies. I stand with the sweat of exertion dripping off my face. My own blood bubbles up from my cheek and decorates any clean space on the enemy's uniform. He is nothing but a corpse now. A dried and withered leaf, nailed to the ground by the giant spike of my gun. I collapse on the gun-butt.

I try to pull the weapon free but it is buried too deep—like trying to remove a fence-post with your hands. I'm exhausted. All the energy has drained from me. I crumple to my knees and let the gun stand as memorial to my fallen foe. I fall next to him, roll on my back, and stare up at the sky through the canopy, where I catch glimpses of it in little patches.

Bugs crawl over me. More buzz over me. The world darkens and a gentle wash of rain clears away the crusty red sediment on my face and mixes it with mud. There's no way to keep yourself clean in the jungle. Already my dead companion begins to stink. It has only been minutes—or has it been hours?

I stare at my partner: he is a rumpled mound, a heap of flesh on earth destined to merge with the surface like a dissolving block of salt. I am alive for now—this time I have won. I await the final judgment of my next encounter. And the next after that (if God wills). But for now I will spend the night with him and pretend the only universe is this space, this time. And I hope the rest of creation can get along without me.

RADEMACHER'S HILL

Rademacher was an old man that everybody liked. He lived on top of a hill on a nice big old gingerbread house. Every day the Postman would come by and say, "How ya doin', Bill?"

And Rademacher would answer, "Fine. And you?" And the old man would be busy puttering around in his garden, fixing things on the house, and keeping himself occupied with all manner of domestic chores. That was one thing about Rademacher, he was always busy.

Many people, by the time they hit 75 become very inactive, if they reach that age at all. But not this guy. Every Sunday he went to church, helped out at various functions, and generally helped everywhere he could. He helped the neighbors, he shoveled sidewalks until he was finally too old to do that; and by that time some of that favor was returned. The neighborhood youngsters came to clear his pathway when the hard winters hit. He thanked the boys, gave them candy and hot chocolate, and a dollar or two when he could. Rademacher was not a rich man, but he was a happy one. Or so it seemed to the neighbors.

And despite his offerings of help, he lived a rather solitary life. His wife had died some twenty years before and no one of the present generation could remember of him ever being with anyone. He knew all the names of the kids in the neighborhood, knew all their parents' names. Rumor had it he was a schoolteacher once but nobody could ever get him to talk about the old days, and so nobody knew for sure what his occupation had been. He was simply regarded as the nice old man on top of the hill.

You'd think there would have been a sign somewhere, some sort of clue—an indication of what was to come; but there was nothing. He was so active, so generous; so helpful to the people next door, down the block, or to anybody who came by. There was that smile on his face—always—even in the dreariest weather. There was his ability to make jokes on any subject, any situation. A kind, gentle humor that was never biting or deprecating to anyone in any way. You'd think there were some indications somewhere in all that but there weren't. Maybe it was just old age. Maybe it was being alone for twenty years. Maybe he just gave up.

It was that day—that warm, bright, sunny summer day. Mrs. Wilkenson stopped by and gave him flowers. Mrs. Wilkenson often gave him flowers.

"And how are you, Mr. Rademacher?" she would say.

And he would respond, "Why, thank you, Mrs. Wilkenson; I'm just wonderful!" He always was, you know. "Oh, what lovely flowers!" he would say, "I love flowers!" And, of course, he did. "Flowers from a rare flower herself!"

Mrs. Wilkenson would answer, "Oh, Mr. Rademacher! How you talk!"

"No, I'm serious!" he would reply. "Mrs. Wilkenson, you have that rare beauty that only someone of divine character could exhibit."

Mrs. Wilkenson would blush and answer, "Why Mr. Rademacher, you're making me tingle! If I weren't mistaken, I'd swear you were making a pass at me!"

Mr. Rademacher would return that by saying, "If I were younger, I *would* be making a pass at you."

And Mrs. Wilkenson would giggle like a schoolgirl, and after a brief conversation of weather and mutual interests, would excuse herself and head on back home. But not before Mr. Rademacher would exchange the politeness by giving her a clipping from his garden. And both would add a flourish to their kitchen tables by displaying their mutually traded botanical wonders for this particular day. Then Mr. Rademacher would return to his beloved garden, which was, of course, the loveliest in the neighborhood; but perhaps not before a quick snack or maybe a cup of tea. Rademacher was fond of tea, no coffee drinker he.

Within about a half-hour later the Postman would wander by with his usual, "How ya doin', Bill?" Then Rademacher would offer up his characteristic response and continue with his garden work. The Postman never seemed to leave any letters. He would just stop by to talk to Rademacher. Lots of people did. It was interesting to note that for all the friendliness that Rademacher seemed to exhibit no one sent him any mail—not even something marked, "Dear Occupant." He subscribed to no publications and never got the sales junk everybody else did. But the Postman would stop by because it was the halfway mark of his route, and he could rest a bit while chewing the fat with good ol' Bill Rademacher. It helped make the Postman's day, and apparently Rademacher's as well. But anytime he ever talked to anybody the old guy gave that impression.

So the Postman would be on his way and Rademacher would fuss with his garden. The kids would wave to him and he'd help out whenever a ball got lost or a bicycle got a flat tire or whatever might occur among the usual mishaps of children. And then he'd tell the kids goofy stories that they didn't believe but liked to hear, and whatever suffering was caused along the way was forgotten.

As the afternoon wore on, Mrs. Grigsby, on the other side of the hill's cul-de-sac, would come up the rise bringing some brownies, cookies, or whatever she had created in her oven. Mrs. Grigsby was always baking something, and she was always giving Rademacher the first fruits of her endeavors. Mr. Rademacher accepted them graciously . . . then the two of them might sit on the porch for a few minutes sharing the bakery—Rademacher offering up his home made tea to help wash down the crumbs—and they'd talk about current events (something Rademacher seemed very knowledgeable of) even though he never seemed to watch television or read a newspaper.

It was sometime after the second cookie that Rademacher broke the news to her. "Don't bother to come around tomorrow, Ellen," Rademacher told her; it was in the same cheery voice he always used with her. It was because they had both been widowed for many years that they seemed to have a mutual understanding that was not always expressed in words. Still, even Mrs. Grigsby couldn't understand what the meaning was behind those words.

"Oh? And why not?" she answered.

Rademacher told her, "I won't be around tomorrow."

And that was all he said. That was the only hint, the only clue he left behind.

"Oh?" said Mrs. Grigsby, "Don't tell me Bill Rademacher, after all these years . . . I've known you as such a homebody. You actually have some place to go?"

"Not really," he told her, "I just have some business to take care of."

"Why, Bill!" Mrs. Grigsby said jovially, "This is shocking behavior on your part! I'll just have to get along a whole day without you, won't I!"

"I'm afraid you will, Ellen," said Mr. Rademacher. "But don't worry, I'll be around. I'll always be around."

"Well then," said Mrs. Grigsby, "I'll have to bake you an extra special pie for the day you return."

Mr. Rademacher answered with, "You do that, Ellen. That would be wonderful."

There wasn't much more to it than that. They chatted for a little while longer, parted company as the best of friends; and then Mrs. Grigsby took her plate of unfinished cookies back home with her to display to her family.

Mr. Rademacher did not continue to work on his garden after that; he just sat on the swing on his porch for the rest of the afternoon. The neighborhood kids came by, waved to him on their way home to supper; and one by one the lights began to pop on within the houses as the sky slowly turned orange to rose to a somber navy blue.

Rademacher finally left his swing and went to the farthest end of his yard—his beautiful garden—and rested his arms on the rails of his fence. He looked about at his lovely work then at the neighborhood—the peace and calm that always permeated the place. He waved to an occasional passer-by: somebody who no doubt knew him very well. And as the street began to settle itself in for the evening, a certain sadness came over Rademacher's eyes. The kind of sadness one gets when saying goodbye.

Maybe it was old age. Maybe it was loneliness for having been alone for so long. Maybe it was just that day—that warm, sunny summer day. Maybe it was too perfect. Maybe we will never know. Rademacher took one last look at the street he lived on and loved, at the garden he tended for so long, and walked up his hill one last time. He entered the house, turned off the lights, and killed himself.

**There is a footnote to this story. The children claim there is a friendly ghost that watches over them in the neighborhood. Long after the Rademacher house was sold, the garden still flourishes, almost unattended. And Mrs. Grigsby left a pie on the grave of Mr. Rademacher, in his memory. The pie found its way back to her house—with one bite taken out of it.

DANCER SUNRISE

Sunlight come out bright and pink,
Dancer take the time to think.
Sky all blue, much darker hue.
Dancer sing a song to you.
"Come bright Moon and bright starshine
move about the light divine."
Dancer move on stretch in rhythm,
find a place in Dancer's Heaven.
Roll upon the grass—delight.
Run atop the hill's great height.
Dancer mimic bird in sky.
Dancer let light limbs to fly.
Dancer play in world below.
Dancer swim the sea to flow.
Dancer swirl to greatest heights.
Dancer keep the world from fights.
Dancer quiver, Dancer bend,
Dancer breathes the things it mends.
Dancer shiver, Dancer shake.
Dancer give the world a break.
Dancer dance the world alone.

Dancer bring the meaning home.
Dancer fill us with delight.
Dancer keep us from our plight.
Dancer slower, Dancer fast,
Dancer purge the shadow cast.
Dancer flicker, Dancer fling,
Dancer twirl through everything.
Dancer help us, Dancer stay;
Dancer, keeper of the day.
Dancer jocund, Dancer love;
Dancer from the universe above.
Dancer Dancer, break our woe,
never let us feel too low.
Fling your fire gentle light;
keep us till the world is bright.

Dancer, Dancer, come again
Show us how the world you mend.
Up above us ever true
Hear this song we sing for you.

PURVIS PEEVIS'S PRECIOUS TINKLE

It was a clear and fulsome day (is there such a word as fulsome?—never mind, it sounds quite wholesome), a day perhaps in May when everything is bright and cheery. And the flowers were abloom, and the birds were a-singing, and the butterflies a-winging, and—oh, you get the picture. In the backyard by the shop of Mister Brindle Brighton Cleary, who was always rather dreary but awfully gifted in his shed with whatever was in his head when it came to gadgets and gimmicks and clocks. Mister Cleary set himself to tinker with his tools among the jewels he felt he built from bits of junk and sheer detritus found within the dump.

Now next door was young Purvis Peevis who was rather egregious when it came to mischief making as his curiosity was so overwhelming it killed the cat. It actually killed the cat. There it was—the cat. And there he was—Purvis Peevis. Young Peevis was busy snooping in places he shouldn't be, and there was the cat in places it shouldn't be. And there they came upon each other. And the cat went: "Yeeoowww!" And young Peevis went: "Yaaaawww!" And with that the cat ran out into the road and got himself run over by a truck. Young Peevis made out much better, having only skinned his knee. Now you could say it was as much the cat's fault as it was for Purvis; after all, the cat was in a place it shouldn't have been either. But a cat is a cat, and that is that. And Purvis is a human and should've known better—even for a lad of ten. Be that as it may, the dear boy was always getting into things, and there was nothing he liked better than to spy on Brindle Brighton Cleary and the magnificent mixes of junk the man made into magnificent messes of after-junk (is there such a word as after-junk?—well, never mind that now).

So it was on this day (perhaps in May, when things were bright and clear and . . . well . . . fulsome) that Purvis Peevis got it into his devious nature to pay a call on Mister Cleary and see what was cooking in the workshed. And there was Mister Cleary amidst the clatter and clutter of the outgrowth of his ingenious (some would say demented) mind and shop. Sparks arose as Mister Cleary, bending over a spinning grinding wheel that was busy wheeling a—whatever—the old man happened to hold in his hand. His face was hidden behind a visor that made him look even more ominous—like the real life Doctor Frankenstein the kids always accused him of being. Well, actually, he looked more like the good Doctor Frankenstein's monster with that thing on his head—but you get the idea.

Purvis crept through the piles and piles of gidgets and gadgets, widgets and wadgets, discards and bit-yards that filled the area around the shop under the tin awning that kept the entire shadowed area hot—thus defeating its purpose. As Purvis peeked through the dusty dirty, cracked and grainy window that allowed some light into the place, he was immediately struck by Mister Cleary's intensity at his grindstone. Okay, actually Purvis was immediately struck by all the spiders and spider webs around the window—and then he was struck by Mister Cleary's intensity.

And there was Mister Cleary, grinding and polishing, polishing and grinding. Exactly what, Purvis Peevis couldn't see. Finally, Mister Cleary held whatever it was up to the light. He switched off his grindstone which ran down with a wrrrrr . . . rrrrr . . . . rrrrr . . . as if it were somehow lopsided. Mister Cleary kept his masked intensity on his whatever, peering and peering, examining and examining. Then he lifted his . . . what actually was a welding mask . . . up and it made him look even stranger, as the visor pivoted on the head-band and gave him the appearance of having two heads—the metal one on top being upside down. Still he peered and peered and peered at his object. And then he said, "Rah!" and with a disgusted snort threw the whatever out of the door of the shop.

Purvis Peevis, standing outside the shop next to the spider-covered window by the door, watched and heard the whatever go blink, blink, blink, as it bounced onto the stones of the old cracked patio floor. Purvis was nervous at the thought of finding out more; after all, Mister Cleary wasn't in the best of moods. And he was right, for moments later, Mister Cleary, the two-headed Frankenstein of rage, bellowed, "Ggrraaah!" as he threw out a whole box of dits and dats that landed on the stones. Mister Cleary also yelled about a son-of-somebody, but Purvis was still too young to figure what that meant.

Then two-headed Frankenstein headed out of the shop himself. Purvis ducked behind the stacks of stuff surrounding the shop, but made a little bumping noise against something or other. It should be noted that some something-or-others are noisier than others. This one was fair to middling. Not as loud as trash can covers, not as quiet as carpeting. It should also be noted that Purvis picked up a few spiders in his maneuver; but not to worry, they were friendly spiders. It, the noise, was loud enough, however, for Mister Cleary to stop and turn his two Frankenstein heads in Purvis's direction. And this was good enough to cause Purvis to take a gulp and hold his breath. Mister Cleary was still in his intense phase. But said noise was not loud enough for Mister Cleary to want to investigate, so Mister Cleary left and took both of his ugly monster heads into his house where he lived alone with his cat—up until the cat died from a truck accident.

Now Purvis was alone (excepting the spiders) and decided it was time to let his curiosity go to work. He crept towards the doorway of the shop, shedding spiders on the way, and surveyed the mess of discards recently heaved through the shop's doorway by Mister Cleary. He puzzled and puzzled over what lay before him. It was nothing but bits and pieces of other things. In a word: junk. He tried to find the whatever that Mister Cleary had been polishing but couldn't identify it from everything else. But what he did find was a tiny bell on a little chain. It was unattached to anything else, and where it could have come from he hadn't a clue. But there it was. Little and precious. *Tinkle, tinkle*, it went—almost like it was waking up, almost like it was speaking to him.

But it was dirty and grungy. Purvis felt it didn't deserve to be treated in such a fashion and it didn't seem to want to be there anyway. The boy felt the need to take it home and do some polishing of his own. But . . . should he go in to Mister Cleary and ask about it, or should he just take it? Mister Cleary seemed awfully grumpy at the moment (of course, he was always sort of grumpy). And then there was that cat thing that might be brought up. Would he mind at all if Purvis just simply took it? Let's not call it stealing, let's just call it . . . claiming discards. Isn't that what Mister Cleary did with all this stuff anyway? *Tinkle tinkle.* The bell was talking to him in the wind. Yup. He would have to take it home with him. Mister Cleary clearly doesn't want it anyway.

And so Purvis Peevis took it home, and cleaned it up, and polished it up, and warmed it up. *Tinkle tinkle!* The bell was so happy! And then came the magic moment, the spooky thing that happened! Is this a story about spooky things that happen, you ask? Why, yes indeed! Else why tell a story such as this?

Now Purvis was a strange boy. You have probably figured that out already. He had the capacity for wishing. He believed in magic. It's not unusual for boys to wish for things. Sometimes boys wish for bikes—and they get them! Sometimes boys wish for snowstorms to close schools—and that happens! Sometimes boys wish their teachers would get sick in order to get a pretty substitute—and it happens! I never said all wishes were good things. Actually, usually when the teacher gets sick, an old fat and ugly substitute with white hair and warts on her face take her place. But usually the old ugly substitute can't catch you when you're shooting spitballs at the back of Susan's head—so it's still a good thing. (Incidentally, every class has Susan in it. And don't you just hate her?) And sometimes boys wish for home runs—and get them! And sometimes boys wish their penises would get real big, and suddenly they do! It's all magic. Spooky magic. But it's all real. It's magic you can believe in.

So why not believe in magic that can do even greater things? That's the kind of boy Purvis was. He believed in magic that can do greater things. He would often wish for things that most people would scoff at—like taking a plane and flying over the world. Or he might wish that the cat was alive again—actually, that one didn't work out so well; but it never stopped him from wishing.

So once his shiny new bell was all cleaned and polished, he put it in his hands, and then put his hands together, and wished and wished it would bring him good luck. And he wished and wished it would do magic. And he wished and wished the bell would do something about Susan. And he wished and wished that all sorts of good things would happen from now on. He even wished and wished Brindle Brighton Cleary would stop looking like a two-headed Frankenstein. He wished all kinds of good things. And then with his last wish, he rang his little bell. *Tinkle tinkle tinkle!* it went. It had such a charming little sound to it—like a little fairy's bell. Who knows? Maybe that's where Mister Cleary got it from. Maybe Mister Cleary found a fairy junkyard and picked it up from there. Then, when he couldn't get it to work properly, he threw it out. You never knew what Mister Cleary might find or do.

Tinkle tinkle tinkle! Tinkle tinkle tinkle! He kept on ringing it. It had such a clear, piercing, and happy sound. He was so happy with it he went downstairs to show Mom. Mom was in the kitchen, because that's where Mom always is.

"Look, Mom!" he said careening into a chair. *Tinkle tinkle tinkle! Tinkle tinkle tinkle!* "Look what I found!"

"My goodness! What have you there?" said Mom. Mom was fascinated by the sound. "It's like a little angel's bell," she said. *Tinkle tinkle tinkle!* Purvis continued to ring it. "Such a pleasant little tinkle," Mom said, "such a happy little sound. Wherever did you find such a thing?"

"Oh. Around," answered Purvis.

"Why don't you show Missus Gaddison Gilbert Gadby the wonderful thing you found?"

"Why would she want to know?" said Purvis peeved.

"Don't you want to make her happy?" encouraged Mom, "she often frowns. I get the feeling that she'll find this appealing, and maybe then she won't come by to bring us down. Meanwhile, I'll bake some cookies: double fudge with chocolate icing, and let you be the first to lick the batter bowl all around."

And suddenly Purvis knew what was his mission—he knew what was his wish. He knew that he had wished a wish and it was starting to come true. He would go about the town with his magic bell spreading happiness around. Isn't that what bells are for? Magic bells, that is. Miniature merry fairy bells, with magic, if you please.

So just within a twinkle Purvis took his little tinkle, and the promise of a cookie and a batter bowl to lick, and out the door he went, towards his goal he now presents, to let his mighty merry magic bell all such unhappiness prevent.

And he went to Missus Gaddison Gilbert Gadby, a fussy old, stuffy old, musty old cuss who lived down the street with her roses and her beets, and was always taking treats away from children in the street when they snatched them from her crabapple, periwinkle, persimmon sweets that she grew in her garden in the Gadby-gated way. Missus Gadby had her nose to the ground and her, *ahem*, in the air, as she examined and examined the little aphids clinging there.

"Missus Gaddison Gilbert Gadby?" shouted Purvis Peevis from the fence.

"Dear me! Whatever could it be? What is this shouting all about? How dare someone approach me while I'm with my garden sprouts!" And she raised her what's-behind-her, fixing specs upon her snout. She had a look to find the crook that seized her from her work. There was Purvis Peevis as usual acting like a jerk.

Tinkle tinkle tinkle! went the little bell in Purvis's hand. *Tinkle tinkle tinkle!* and against it no hard heart could stand. "Good heavens!" Missus Gadby cried, "what is that delightful sound?!" *Tinkle tinkle tinkle!* "I do believe that's quite a lovely little bell. And it seems to me you play it unusually well. May I chance perchance to see it? A little closer if you please, aren't you the boy, that Peevis lad, who always scrapes his knees?"

A hop across the fence was Purvis's own style; but sensing she would frown again, he took the gate the while. And Missus Gadby had a talk, and lemonade to offer. Before he left, Purvis saw for himself the frown within her brow decay away and in its place at the corners of her face were kindly grandmotherly wrinkles, one for every tinkle, and a flushing complexion beneath years of callused expression. Magic, pure magic. It had to be. Why wouldn't anyone believe?

"That is a precious little tinkle!" she said joyously to the boy. "You must immediately take this bell to Missus Finkle," Missus Gadby claimed, "and let it do for her what it did for me."

So off he went to Missus Finkle, a lonely widow without a wrinkle, to give to her a little tinkle from the magic of his bell. She sat somberly amongst the dishes of her kitchen, often unwashed because their filth reminded her of her own condition. *Tinkle tinkle tinkle!* went Purvis Peevis without much ado.

"What a precious tinkle!" said ecstatic Missus Finkle, "what a thoroughly charming bell! It's made me happy as hell—or rather, I should say as pleased as pandemonium—to be in its spell. Thank you for coming, my dear dear boy. And thank Missus Gaddison Gilbert Gadby for thinking of linking us up. By all means, go to Mister Winkle, that poor, poor deserted man who has spent his days in a bewildered haze since ever that war began. The dear soldier lost his brother—that and at home again his mother, and another he was all but married to in the end. He is in such a need of comfort, by all means be off and run quick. Bring your precious little tinkle to him and all who need a lift!"

Without a clue or inkle, Purvis went to Mister Winkle where he tinkled for the maudlin man out sitting on his porch. "By Jove!" said Mister Winkle, "There is magic in your tinkle! I feel as though the war I fought had never been begun. Go off to Missus Beavis," said the man to our young Peevis, "let her hear the joy you carry in your hand this time around!"

So off to Missus Beavis, bell in hand, did Purvis Peevis, tinkle for her did he roundly soundly ringing his jingling song. Missus Beavis looked at Peevis and momentarily cooed in pleasure at the tingling ringling noise. "Purvis Peevis," said old Beavis from her rocking chair and shawl, "for these many years I'm shedding tears at all the memories gone. You see, when you reach my age, you reach a stage where memories escape you. They give it names but all the same it means you're losing your long held faculties. With your amazing tinkle, even with its slightest sprinkle, you remove the sullen stinkle that simply clutter up my mind. You bring the world of joy to me, the thoughts that can employ for me the memories of the life I've spent as clear as day today. You've no idea what this means. It's magic, or so it really seems. I bless you, son, for making this a most enjoyable stay. Do, by all means, visit Mister Treacle, whose accident in his vehicle, has made him a most inconsolable mess."

So thence to Mister Treacle, went our lad upon his be-cycle, and offered up a voluntary tinkle at his best. "Lord Almighty!" said yon Treacle, "Why I've scarce heard such a sequel to an angel's choir—as such I heard when crashing through a wall! And how absurd—you may have heard my accident was foul—to wait for such a lad as this to offer simple bliss to clear my mind with such extraordinary sounds! I must confess," the man protests, "my innards haven't been the same. Since lo these days, in so many ways," a blush came over Treacle, "I haven't been able to enable a fecal. My intestines are blocked, my digestion has stopped, and oh how I feel miserable. But you with your bell which you tinkle so well, have invigorated my system. Your tinkle has worked its way inside," said Mister Treacle with pride, "and I now feel compelled to reside in the privy to take care of some business that's long overdo."

Purvis Peevis did not wish to see this and excused himself out of the door, but not before a wish from Mister Treacle. "There's magic healing in your tinkle!" said the man on his way to the mail for a long, thoughtful read, "Go and heal some more! You've a gift, young man, a gift! Make use of it what you will. But all of the town and all of the county will be at your feet to fulfill their list of needs. Take heed, for your bell now begets responsibility!" And with that he closed the door on his treatment. And Purvis rode off on his way.

Word spread among the townsfolk and it wasn't long before the stroke of politics entered into the actual fray, as Mayor Brinkle heard about the tinkle and had the youngster brought before him as he traveled through the day. Mayor Brinkle was tickled pinkle as the tinkle came from Purvis Peevis' precious bell.

"Young Peevis," said the Mayor, "why I'm absolutely speechless" as he cleared his throat announcing that a speech was on its way. "Your bell is really quite astounding, as its spell is so unbounding. All of us around you are now so resolutely well. You have shown us quite a measure and should be declared a civic treasure, as the tinkle of your bell has brought us joy to fill a well."

Wow! Amazing! The truth of it's engaging! The magic really worked in it. So wishes can come true! And everywhere young Peevis went his magic bell would leave all spent in serenity and joy. And even Purvis Peevis had the benefits of his fine gift as double fudge cookies chocolately iced were on the menu every night for a week at a time. People soon regarded Purvis not as that troublesome boy whose curiosity once killed the cat, but as the boy with the precious tinkle that made the town the happiest place on earth.

As the days went by, there was little to sigh about, as everywhere Purvis went, happiness was sent. Missus Beavis passed peacefully, and all the town was there. Missus Gaddison Gilbert Gadby sang, "O Blessed Art Thou" and no one complained. She even shared her persimmons with the local children. Missus Finkle married Mister Winkle, and the Finkle—Winkle wedding was the talk of the town. Mom baked cookies for everybody.

Even Brindle Brighton Cleary gave up his two Frankenstein monster heads as people finally found out what he was building all those years—his own helicopter. And off he went into the wild blue yonder, sending back postcards to Purvis, of his travels (he never did find out it was Purvis who pilfered the bell from him—and Purvis never told). Mister Cleary had a lifelong ambition to see Canada from the air and took his helicopter there (nobody knew why he wanted to see Canada from the air; but then, the alternative is seeing it from the ground, and who does that? It's Canada, for Pete's sake). Actually, not, because he crashed soon after he began and that was the end of him (he didn't die from the crash, but was attacked by furious prairie dogs when his chopper plowed into their town). But this is too cheery of a story to end on so gloomy a note.

And as to Purvis Peevis, what a story he'll bequeath us as he goes along through life giving refuge with his bell. He opened up a clinic despite the talk of cynics who felt a boy his age had no such business doing business in the town. And whenever someone needed a lift, there was Purvis with his gift (he was not the one to decline a house-call just in time). And off he'd go upon his bike when someone couldn't make the hike to his house where Mom made cookies for all to take. So let us hope he stays the course as he ages without remorse. Perhaps he'll be a doctor or a counselor or a teacher or a guide, where he'll tinkle out the pain within the hearts where pain resides. For magic often happens in ways we don't expect. And there is nothing that a man who has a precious tinkle can't affect.

THE MAN WHO WAS A TREE

He loved green things. His house was surrounded by a sumptuous garden. Even his name was Branch. Marvin Branch. He had always been interested in plants ever since he was a little kid. As a boy, he would stop off after baseball practice—little league (which he was never really good at)—to examine the foliage of bushes that hung over the sidewalks and alley-ways on the way home. He saw the bees and the flies buzzing in and out of the petals and the buds that hung off the vines and stalks. The other boys would be annoyed by his departure—turning around to see where Marvin was now. They'd call to him, and maybe he'd hear them on the first go around, maybe he wouldn't. The boys would wait, far up ahead, pained expressions of impatience on their faces. *"Marvin!!"* Maybe on the third or fourth try they'd get him while leaning on baseball bats, hands on hips, twirling fielder's gloves in the air.

Marvin might finally respond and run to catch up. "You should see what the rhododendrons are doing!" he'd exclaim as he rejoined them. The others would just sigh and move on—as if they cared about the rhododendrons . . . as if they actually knew what a rhododendron was. Not only was he lousy at baseball, but he'd talk to the stupid plants. Quite frankly, in their eyes, Marvin was a little creepy. But he seemed oblivious to their stares of consternation and their overheard jokes and criticism. He was an innocent. Totally in love with his plants.

And then there was this rumor . . . that when he was born, the afterbirth came out looking like a seed pod, and the umbilical cord looking more like a green leafy vine of some odd sort than whatever it was supposed to look like. Rumor had it that the doctor and medical staff who helped in the delivery were the ones who started the tale—and after that the doctor himself swore his staff to secrecy. At any rate, no one talked about it much after Marvin's birth. And it soon could be attributed to one of those urban legends you hear about. Or maybe it was something made up due to Marvin's peculiar and somewhat asocial behavior. Marvin's mother never admitted it, if she even knew about the story at all.

As he grew older, he developed a love for biology and did a lot of extra assignments in his high school class. It was one of the things that got him in good with girls during those teen years. It also didn't hurt that he was a rather good-looking boy as well; however nerdy his behavior might be. He would do other students' biology homework for them, whenever they were stuck. This eventually ended up being a kind of business, as he would trade goods and services for other people's homework. At first it came as an offer, "if you do my homework, I'll do your paper route on Thursday." It wouldn't take very long before he had everybody in the class working for him in one capacity or other—from mowing lawns to sweeping out garages, to filling in for him at band practice (music was something he was not good at despite his mother's encouragement). But it was the girls who saw potential in Marvin—and Marvin's homework capabilities. Soon other boys became jealous, but there was nothing to be jealous about. Marvin seemed to have no interest in girls—something the girls became acutely aware of. Still, every new semester brought new possibilities.

It was the school principal who put it all together and took disciplinary action. Report after report came in from Marvin's various teachers. Too many students were getting A's—especially in biology. And all with conveniently similar answers—even on essays. Marvin was smart enough to vary things from page to page, student to student; but even the best of criminal types leave behind enough traces to end up in jail—or in this case, the principal's office.

And so Mom and Dad and Marvin were there, looking at a stern, glowering principal. Soon Marvin was back to mowing his own lawns, taking out his own garbage, and being his own partner in biology lab.

Actually, Dad was proud of his ingenious and enterprising son, but felt his energy needed a more socially acceptable outlet. So he built Marvin his own greenhouse in the backyard. Marvin gave up baseball and band, and basically moved into the greenhouse, filling it with all sorts of exotic plants from jungles halfway across the world. He began his own program of crossbreeding types of corn and other grains. Best of all, he began to plant trees. He started them from seedlings, grew them to healthy pot-sized stubs, then wondered what to do with them. It was a mere mental hop from tree sprout to birthday gift. He started giving away trees to people for birthdays, for Christmas, for anniversaries, for no reason at all. He found bare spots on empty lots and put trees there. He added trees to the local park—behind the bleachers of the baseball diamond. He even put them along the river after a storm and subsequent flood knocked a few of those old wooden monuments of pre-development days to the ground. People found him on the shoreline sobbing after all that tree crashing happened. Somebody had to take him home. They listened to him bellow that his oldest friends were gone. They weren't exactly sure what he was talking about, but the assumption they could make was a little too weird for them to stomach.

This is where Germaine entered the picture. Marvin lived in a city of about 50,000. Big enough not to be a town, but small enough to still be considered sort of rural. And what better place for a tree fanatic than in the heart of the American midwest's greenery nestled between farms and fields in all directions. This meant that the city shared a school district with most of the rest of the county. As such, high school can expose one to people from all over, including those not only outside your neighborhood, but outside your community. One such person was Germaine. Germaine did what every other girl in her class did, she asked Marvin for help with her biology homework. What was different about Germaine was that she was willing to except Marvin for all his insulated weirdness.

Germaine was pleasantly attractive, but no beauty. She could overcome her alleged plainness with just some modest touch-ups when she felt inclined. However, she seldom felt inclined. Germaine's biggest problem was low self-worth. She was never popular and never considered herself pretty enough to make it in the big leagues like the cheerleading squad. This attitude was probably due to a slight lisping sound she made when she spoke as a result of an overbite her parents were too poor to provide orthodental care to correct. She was actually smart and personable enough, but hid it under a "poor me" façade. In a sense, she was another Marvin—just without Marvin's outlying obsession. Perhaps Germaine's obsession was herself.

Germaine struck up a much more permanent friendship with Marvin—a boy who didn't have many permanent friends. Even though she lived out of town, she was willing to bike in from her home and spend an entire Saturday or Sunday afternoon watching Marvin putter in his greenhouse, even helping him scrape seeds, pollinate flowers, or shift about bags of fertilizer—whatever Marvin ordered her to do. She would talk, and Marvin would say, "Uh-huh," and it didn't bother her if Marvin actually paid little attention to what she was saying.

But the surge in female hormones in a young body can affect even the most timid. It was inevitable that someday one of those adolescent admirers of Marvin's would play out her hand. It happened to be Germaine. It was a Sunday afternoon. The two of them were engaged in pollinating corn—the result of which Marvin was writing down in a book he was intending to publish (Marvin was not shy about his belief in his horticultural skills). Germaine got the idea in her head of: why not pollinate each other? She stared at him for awhile, watching him fuss with his plants. Then she just came out and said, "Let's kish."

Marvin looked up at her as if she had just said, "Let's build a zeppelin." "Why?" he asked after first receiving a conformation of what she had asked.

"Becaush it would be intereshting," she reasoned out. "It'sh biology. Don't you like biology?"

"Yes, but—" she didn't give Marvin time to finish his thought. She just grabbed him and planted one on him (no pun intended). Marvin was not only surprised by the action, he was surprised to find out he liked it. It was kind of like sticking your face against a wet sponge, but for some reason it was exciting. After that, Marvin and Germaine spent a lot of time kissing in the greenhouse. And so they were boyfriend and girlfriend.

And then there came graduation. It came the same year (senior year) as the year Marvin won all those prizes: first in the school fair; and later, the state science fair. Marvin filled tables with hybrid corn, wheat, sorghum, dwarf plum trees and apple trees, and so on. One table was filled with nothing but compost. Marvin had discovered a new way to make compost and wanted to show everybody. The fact that it smelled to high heaven didn't deter somebody from giving him a blue ribbon.

At graduation, the principal reminded everyone, as Marvin stepped up to receive his diploma, of Marvin's biological accomplishments. And the other girls were reminded of Germaine's biological accomplishments in having snatched away the dorky but handsome future bio-engineer. And dorkiness can be overcome with a big paycheck—which Marvin seemed destined to obtain. This fact alone perhaps won Germaine the esteem she had been craving throughout her high school career. And no one noticed her lisp anymore.

Marvin would spend his next few years at a community agricultural college. He stayed at home. He fully believed in the words his father had always told him—and that was: to be fully stable as a person, one has to establish roots. For Daddy Branch, and for young Marvin, that meant staying home. Dad had made enough money in the packing business to buy a nice house with a nice big yard in a nice semi-urban/semi-rural community. And once planted stayed put, never going anywhere. Marvin, who came to be the only child (perhaps due to those ugly rumors about his birth) shared father's lack of wanderlust, and only pursued an education that took him to a school within a morning's commute and no further. The rest of the time, he stayed in his garden and his greenhouse, and let Germaine come to him—which she did. Having found the ways and means to drive a car to Marvin's house, she spent as much time there as anywhere, helping him on his projects whenever he saw fit.

Now one would think that someone as bright as Marvin wouldn't find easy and lucrative access into a professional field to his liking. And he did get his offers as college graduation approached. But that was when the change began to happen.

By this time Germaine, though more confident than ever, had given up her search for a prospective mate—or rather, find an alternative source for her youthful hormones. As far as she was concerned, Marvin was it. There was a certain immovable comfort zone buried in her as well, which is no doubt why she and Marvin got along so well. They both believed in planting roots. In Germaine's case, her roots were buried in Marvin and she was not about to pull them from that plot. Marvin never did become more sociable despite his advance into higher education. In fact, he got nerdier; more obsessive about his plants. No one new would or could enter his life, and only those imbedded into his existence could possibly tolerate the self-absorbed brilliant nitwit he had become. So Germaine and Marvin got married.

While Marvin was smart enough to know how pollination occurs in all species—including humans—it remained for Germaine to show him how humans occupy their time with it. And while Marvin was a dutiful lover, he remained distant as the whole procedure unfolded. It was not out of any displeasure in Germaine, whom he loved dearly in his own peculiar fashion, nor any distaste for the act of procreating itself that might have kept him a bit aloof; it had more to do with the fact that he was not engaged in the same way as he was with crossbreeding grain. Germaine found a solution in placing as many green plants in their bedroom as possible—which seemed to encourage her husband to greater heights. She even covered herself in foliage and asked him to find the flower.

They lived in a small apartment away from home. And that probably had a lot to do with Marvin's distraction. He still spent most of his free time in his greenhouse and his garden, but often found it difficult to sleep at night, since he was no longer in his old lodgings.

Two things happened, one on top of the other: father died—a sudden heart-attack; and Germaine found herself pregnant. Mother offered the newlyweds a place to stay in the old home—which Marvin immediately jumped at. And the baby was born in that house. A girl. Why have a baby any place else but home? . . . was Marvin's argument. Not a fashionable concept in the day, but one both the new mom and the new grandmom were willing to concede to. And while there was nothing unusual about this baby's birth (no weird rumors), there was something unusual taking place about Marvin. His hair was turning green.

College graduation over, and a promising career in front of him—the future was bright; yet the family grew worried over Marvin's green hair. So before he started work to bring in that prize income everyone expected of him, he went off to a clinic to see about neutralizing those green hair folicles.

The doctors were stumped. Nobody knew what to do about a guy with green hair. After a few days, Marvin returned home with a hand-full of antibiotics and regulations for a new diet. The Branches followed the diet dutifully. And Marvin got greener. And weirder.

Germaine was the first to notice it—as might be expected. For once the baby was quiet. For once Marvin was not distracted by his plants. For once Germaine could interest him in a bout of love-making in the middle of the night. But Germaine herself stopped it with a scream. She found little sprout-like leaves extracting themselves from pores in Marvin's skin, and peeling their way off of his body hair.

Back to the doctor. This time it was a specialist somebody imported for the clinic. The specialist went, "Hmmm." Then he went, "Huh." Then he said, "Let's take some X-rays." Then they took X-rays. Then the specialist examined the photos on a big electrically lit screen. Then the specialist said, "Hmmm." Then he squinted and rubbed his eyeglasses and looked closer. Then he said, "Huh." Specialists are known for reticence.

"Well, doctor?" Germaine nervously inquired.

"My dear boy," the specialist began in addressing Marvin, "you have a plant growing inside of you."

"What kind of plant?" Marvin said with interest.

"Never mind what kind!" Germaine snapped, "What's it doing there?"

"I don't know," the specialist responded. "It's not supposed to be there. By all accounts, a plant cannot live inside a human being—unless that human being is dead. You're not dead, are you, Mister Branch?"

"No," Marvin said, certain of his liveliness.

"How do we get it out of him?" Germaine returned, "I assume we want it out?"

"Oh yes indeed!" the Specialist said. "It's not doing any good being there. I suppose we could give you something that will help dissolve it; like any other parasite—tapeworms for example."

"And if that doesn't succeed?" Germaine questioned.

"Operate," said the Specialist. "Hopefully in time."

So Marvin was put on an even stricter diet, and had to take yucky medicine twice a day (besides the occasional shot in the butt, which specialists prescribe for everything). And Marvin got greener.

So they were forced to operate. It was no good starting up that new promising job in that new promising career. Marvin couldn't show up green and not scare away his co-workers. So Marvin sat in the house all day. His skin was now turning green, and leafy appendages were growing out of his head. And Marvin was becoming more and more morose.

"I'm becoming a plant," he'd say somberly, sitting in his favorite chair. Germaine would wrap her arm around him, snipping off a frayed leaf or two in an attempt to keep him neat. Pulling on the stems or the fresh green leaves apparently was painful; but the older twigs and leaves were okay to pinch off—just to keep up appearances.

So then came the ten hour operation. They removed the root cause (so to speak) of his affliction. Marvin spent a month in bed recuperating. And Marvin got greener. Marvin never left the house. Neither Mother nor Germaine left the house except for necessities. And they never spoke of Marvin to anyone lest more rumors like the birth one get started. If anyone asked, they said Marvin was out of town at his new important job somewhere and doing well.

Specialists, however, came to visit. And they scratched their heads and puzzled and puzzled. Marvin sat motionless in his chair like a big bush with a face in the middle of it. And the specialists went home, writing notes in their notebooks and discussing what they would print in the medical journals—and whose name would come first.

The little girl crawled around Daddy, occasionally playing with Branch's branches. Marvin just sat and looked sad, for he was no longer able to engage with his child, his wife, or his family. He was also losing his voice. He seldom moved. His feet began sprouting roots so he could no longer wear slippers.

Mother died—perhaps of a guilty conscious and a broken heart. Germaine went alone to the funeral amidst the talk of the town. Late at night, Germaine, with the help of some medical students, carried in Marvin to the funeral parlor at Germaine's special request. Marvin sat and stared at his mother. Some of his leaves began to shed. Then he was carried back home and Mother was buried. The house and its garden were now theirs.

Marvin's last request, his last vocal response, was that he be placed out in the backyard near his greenhouse. Within a year all traces of Marvin slipped away. Where he was placed was now the site of a beautiful growing tree. Visiting neighbors would come by wishing Germaine and her girl well. They would comment on the beautiful tree in the backyard. Was that one of Marvin's latest experiments? It was always so lush and full. And it had many different types of leaves—oak, maple, willow. Through the years it even bore fruit: plums and apples, peaches and grapes. That Marvin was a horticultural genius! What kind of tree did he say that was?

An excuse was made that Marvin met with an accident out of town, leaving Germaine a widow. Their daughter grew to school age, and all the kids used to come by and play by the great exotic tree—tugging at its flowers, pulling off its juicy fruits, climbing its limbs.

Then came the summer of the storm. Daughter Lucilla was out playing the in garden when the storm hit. Actually, she had been investigating the haunts of her barely remembered father. She had studied the insides of the greenhouse, now left in a state of decay and disrepair. When she was very little, Germaine had forbidden Lucilla to step inside the greenhouse. But as Lucilla got older and the greenhouse fell into ruin, the lock eventually fell off, or rusted off, of its own accord and Lucilla one summer afternoon found herself exploring its insides.

Lucilla always felt a kind of presence when she was playing in the backyard, but it never frightened her—not like some ghost. But she grew up with a sense that someone was watching over her. Sometimes when it was windy, she felt as if she heard someone calling, "Lucilla" through the leaves. She always wrote it off to her imagination.

But that day in the greenhouse was the day she wanted answers about her father. Who was he? Where did he go? Will he ever come back? Her mother had mumbled things that sounded like excuses, but those answers never satisfied her. Finally, she found the lock on the greenhouse open and she began snooping around. Mother had thrown out all the plants that used to inhabit the place. It was now just a containment for empty pots and tools and piles of unused supplies.

Then the storm hit. Lucilla had been so preoccupied with her investigation she never even noticed what was going on outside. She thought she even heard voices inside. Perhaps that was the storm brewing and whistling through the cracks. And the storm did come up suddenly. BOOM! And there was lightning and thunder—and rain! And the greenhouse door blew open.

Lucilla ran out just as a power-cable snapped off a telephone pole. And at that same instant, one of the biggest limbs off the exotic tree came crashing to the ground. But not before its tangle of branches caught the cable, knocking it back out into the street. Lucilla had tripped when all this exploding of limbs happened. It seems a funnel cloud just touched down near the yard before springing up again. No other funnels were reported that day.

"You're lucky, little lady!" said the repair man surveying the damage. "If that tree limb hadn't come down at the right moment that cable, hell, that whole telephone pole hadda come right down on top of you where you was!" The exotic tree was nearly split in half and so partially destroyed. But Germaine always considered that day the day of miracles—even more so than Lucilla did. But Germaine never mentioned anything more than that, and never did explain to her daughter about the tree. Time and new activities made Lucilla forget all about the tree and the greenhouse in the backyard.

In the end, Marvin's daughter went off to junior college and married an aviator. She couldn't remember her father. Germaine stayed at home and did laundry and domestic chores for money. She never remarried and she never did get that overbite lisp fixed.

Germaine outlived her one and only husband by nearly fifty years. At her request, she was buried next to the big exotic tree in the backyard (what remained of it—for however shabby looking, it continued to live and even prosper). Lucilla came back to see to her mother put to rest. She raised two girls of her own—Marvin's granddaughters—and they decided to live in the same old big house she was raised in . . . in the old familiar town in the old familiar neighborhood. A quiet, friendly place where they could play in the backyard on the big exotic tree that grew there and never ceased to yield its many fruits. A place where a vine grew up out of their grandmother's grave to wrap around the big tree and yield fragrant smelling blossoms of its own exotic variety. A place where they could have the best tree house in the county.

Sometimes it's good to lay down roots.

JIMMY'S IDEA OF SEX

Jimmy was the smartest kid on the playground. Jimmy was smart because he knew something about sex. The rest of us were as ignorant as tar paper in the summer sun. So we all went to Jimmy. Jimmy knew.

Sometimes the teacher who was out on patrol covering the playground as a kind of chaperone/policeman during recess would catch us gathered around Jimmy spinning his stories about matrimonial bliss. This was not allowed on the playground. Sex was not something to be condoned at school, even in verbal form, even if it was somewhat mythic in content. He (or she) would be wandering around the asphalt as jumping, screaming children were busy chasing each other, bouncing huge, slow, flabby rubber balls off each other's heads, and basically engaging in dispersing child energy in random ways, when he (or she) would come upon Jimmy and his infatuated listeners. The teacher would swoop up like a ghost rider—only a ghost rider with lampreys in the form of brown-nosers who walked with her (or him)—and break up the latest sex lesson.

And Susan was always with him (or her). And you *had* to call her Susan. Not Sue. Not Suzy or Suzie Q (you'd be spit on if you tried Suzie Creamcheese). She was Susan. And she was one of those who always took the teacher's hand and spent the entire recess (along with a few other ass-wipes) escorting the recess patrol, hand in hand, to make sure all the other children were behaving, and that Law was enforced beyond all measure. Susan would even spy on Jimmy and the rest of us and report her findings with lightning speed to the nearest grown-up—and sometimes that would be the janitor.

We—we boys, that is (Heaven forbid a girl would join us; Hell prevent us from allowing a girl in)—would gather in some (temporarily) obscure corner and let Jimmy talk. Jimmy convinced us he was the smartest. Hell, he knew what sex was.

"Girls don't have a wee-wee," he would say.

"Aw, come on, Jimmy! What are we, little kids? Nobody calls it a wee-wee!"

"Hey, I need to know the level of the crowd here," he said confidently, as if he were some master emcee of some high-class gala.

"Go on . . . before Miss Dempsey sees us!" we encouraged. And you wouldn't want Miss Dempsey to know what you (we) were doing. Miss Dempsey was as big as a pro fullback and a hundred and fifty years old. You know Miss Dempsey wouldn't want kids talking about sex. You know Miss Dempsey never had any. Miss Dempsey was the one usually picked by the school as the he or she (in this case, a bit of both) on guard on patrol on the playground at recess.

"Okay, so girls don't have a thingey."

"What do they have?" somebody stated—obviously the new guy. The rest of us were past this point.

"They have a bush and a bear trap!" Jimmy came from a family of outdoorsmen.

"What's that?"

"If you look where a willie is supposed to be, they've got nothin'. But if you look close enough, they've got a bush and inside is a bear trap."

"Get out. Why would they have that?"

"To trap bears, you ninny!" I hollered, somewhat facetiously (not really, it could've been a bear trap for all I knew). I've heard Jimmy's stories many times, and he does change them a bit to gear it towards his audience; but I always love how they turn out, so I always listen.

"Go on."

"Why would they need to trap bears?"

"It just looks like a bear trap. They don't really trap bears, they trap your wiener," Jimmy answered his skeptics with aplomb.

"Why would they do that?"

"Because that's what girls do."

"I don't want anybody trapping my wiener!"

"Oh yes you will! You can't help it. Girls have this power, it comes from this smell they give off."

"What kind of smell?"

"It's like raw bacon, only coated in honey. It's the kind of thing a bear might want."

"Why do they need to bother us with it? Why can't they just go out in the woods and catch bears?"

"Because they don't want bears, you bonehead. They can't make babies with bears."

"They can only make babies with boys?"

"Yeah—otherwise we'd be walking around with bear heads and tails right now; because we'd all be part bear and part people."

"Oh."

"Why do they want to make babies anyway?"

"Because that's what girls do! If they didn't, we wouldn't be here. Who invited him anyway?"

"Leave the kid be. He's in Mrs. Parker's class. Go on with your story, Jimmy."

"Okay . . . so once you get a whiff of their smell—"

"I still don't get this whole bear thing."

"Shut up. Jeffy, he's too young for this, have him stand lookout."

"You heard him, kid, go over there and watch for Miss Dempsey."

"Aw, crap!"

"Go on. All right, Jimmy, go ahead."

"Anyway . . . as I was saying, when they let you smell them, they want you to get a boner."

"What?"

"Why?"

"Because of the bear trap in the bush. You guys are so slow!"

"Why do we have to get a boner?"

"You can't help yourselves. It's what they do to you. It's their plan."

"It seems silly to me."

"Maybe, but it's what happens."

"All because of the bacon smell? I smelled bacon all the time, and I don't get no boners from it."

"This is different. This is girl bacon."

"You're not old enough yet. But it'll happen."

"Okay, Jimmy, go on. After the boner, what happens? Wait! Miss Dempsey . . . pretend like were divvying up for basketball."

"We ain't got a basketball," Jimmy acknowledged.

"Wait. Steal a kid's dodgeball. Hey, kid come here. Gimme that thing." That was Tim. Tim was always getting us into trouble whenever Jimmy wasn't.

"Hey!"

"Now beat it."

"That's my dodgeball!"

"Go on, get lost!"

"Miss Dempsey! . . . Miss Dempsey! . . . They took my dodgeball!"

"Oh great, why'd you do that?"

"I didn't know he was going to whine like that."

"Quiet, here she comes."

"What's going on here? What are you children doing?" Miss Dempsey had the worst breath imaginable. And it always blew out of her every time she spoke like a whale blowing steam. Standing next to Miss Dempsey was like standing in a tomb full of mummies.

"Nothing, Miss Dempsey."

"Did you take this child's ball?"

"He gave it to us. He said it was going flat and wanted us to check it out. Here you go, kid. It's all right, just needs a little air." Tim tossed the distressed child the ball.

"You're Timothy Gaines from Mrs. Bruder's class, aren't you?" Miss Dempsey scrutinized him through her antediluvian eyesight.

"Yes he is, Miss Dempsey," Susan spoke up—as always. "Mrs. Bruder always has trouble with Tim."

"Mmh. And what are you boys doing?"

"Nothing, Miss Dempsey."

"That's Jimmy Sample, Miss Dempsey," Susan added smugly, "He's the one who—"

"I am acquainted with Master Sample. I suggest the lot of you decide to do something instead of nothing. Wear out some of that unbridled energy in a more healthy and constructive manner while you have the chance. I'll be watching."

"Yes, Miss Dempsey," we all chimed in a once.

Susan wrinkled her nose at us, and then like a steamship turning and passing in the night—complete with an escort of bobbing porpoises—Miss Dempsey walked away. Susan, of course, eyeing us suspiciously from time to time in parting.

"Rats."

"I hate Susan. You think she's got a bear trap?"

"Oh yeah. They all do."

"Well I'm not going to have my willie trapped by her!"

"Hey, here comes Ted. He took out a softball. Let's toss that like we're playing keepaway!"

"Hey guys, what's up?"

"Quick, toss me the softball. Jimmy's telling us about girls' parts!"

"Hey, I want to hear this!"

"Okay, Jimmy, go ahead!"

"Where was I?"

"Girls smell like bacon and give you a boner."

"Wow, did I miss all this?"

"Shut up, Ted. Go on, Jimmy."

"Then you have to take off all your clothes."

"What for?"

"She has to too."

"Really? Hey, that doesn't sound all that bad."

"Why do you have to take your clothes off with her?"

"Well, this is the big test. You have to stick your boner in her bear trap."

"Yuck!"

"That's disgusting!"

"You mean you *have* to?"

"She wants you to."

"All girls are like this? I really don't like girls that much. Especially Susan."

"You don't have to do this with Susan."

"Thank God."

"But you have to do it if you want babies."

"I don't want babies."

"Well, maybe you will when you're older, jughead! I'm just telling you, this is how it happens. You stick your wiener in her trap."

"Doesn't it hurt?"

"No, cuz it's mushy like the inside of a pumpkin."

"Eeeyyyeww!"

"Wouldn't it be slippery then?"

"Yeah. That's why they get these puffy chests. You have to climb on top of 'em, and so that you don't slip off before you get stuck in her trap, you have to hang on to these chests they grow like big pillows."

"Oh, that's why they have those things!"

"Yeah. And then when you're there you pee inside her."

"What?!" "Why?!"

"This gets worse and worse, Jimmy."

"Hey, it's what happens."

"Why would you pee in her? What's the point of that?"

"And they let you do that?"

"Yes."

"Why?"

"Because you have magic pee."

"Magic pee?"

"Yeah. Whenever you stick your thingey in a girl's trap, you get magic pee."

"This all sounds really stupid."

"Who came up with this idea?"

"Hey, I'm just telling you what happens!"

"And then what?"

"Well . . . then you're done and you go away."

"That's all?"

"That's not enough?"

"This is how you make babies?"

"Yeah. Well then once you're done, then she goes and makes a baby in her belly."

"Couldn't you just kiss her and that would be enough?"

"No. She's needs the magic pee from your willie. God, you guys are thick."

"Then what?"

"Then she goes to the hospital, and a doctor sticks his hand up her butt and pulls out a baby."

"Eccch!"

"You're makin' all this up, Jimmy. This is all so gross!"

"I'm telling you, this is how it happens."

"There's the buzzer. We gotta go in."

"Susan is still looking at us. So is Miss Dempsey."

"You think Miss Dempsey has a bear trap?"

"They all do. Even Miss Dempsey."

"YYYUUUUUUUUUCKKKKKK!!!!!"

I can't explain it. I heard Jimmy's story again and again. It changed a bit each time he told it, but overall it stayed the same. I found it as repulsive as the other guys did, but couldn't pry my ears away—I was so gripped by his story's power.

I haven't stayed in touch with any of those kids since school. I grew up and moved away, got married and had two children of my own. Somehow the whole facts-of-life thing ended up to be more pleasant than I originally thought. I heard Jimmy eventually became an OB-GYN. I can only hope the story he tells his patients has been refined a bit since those days on the playground with Miss Dempsey watching.

TITS OF PLEASURE

He was the kind of guy who liked watermelon for breakfast. He seemed to like big round objects as a child. He loved the way bath sponges squirted when you soaked them for awhile and then squeezed them really hard really fast. He grew up to love tits. It was on his mind constantly. He dated big buxom girls in high school and college. Afterwards, he went online and dated big buxom women. If he showed up at the door or at a scheduled meeting place, and the evening's sample was not ample enough for his tastes, he would quickly turn around and exit. It was just the way with him.

He picked up magazines featuring women with the biggest mammaries (one usually finds such literature at truck stops). He studied art and took drawing classes so that he could spend hours drawing breasts from all angles. Just breasts. He never got around to the rest of the torso. As for arms and legs—well, forget it. He had dreams of rolling around on the great plains.

It somehow never occurred to him that a person was attached to the other end of those luscious globes he coveted. He would stare directly at women's chests when talking to them and not think anything of it. They, however,

did. It got to the point that no woman wanted to deal with him. So he had
to come up with an alternative.

He started with blow-up dolls. He could scrunch away on them as long
as he pleased, and no complaints. Still, the sensation was plastic not flesh.
Then one of those catalog companies that deals with "marital aids" as they
are called, sent him a copy of their most recent issue. It turns out they were
selling just tits on some random page inside. And that's what they were
called too: "Just Tits."

So he sent away for a box of tits and waited an impatient 3 weeks for
them to arrive. Arrive they did in a brown box with glaring fluorescent
orange letters on it stating: "Sexually Explicit Material Inside—To Be
Opened By Addressee Only." This is, one presumes, a way of keeping
other people away from opening the box "accidentally". Or maybe it is
intended as a way of keeping one's dirty little secret a secret. Whatever
the thought behind the person who put that stamp on the box, it had the
effect of putting fireworks and bicycle horns on the package. Everyone
in the building knew that he was getting something obscene in the mail.
And of course they whispered to each other about it—behind his back,
and sometimes in front of it. But beyond suspicious looks they never said
anything directly to him about it. They just knew he was the odd little
man who sent away to New Jersey for masturbation gear.

He occupied a room on the third floor. Opposite him was a librarian. He
had fantasies about what was behind that librarian's blouse. The librarian
had fantasies that he had fantasies about her, and it repulsed her. She
avoided him at every sight. She felt he was always staring at her shirt and
that he would then run off to his room to play with his obscene material
from New Jersey. It was a dirty spot in her mind she couldn't erase. She
actually over-exaggerated her pull on him. He kind of took turns doing
such a thing with everybody; but he was not obsessed with her. Just tits.
Actually, she was right in the long run.

He spent long evenings with his "Just Tits" thinking about just tits. They
came out of the box and their plastic wrappings smelling like plastic. They
felt rubbery, but were the right size and shape. They may not have been
real, but he had a vivid imagination. He woke up smiling and it carried

him on his way to work. He placed "Just Tits" by his home phone and during his coffee break would call in on them to make little cooing noises to them by voice mail. He played back his own message that night to get himself back into the mood. On occasion, he was able to sneak "Just Tits" into work with him and play with them in the men's room on his coffee break.

Then one day his housemaid was there during one of the phone calls home to his beloved tits and quickly resigned, not wanting to work for a pervert. His laundress also quit, being the mother of the housemaid. Word got around that he was nuts, and complaints were registered with the building superintendent. He said he couldn't do anything about it. Everybody was entitled to live the way they wanted in the privacy of their own home as long as they didn't harm anybody and didn't do anything illegal. Since this pervert always paid his rent on time everybody, in the super's opinion, should mind their own business.

This did not sit well with some of the tenants—such as the suspicious librarian. They finally complained to the building's owner. He said much the same thing, which brought on a bit of a row. To get everybody to shut up, he said he'd look into the matter. After some hemming and hawing, he confronted the tit-lover with a series of ongoing issues and problems (mostly made up and none addressing the truth) to ensure that the little man with the rubber tits would find some other place to live.

The issue came to a head when he was caught on the old wrought-iron fire-escape hanging up laundry in the middle of the night—while wearing "Just Tits." The fact that he had now taken to wearing rubber tits in public (even if at night, even if at the back of the building on the fire-escape) was now good enough for the building super, under orders from the owner, to send the cruddy little man packing.

But he had not learned his lesson, as once he found a new home in another building on another street in another part of town, he couldn't keep his tit passion down. While he was scrupulous about being quiet and apart from all others in the building; and he certainly did not give out his secrets to anyone, he was not averse to being seen inappropriately in public. He wore his "Just Tits" to Central Park on a Sunday afternoon and could be seen squeezing himself while humming a happy tune in front of children, dogs, and constables on horseback. And this led to a disturbing the peace charge brought against him.

It finally got filtered around to what few friends and family members he actually had; and they, as a group, decided he had a problem. They sent him to a therapist. It was a female therapist—with a big chest. And this led to his second disturbing the peace violation. It also led to a restraining order. His first. He then went on to collect several more. It got so bad he was not allowed back at work. Finally somebody got the bright idea to put him into some kind of rehab center. A place with all males. His rubber tits were taken away, and they had him making baskets and hooking rugs—anything to keep his hands busy. The last anybody saw of him was of him keeping busy in his room or in the crafts lounge making throw rugs for people outside the hospital. They were formed in strange abstract patterns of round shapes. People got them for Christmas, Easter, any time of year, any occasion. It turned out that he enjoyed making Jell-O molds in the kitchen and he made friends easily with the turtles in the creek that ran along the hospital's backlot.

No one goes to visit him. The doctors were thinking of making him assistant janitor.

SEX WITH ALIENS

I'm a high-flyin' hip kinda guy. I drink, sure. Spend my time with the ladies—you betcha. I have a nine foot hookah in my bedroom—and its not filled with ordinary substances . . . if you know what I mean. I go to all the with-it places. I've danced in the anti-gravity bars that circle the planet. I've done double-shots with the Weeron Warriors on Rigel II; hung out on glaciers in Aldebaran VI; did the voodoo like ritual with the Gammaruns on Sirius V. I've been round and about this end of the galaxy and did it all within my first hundred years. I'm a pilot by profession. A merchant by trade. I was born on an interstellar voyage in a bus between old Sol and Alpha Centauri (I can't believe people still go there—it's a dead zone). But above all . . . I'm known to be a lady's man. And they don't even have to be the same species. They don't even have to be human. They just have to be a lady.

I once met this Trucanian at the Moon Bar in Copernicus crater—Della Luna—as they say. Trucanians are fascinating chicks. All blue. Blue hair spiked up into a blue pony tail at the tops of their heads. Blue eyes—even what should pass as the whites—with their odd double pupils in each eye. Those long blue fingers and lanky limbs. And their skin, soft and spotted with darker blue patches as it is, peels every few weeks so that they don't need to wear clothes. Now that's freaky. And cool. You don't want to catch a Trucanian on a peel day (temperamental bitches to say the least) but the rest of the time is play time. It's the double vagina that makes them a prize. Double-freaky.

The first Trucanian I nailed was a glerk (they call them glerks instead of girls or women) who was outward bound running as an ambassador's aid. She was on her way to Vega with her boss and just stopped in for a fligg. I had a margarita. They can't get used to the salt, though I offered. Trucanian glerks like human men because Trucanian shlerffups (men) are basically a lump of meat with a penis. Okay if you like that sort of thing, and apparently Trucanian glerks did for millions of years; but glerks have all the brain power and do all the mental work in Trucanian society. The shlerffups are just basically beasts of burden doing menial physical labor and haven't learned to speak yet. Human males are fascinating to glerks because we can speak and operate machinery at the same time.

Her name was Xxxggmmllrr (I'm guessing at the spelling). I spotted her the moment she came in. I went over to her and said, "Yyppllff" (hello). She liked the fact that I spoke a little Trucanian (with a darling—so she said—Earthian accent), and I offered her a drink. We danced to the music of The Pitchpipers and then we headed to my hotel. I don't waste time when I'm on the move, and as long as the subject is willing . . . and she was willing . . . willing indeed.

We spent a little time giving lip service to a Trucanian mating ritual. Xxxggmmllrr was not a stickler for conventions, but she felt she owed it to her mother to at least do a little bit of homage to the ancestors before we got started—seeing has how I was a different species and all. I didn't quite understand it, but it had something to do with shaking our heads and howling while stamping our feet for about a minute or two. After that, it was all Ya-Ha time! I'm amazed at what an extra orifice can do to a brief bit of canoodling. Trucanian glerks are used to being on top, too. They have to, the shlerfupps don't know what the hell they're doing. I convinced her to do a flip-flop—which she seemed amazed by (imagine a male interested in sex in the first place!)—but that was only after the first hour of doing things her way. Trucanian glerks seem to have a built in cock-ring so that they can get the most out of whatever poor sap they happen to have under them. Thank God for that. I can sustain myself for awhile thinking about

Mesmegomian algebra, but sooner or later I'll lose out. But this glerk had me going for hours. And in the morning—she was the one who left early. She had to be to Vega. I needed a couple more hours of sleep.

*   *   *

Then there was that space station that circles the Sun from the Oort Cloud. The Sun is just a dot from there, but there is plenty of traffic through it coming from the Galactic arm—especially from Orion's belt. Nearly all of them merchants like me. The Oort Cloud has sort of a wild-west atmosphere—as does much of the galaxy, for that matter. There is a small police force on board, but who pays attention to that? Besides, they can all be bought off any way.

I was in the bar (you may have noticed I spend an awful lot of time in them when I'm not traveling) when a red shaggy came in—all hot and bothered. Red shaggies are what we call them out in the cloud. They're really Zets-zallows from Procyon VI. We call them red shaggies because . . . well, they're red and shaggy. Like Trucanians, they walk around nude, but not because of delicate peeling skin, it's because of the growth of vermilion hair. It's on the outside of their arms and legs like marching band stripes. And they have another strip going down their backs. But their heads have this big poof of flaming hair that juts up and out around their heads like a lion's mane. And like humans, they have pubes, but the rest of them is bare yellow skin with very large freckle-like reddish-brown spots. And, of course, they have those famous yellow eyes.

So this female red shaggy steps into the bar, looking around like she lost somebody. Real smooth, I went up to her and said, "Looking for a dream?"

She laughed her yellow teeth at me and said, "Vvrrhhxxtu oi oi?"

I don't speak Zets-zallow, so I said, "Does that mean—you're on?"

"On what?" she converted to English. Everybody speaks English outside the solar system surprisingly. Everybody seems to have picked up on our tv broadcasts about the time they began adventuring out into the stars themselves, so everybody learned to speak English when they came to our space stations. It's surprising how illiterate it is possible to be out in space.

"It's an Earth expression. It means are you game . . . are you up for it . . . do you want to parley . . . to . . ."

"Make love—they say?"

"That's very good. You pick up on things real fast."

"As you are the male of the species and I am a female of my kind, I assumed that was what you were asking."

"Your English is very good."

"Thank you. I learned it from your TV. Your 'Mister Ed'."

"A talking horse."

"He looks a lot like our leader."

"Your leader is a horse?"

"No. In Zets-zallow society, we let governmental decisions be made by another species. They are immobile. They are actually what you would call sponges. But they have heads that look like your horses. They make the decisions that run our planet. We do everything else."

"Well that's kind of handy. Were you looking for someone?"

"My sister. She often gets lost."

"Ah! Shall we go find her?"

"You will help?"

"Why not? Maybe we can convince her to come out and play!"

"Then we will do the sex thing, yes?"

"Only if you want to. I wouldn't want to be accused of forcing someone to do anything against their will."

"No. That will be okay. I have a three cycle layover. I find drinking in bars boring."

"I have a room at the other end of the station."

"That's fine. But first we find Jkljkl-a."

"Who?"

"My womb-mate. Sister."

"Ah, yes! We wouldn't want to forget her!"

We did find Jkljkl-a in the arcade. She was busy killing aliens on the holodeck. It would seem red shaggies—at least this pair—are surprisingly easy to talk into bed, even with their womb-mates. And let me tell you—you have never had threeway until you've done it with a pair of twin red shaggies.

*   *   *

One of the weirder species to have sex with are the Mrrgrrvrrs from Algol III. They look like tube worms standing upright with a little pair of feet. They're about as long as your forearm. They only have sex in clusters. No one knows why. Even on their home planet they've only been seen to reproduce in bunches, never pairs. But they've become very popular on the various stations in the Oort Cloud region where they've been imported (illegally) to the backrooms of fashionable salons.

What you get for your money is you lay down naked on a mat on the floor as they release them from some kind of cage. Then 20 or 30 of the little tikes come running up on those funny flat feet and start kissing you all over at once. Nobody actually understands what the Mrrgrrvrrs get out of it. But I can tell you what the humans get, and it's worth the price.

*   *   *

Perhaps among the weirdest species I've had sex with came in the form of a plant. On Earth, it's not unusual to see flowers shaped in such a way to give a bee, a beetle, or a hummingbird—whichever the plant likes to pollinate with best—not only the best access to its pollen, but also the best reason for doing so. It supplies said pollinator with the finest scent, the most striking colors, the sweetest nectar, and perhaps the best rubdown said pollinator is going to find—ergo, it will keep returning.

Well there's a plant just like that out on Castor VII, I forget the name of it. Some asshole gave it a big Latin tag like we need Latin words for junk in outer space. Anyway, it's a kind of cactus. But its primary pollinator was a kind of humanoid type animal which in time became extinct—who knows why. The cactus thing was on the verge of dying out—until people arrived. Humans, that is.

It seems the ancient critters used to mate with the plant. The critters got their rocks off, and the cactus spread its pollen around to other plants. These things happen to be big suckers too. One plant would fill out a suburban patio. Like a strawberry, it has a central pod-like base with leaves on it, and shoots going out to flowery buds. Once the planet was discovered, humans began basing permanent stations and science labs on it. For the first ten or twenty years, they watched as these cactus flowers opened up into curious, almost monkey-like shapes but then withered and died.

Then one growing season, suddenly these buds opened up to form a naked woman (since most of the lab scientists at that particular station were male). And since they were human, and male, and stationed light-years away from civilization, and they were lonely and bored and drunk on an off night, some of the scientists began to curl up with one of these pod women to have a little fun.

Next morning, the guys awoke to find they were covered in some kind of orangey soot they had difficulty removing. When they snuggled up to another pod woman, voila, the soot came right off. And *boom!* cactus population explosion. The planet's covered with them now where as when Earthlings arrived there were only a few withered descendants left.

So far no human has had any ill-effect from the plant pollen (or from plant canoodling). But they are still outlawed pending more research (I'm told the research is quite fun and there are long lines to get into the field—or to even visit Castor VII). However, there is always the black market, and there are always those illicit stations in the Oort Cloud with their notorious salons—one of which I myself visited.

And it's true! It's true! It's a cactus flower in the shape of a naked woman. And a damn fine lookin' woman at that. These cacti have taste—or have researched their scientists' brains well. It's a bit odd because the plant is not as warm as a human (they put heaters in the salons to up the temp a bit) and it doesn't move or make noises; but it looks right and feels right. And a little bit of vodka and a little bit of imagination—what's to complain about?

Incidentally, the pollen is like flour, and it takes a week to wash off—or another night with another cactus flower. You almost have to do it twice to make it worthwhile and get the full effect. Oh, and by the way, deposits in the plant made by human males (you know what I'm talking about) apparently work as fertilizer on the cactus. So it's kind of a win-win. I haven't heard of any cactus flowers looking like naked men yet; but I hear there's a group of serious-minded women scientists (or a group of gay ones) who are devoting a lot of time and energy to this research. We'll see what they come up with.

*   *   *

Right now I'm on my way to Barnard's Star—which is a big nothing. A monster gas bag. I giant version of Jupiter with no planets, no satellites. But there's an exchange station nearby set up by the original Grays who hit Roswell centuries ago. They have a lively skin trade. Technically we're going there on an equipment delivery deal. But I want to find out what they really keep in those cages on those ships of theirs. And then there's always their infamous probes. Maybe not my kind of thing, but you only go around once in life, and you never know what's going to make it worth your while.

SEX WITH ROBOTS

"You're appointment is at one o'clock," my personal servant, Oom-Vac-Voom, stated in that mechanically nasal voice of his as he entered my bedroom.

"What time is it?" I grunted. Actually, that's what I wanted to say. It probably came out sounding like, "Mrrrmmrrrnnngggfff." Luckily Oom-Vac-Voom has been programmed to interpret all of my grunts into meaningful messages.

"Noon, sir," Oom responded. "Shall I open the drapes?"

I'm a nightowl. I often work late so it's a force of habit, a lifestyle choice, and it comes with the job. I shut off the drapes knowing I wouldn't want to get up right away. They're programmed to open at noon everyday. My first appointments don't usually occur until somewhere around three, so noon is good enough for waking up. But even with them shut off, steady Oom is ready with his inner clock ready to yank me out of bed.

"No . . . yes," I answered. Oom knows me and knows to respond to my second cue. He opened the drapes and let the sunlight wash over me. I squinted and groaned. This was a regular groan, without meaning.

"I have coffee ready for you, sir," Oom said pushing a tray in front of me next to the bed. "Do you have any preferences for breakfast?"

"No. What do I usually eat?"

"What you usually eat, sir." He wasn't being a smart-ass, that's the way robots usually think. And he does have a better memory than I do, particularly first thing in the morning.

"Well then, make that."

"And shall I run your shower, sir?"

"Yeah, sure. Whatever."

Oom left to see to his tasks. I got up and stretched. I live on the top floor, just under the penthouse. I can see a lot of the city from here. I don't care if I stand in front of the windows naked, I'm pretty high up from the streets. Apparently, the neighbors don't care if I stand in front of my windows either as they never complain—probably because they're never around when I do that.

I grabbed the coffee and started sipping. I could still barely open my eyes. The city vista stretched beyond the horizon. Flying cars zoomed every which way. I was always amazed there weren't more accidents. I couldn't see the bottom of my building or the streets for that matter because of all the freeways down below for the slower trucking traffic that wrapped around everything. As far as I knew, the original streets were mere fossils, buried under centuries of debris from above.

"Your shower is ready, sir," Oom piped in from the doorway.

"Thanks, Oom. Anything on the news today?" I padded barefoot to the bathroom, coffee cup in hand. Oom followed with my robe made of white glerron fur. I never found out what glerron was. Some product synthesized from plant fibers and animal fur made in the foundries on the southernmost tip of Argentina. It's warm, cozy, and absorbent. That's all I know about it. And it's not supposed to give you cancer. That's what the tv ads say, anyway.

"Italy has a brand new volcano. It killed thousands. The new space station in the asteroid belt was hit by a meteorite, damaging two compartments. Detroit is in flames again due to rioting. The mission to Jupiter was postponed again due to weather. And here there's another garbage strike by the city workers." Oom was good at summaries.

I stepped into the shower, handing Oom my coffee cup. Oom saves me time going over all the news channels that believe in overkill of every story. Ten seconds worth of headlines is about all I can take. I showered, shaved with that new foamy electric thing somebody gave me for some occasion, smothered myself in that glerron robe Oom held for me, and headed out onto the breakfast nook overlooking the city for my meal.

Oom had done his best as usual with the morning digestibles. Of course, Oom is just a machine who presses buttons on other machines, but he does a nice table layout. Two minute egg standing in a cup, toast, sausage links from some dead animal or other, two strawberries and a bit of cream cheese on a biscuit, and lots of vitamin pills. I hate to say it, but I'm now at the age where the vitamin pills are the thing that does the trick to keep me going during the day. And, of course, lots of coffee. This stuff comes from a hothouse in Sweden. Who'd have thought the Swedes would be good at growing coffee?

I left the television off (it annoys me no end), read a print-out of selected e-messages (so I wouldn't have to turn the damn machine on and be bombarded by requests, ads, and complaints about my last review) and listened to the traffic noise from the half-open louvers that surrounded me. It was going to be a warm day. Good. I don't have to worry about what I wear—or rather Oom doesn't have to.

"Your appointment book," said the screen on the table, and up popped my day-planner. I had three reviews today. Take extra vitamins. I'm getting too old for this kind of work. Still, I hate that snot-nosed kid at the office who is trying to horn in on my territory. "Let's get some fresh blood in here," said the editor, "get a fresh perspective on things!" He was waving his hands in the air as if he was making a grand generalization, but I knew he meant me. I'm not hip enough. I don't appeal to the younger crowd. I bet the boss deliberately scheduled three reviews for me in a single day just to prove I'm worn out. He wants that kid to take over—take my job. Not if I have anything to say about it.

"Your day wear is laid out for you," said Oom, coming from the bedroom. "Are we to be business-like or do we prefer casual wear today?"

"Since when have you known me to be business-like?"

"Well . . . with those meetings with the boss, you usually—"

"Not today. Reviews only today. No meetings—particularly with the boss."

"I understood there was lunch . . ."

"That's not a meeting, that's just lunch."

"Very good, sir. As today is Wednesday, I laid out a selection I thought would be more Wednesday-ish."

"What the hell is Wednesday-ish?"

"You tend more towards browns, tans, and subdued orange and yellow patterns on Wednesday, sir."

"I do?"

"To my observation. Perhaps something with a few tasteful stripes?"

"Sure, fine. Just as long as I'm not sent out naked."

"I believe there are still ordinances in place prohibiting such measures." Oom clunked off to do whatever he does when he's not around me. They've never bothered to install a sense of humor in domestic bots. Seems to me humans and machines would get along better if they had.

I finished off my breakfast, dressed in something brown with tasteful yellow stripes, and rode down to the car-loft. They just installed a glass-enclosed elevator into the building recently, but I never take that one. I'm usually still partly dressed on my way out and don't want people to see me fiddling with my shoes or scratching my butt.

In the car-loft was Nak-Pik-Zom, the oldest robot I have ever met. He had originally some civil maintenance kind of job—working in sewers or cleaning gutters or disposing of autumn leaves—something like that, before they reprogrammed him for the car-loft. The cheap bastards who own the building didn't want to buy new, and the city was giving away its old robots for practically nothing.

"Good morning, Mr. Anderson," Nak called as I stepped off the elevator. His voice always sounded like telephone operator trapped inside a toaster.

"Hey Nak, how's it goin'?"

"I noticed you had a little dent in your car when you came in last night."

"Did I?"

"You seemed a little inebriated."

"Mmh." I don't remember running into anything. Or did I?

"Must've switched on autopilot somewhere along the way. Got in safe. I didn't have permission to bang out the dent, but I did give it a polish this morning to make it look a little better."

"Thanks, Nak; I appreciate it."

"No trouble at all. Good luck on your rounds."

"I'll need it." Nak wasn't kidding. There was a big old gash on the left front of my Mitsubishi. Good thing I don't invest in expensive cars. I fired it up, pulled it out of its space, gave Nak a parting wave, and off I went into the sky in search of appointment number one.

∗   ∗   ∗

First up was in some boutique on the 20th floor of the Rembrandt Building. It's in the fashion district and it boasts a number of couturiers mostly midline for the barely bourgeoisie. It was Madame Celec's Shop. I always think of celery when I think of Madame. Not only because her name sounds like celery, but she often eats it in front of your face.

"Monsieur Andersoanne!" She's from Brooklyn. I don't know why the fake French accent. Well . . . actually I do know why. Would you buy anything from Brooklyn? "How are you today? We are so 'oppy to 'ave you 'ere! It's been too long! When was the last time?"

"Three weeks ago."

"Ah yes, how stupid of me! But before that we had barely seen you, yes?"

"Yes. You haven't offered much in my line of work."

"We will change that right now! We 'ave a new model for you, all lined up! You will print a great review of us, Oui?"

"That depends on what you've got. What've you got?"

"Right zis way, Monsieur Andersoanne! In our private collections. A new model off the Kilgar line—custom adapted. Our own label on the merchandise. You try, yes?"

"I'll give it a whirl."

She led me to a back room, covered with a velvet curtain. Couturiers liked theatrics, as if they we unveiling the Venus de Milo with every new product. Inside was a machine dressed as a French maid (no kidding—talk about antique sensibilities).

"Zis is Demura." (Ugh!) "She will be of service to you, no?"

"Oui, Madame," the machine sounded like an airport terminal voice through a comb covered in wax paper.

"I shall leave you alone so that you two can do your best!" Madame Celec left, and there I stood in front of a French Maid coat rack wearing a big pasty smile on its "face". Sex with robots is not illegal (after recent court rulings) because there really is no injured party—except the sucker (sorry for the pun) who likes to throw away money on stupid items. That's why I have a job in the first place. I don't remember how I got into this business. If I did, I wouldn't tell you.

"What vould you like done, Monsieur?" Good God, a phony French accent in a machine yet.

"What are your specialties . . . um . . . Demura?"

"I am programmed to zatisfy all Monsieur's demands. You 'ave only to command."

"Uh . . . okay. Let's start with the usual and work our way up to something."

"As Monsieur wishes!"

"You can drop the "Monsieur" for my sake. That's not going anywhere."

"Oui." 'She' clunked over to the mattress in the corner and stood politely waiting for commands. "Shall it be Americaine or European to start?"

"Beg, pardon?"

"Americaine or European?" When I still didn't follow she showed me by opening 'her' arms and legs straddling the corner of the mattress. Then, demonstrating again, 'she" turned around and presented her/its posterior to me. "Americaine or European?"

"I guess we'll go American. One should walk before one runs."

*   *   *

I was given a half-hour, with an extra complimentary time to take it up to an hour. I didn't use all of the hour, but I spent a good 45 minutes perhaps. When I came out Madame Celec was at the bar, eating celery like Bugs Bunny with a carrot. I half expected her to say, "What's up, doc?"

"And 'ow was it, Monsieur? Did I not tell you I import high-quality?"

"Now Gertie, you know I never give out reports pre-review!" I used Gertie, short for Gertrude, which is her real name. Her face soured for a brief second before regaining her composure and replacing that with her smiling public (French) face.

"Aww, zat's not fair! Not even a little tip for old time's sake?"

"Not even for old friends. Thanks for the invite. See you again soon, I imagine."

"Let us hope so, Monsieur Andersoanne. Visit us often—even if you're not on za clock."

I left her and her cotillion of humans and near-humans behind as I boarded the elevator, and kept Madame Brooklyn worrying until tomorrow when the review came out. She was a good egg, after all, but I had my professional ethics to abide by (I hear you laughing). For all its pretence, Madame Celec had a clean and reliable service, and her fem-bots—while perhaps not state of the art—were rather highly rankable. Perhaps not Dom Perignon quality—but certainly a good Tattinger. I gave the little 'French Maid' a (***)—three out of four stars. Madame Celec will be pleased and feel the wait was worthwhile.

*   *   *

Next on my list was a luncheon with the Editor. He was a craggy-faced man with a craggy personality . . .

"It's the new downloadables the kids want these days!" he was saying as he was spitting over his glass of Lambrusco. "The kids want downloadables! They don't want to go to some goddamn shop or some goddamn synthetic whorehouse or even some goddamn mall to get some goddamn robotic piece of ass! They want it right in their own homes now off their entertainment centers! Even home delivery is losing its charm now that they found a way to send robot sex programs over the internet. You've got to start reviewing more downloadables! Chrissakes, this is a goddamn business we are in with a goddamn competitive market! Our publication is falling behind everybody else, goddamn it!"

"You know my reaction to downloadables is the same as my reaction to condoms—whatever they boast, it's like having sex while wearing a weather balloon. There's something artificial about it!"

"Artificial? Hell! You're in the goddamn artificial sex game! It's going to goddamn well seem artificial, no matter what you do! But I'm not paying you for your goddamn philosophy, I'm paying you to review those goddamn sex machines for our goddamn entertainment section! If you can't do that properly, I'll get somebody else!"

"Now, you don't mean that." Brassley—that was my editor's name, and appropriate his name was too, as he was never one to mince words—or use efficient grammar.

"The hell I don't! And what about the home visits? You were doing some of those but stopped."

"I kept getting all kinds of perverted engineers with new ideas showing up at my door at odd hours when my address got out as excepting home visits. That's gotta stay out."

"But a full 33 percent of those who rent sex robots use home visits! That's a sizeable readership who search for your column!"

"All right, but we have to make other arrangements. Send them to the office. Send them to a hotel room. They just can't come to my apartment anymore."

"As long as they subscribe to our site, you can send them to the fuckin' Moon for all I care. But you've got to review more of them—and those downloadables!"

"Jesus!" I made Brassley pay for the check—which sent him off on a tirade. Sure I hate him, but I also love him. And he loves me. We've worked together for 20 years now. I was one of the first to start to review sex-bots, first in print and then on video on the company's own channel. I'm still one of the most followed and highest paid reviewers in the industry. Hard to believe, I know.

*   *   *

Next was a visit to a public utility where they offer way-stations for guests of the city. It has become mandatory to have booths set up for visiting state assembly. Being a municipal project—they aim for the cheap, but at least they've got accommodations. I was introduced to a little room that had a mechanical torso on it with head and arms.

"Hellaoh," the thing said. "I'm Waverly," it spoke with a British accent, like somebody's butler from an old movie. Foreign accents seem to be all the rage these days in sex-bots. It's a fad. And like all fads there is no rhyme or reason to it. "Actually, I'm Universal 3-115-12. But you may call me Waverly."

"That's fine . . . Waverly. Do you come with a female voice?"

"I'm afraid my vocal program is stuck from the last gent who made use of my function. It seems he jammed something out of correspondence in my circuitry."

"Actually, I didn't need to know that."

"I'm sorry, sir. Will there be a problem? After all, I am programmed to do all the same functions regardless of voice. And I assure you, all my other operations are running splendidly."

"I guess that should make me happy, shouldn't it."

"Would you prefer oral, anal, or manual manipulation?"

"Anal? You have half a body!" 'He' looked like a miniature juke-box stuck on a post on a countertop.

"My manufacturers have an answer to that. You see, Universal 3-115 models were built for quick appliance use. But I was engineered for various types of stimulation."

Out of its back sprung a long crane-like winch, the kind one might find in an old-fashioned dentist's office. On the end of it was something that looked like a candy-cane stick with colored lights in it. It began to spin like a power-drill.

"Would you like to be probed, sir?" Waverly said in that polite English way.

"I'll pass," I answered. I settled for a hand-job from that clunking arm of 'his', and gave 'him' (**) two stars. That was the best it deserved, polite English manners and all. But then, it was bought with municipal money—your tax dollars at work. What would you expect?

*   *   *

I wrapped up the day at Bell Lab where they were showing off their new line of super-conducting super-cocksuckers. Only an engineer would think a faceless hose would be erotic. And what happened to Bell Lab, incidentally? Didn't they used to make phones?

The exhibit hall where they held press events was covered with the press and people within the industry. The various super-cocksuckers were displayed on platforms of different heights (they had six different models and price-ranges to choose from). They all looked like state of the art vacuum-cleaners to me. Tell me where the designers got the inspiration for this gizmo from! I bet there are still a bunch of old Hoovers and Kirbys lying around in people's basements that still work—and that teenage boys probably played with before heading off to M.I.T.

There were girls (real ones—humans that is) in glittering scant costumes and metallic makeup draping the hoses around themselves seductively to show off the product. People snapped pictures like the unveiling of a new product-line of cars. Everyone was served complimentary champagne and cheese something-or-others.

Anyway . . . we were all invited to a free suck (they even had adapters for women). The smallest gizmo fits on the dashboard of your car (isn't it tough enough to drive a flying car?), and the biggest was apparently aimed at conquering nations. It was like a hookah that a party of twelve could enjoy together. The central unit looked like it would clean a football stadium. From what I hear (literally—by all of the squealing), the women's modal unit was a big hit.

I took the more moderate home-sized version, the one they expected to be their biggest seller. As long as you don't mind the noise (it could get awfully loud), and as long as you don't mind its impersonality (it does come with an I-Pod and eyescreen for downloading your favorite porn—which I did take) it actually isn't too bad. I gave it (**`) two and a half stars.

*   *   *

When I got home it was late. Oom-Vac-Voom brought me pipe and slippers. Somebody who designed him also designed pet dogs. Luckily I live in a tobacco optional building. A rarity that one pays a high price for. I'm not a big smoker, but the quaint notion of a tobacco pipe does help me relax, so what the hell, what's a few extra hundred credits?

I went to my apartment's studio, wrote up my reviews and sent them to Brassley. Then I added a few extra paragraphs to my blog (after checking the insidious comments I usually get from people), and then finished up my tv review with my home studio camera and sent that in to CNN. Oom-Vac-Voom entered just as I wrapped up.

"Shall I turn down your bed, sir?" Oom asked.

"Fix me a Brandy Manhattan first," I answered.

"Very good, sir. And were our excursions successful today?"

"Enough to keep you well oiled for a few more months."

"I shall take that as a yes. Is Mister Brassley still being crotchety?"

"He was born crotchety. But I'll keep him in line. I'm still too valuable."

Oom handed me my I-Book. "I clicked on the Collected Works of Emily Dickinson for your night reading," Oom stated, "You seem to prefer her on restless days."

"Thanks, Oom. Emily. She lived in a simpler time."

"And unattached to men."

"I wonder what she'd have thought of my business. What I write. What I do."

"Do you still intend to write that novel of yours?" Oom asked, leaving for the bar.

"Some day. Some day. When words count for something again."

I went to my bedroom and shouted, "December." The ceiling over my bed immediately exploded into a planetarium's view of the December night sky—Orion poised in the south just as it should be. I undressed and crawled into bed, my I-Book alight with Emily Dickinson, my drink on the bedstand where Oom placed it. It's a weird sort of life I lead, I thought to myself. I guess it's no weirder than anybody else's these days—just different. Twenty more years to retirement. I need to go to the vitamin store.

BLISS ACADEMY

"Have you been Blissed?" she said, eyes staring wide.

"Blessed?" I asked her in all innocence, trying to correct or clarify.

"No, Blissed," she said again.

"Uh . . . no," I answered, unsure of what was expected of me.

"Welcome to Bliss Academy," she extended a formal greeting. "Come and be Blissed."

She . . . here listed, was a member of the academy: maybe 40 years old, thin and drawn, eyeglasses, plain, short dirty brown hair, completely invisible in a crowd of say, 6 people. She was the type who was somebody or other's sister, never dated, never got invited out with friends—basically had no life beyond her job as an accountant's secretary—until Bliss Academy. She wore jeans and an old sweater, stood at the doorway with a clipboard in her hand and scratched off my name. A friend had invited me and said, "You have to check this out! It's better than sex—only without the mess!" Humoring him and always up for something new, I agreed and found myself here. She handed me a cushion. On her sweater was a nametag that stated: "Hello, My Name Is . . . Sarah." I was given one too that said, "Hello, My Name Is . . . Bill." Somebody sharpied my name in for me—apparently that is one of the services at Bliss Academy . . . you will never have to spell your name again. Along with the nametag I was given, of course, the little, round, blue cushion. Stenciled on it in blazing white letters was the phrase: "Tush-Cush." And underneath that was written: "To Be Blissed Upon."

"We're so happy you came!" Sarah said, apparently meaning it. "You'll like it. It's better than sex—only without the mess!" I wondered what Sarah actually knew about sex, assuming she had never had any; but didn't say anything. I just smiled politely, took my cushion, and entered the room. With the exception of Sarah, I was the skinniest person in the room—and I'm about 10 pounds over what I should be. I actually eat right, exercise when I can; but I do have an office job, I am middle-aged, and weekends are spent mowing the lawn—and that's about it. In my clothes I look fine. Out of my clothes—well, you can see the love-handles (that's where the 10 pounds lie) but you couldn't even call me plump . . . maybe out-of-shape. The people in this room, however, had asses the size of steamer trunks. I imagine all of their energy was routed towards being spiritual (in between meals), and except for that gustatory indulgence probably had little to do with the earth plane.

The room was a big empty office type with no furniture with the big overhead fluorescents turned off. It was probably a real estate office before Bliss Academy got their claws on it. There were possibly 50 people in the place, all on Tush-Cushes. It seems there were even super-sized Tush-Cushes for the super-sized tushes. The smell of incense was everywhere. Each person had a little plastic bottle of water—Evian, I think—perched next to them. Spirituality is thirsty business, and who cares if you fill up the landfill sites with hundreds of plastic water bottles. The earth will dissolve them in 500,000 years anyway.

Everybody seemed to know each other, as there was a lot of low-level buzzing going on while people re-acquainted themselves with each other. Some were steady members of Bliss Academy. I was just a visitor. One woman (they were mostly middle-aged women here) leaned over towards me, seeing me sitting alone, and said, "Your first time?" I just nodded. "You'll like it. It's better than sex."

"Only no mess," I answered her. She laughed like it was the first time she heard that. I began to wonder if this was a standard sales pitch—a slogan of the school. I looked up and at the top of one of the walls was a banner that said those exact words. I picked a spot near the front. I didn't know it was the front until everybody looked towards an extra large cushion at one end of the room. Two women in frumpy long tunics and yellow buck-teeth were placing flowers around it. That's when Dale arrived. Dale is my friend from work.

"Sorry I'm late," he said, setting his Tush-Cush next to mine. "I got hung up in traffic. How do you like the place?"

"It's alright, I guess. I don't know. Nothing's happened yet."

"You'll like it, it's—"

"Better than sex?"

He nodded, "Only without the mess."

Somebody rang a bell, and all the buzzing in the room stopped. They turned to the "front". A barefoot woman with thick glasses and long gray-streaked hair came out and stood before the crowd. "Welcome to Bliss Academy!"

They all said, "Hoo-hah!"

"This is a place where one can feel at home, at peace, and truly feel your connection to the universe!"

"Hoo-hah!"

"For you are a child of the universe. The universe is there for you to play in. The universe loves you. And tonight play in it we shall!"

"Hoo-hah!"

"I would now like to bring out the Academy's supervisor, Dr. Embert Tranquility! Dr. Tranquility? . . ." Applause.

A little bald, wizened man came shuffling out in slippers with a colostony bag strapped to his side. "Thank you, Eleonore," he said, "Our academy's secretary, Eleonore Peace, everyone." More applause. "When I first formed Bliss Academy," he continued, "the goal was to find a place where spiritual pursuits would take precedence, and that we could commune with each other, with nature, with people from outer space, and with the universe itself in total peace and harmony."

"Hoo-hah!"

Now I was starting to feel uneasy. I think it was the mention of the outer space people that did it.

"And after two years of work," Dr. Tranquility continued, "we have finally achieved that. We have our own place. We have our own nature preserve just outside the city. And we can attract some of the best spiritual teachers in the country!"

"Hoo-hah!"

I wondered what Dr. Tranquility was a doctor of—but I wasn't going to dwell on it.

"Tonight, such is the case. We have a large assembly of like-minded individuals here . . ."

"Hoo-hah!"

"Outside, we have beautiful weather. The Moon has come circle to its full beauty . . ."

"Hoo-hah!"

"I have conformation that our interstellar travelers are orbiting just over-head and are wishing us well . . ."

"Hoo-hah!"

"Interstellar travelers?" I whispered to Dale.

"Outer space beings. They're orbiting in a ship overhead."

"What? Where?"

"They're invisible. They have a force field that repels light."

"Why . . . if they're friendly?"

"They have a prime directive just like in Star Trek."

"But they communicate with these folks anyway?"

"They've been properly prepared."

"How so?"

"You're missing the lecture."

"How does this guy confirm this stuff?"

"Telepathy."

". . . and we have one of the best teachers around willing to share his experiences with us all weekend at our retreat, if you care to join us," Dr. Tranquility was saying. I had missed a few other things on his list he was praising, followed by one or two hoo-hahs. Dale shooed me off indicating he wanted to listen, so I stopped asking questions; although I had more coming.

"Tonight, I'm proud to present one of the finest in his field *(field of what, was one of my questions)*, and the author of many books, including his most recent—"40 Ways To Bliss" *(I'd have been satisfied with one, but I didn't read the book).*

"Hoo-hah!"

"I give you, Professor Wow!"

Applause.

Professor Wow stepped out of the shadows of the dimly lit room (the sun had set by this time and we were under candlelight) and shook hands with Dr. Tranquility. Eleonore Peace helped Tranquility shuffle off to a chair as Professor Wow took the 'stage.' The 'Professor' (again, I'm not sure what he was professor of) was tall and lanky with a bad comb-over. He had that look of a 55 year old virgin who read comic books.

"Thank you, Dr. Tranquility," Wow began. He had an annoying, nasal voice. "It certainly is nice to be here in your lovely center with all you lovely people. I checked out the retreat where we will be spending the rest of this coming weekend for those of you participating in our Spring Bliss Weekend. It promises to be heavenly. And our friends from above have promised to stop by for a brief moment or two with some trenchant words of advice."

"Oooooh!"

"So I hope you can all make it. For those of you who can't, we hope to get you started on the right path this evening. I understand there are a few newcomers to the group. Let's see you stand up and show us who you are."

Okay, this is something I did not want to do. Dale kept nudging me, and at his instigation others nearby took to poking and prodding me as well.

"Come on, don't be shy," Wow insisted.

About a half-dozen of us stood, I was the last to push myself into a standing position.

"Very good, welcome, nice to have you with us!" Wow stated. Then he added, "Bliss you!" This was followed by a round of, "Bliss you! Bliss you!" from everybody in the room. It sounded like one gigantic, extended sneeze. I didn't know what to do, so I bowed graciously. The other newcomers seemed to take my lead and do the same, and then we sat down.

"Very good. It's always good to see new blood." I didn't like the way he said that. "You know, I've been all over the world *(he looked like he had never left his basement—or his computer)*; I've studied with Tibetan monks in the Himalayas *(he pronounced it: Hi-MAL-yahs)*, witch doctors in the Amazon, medicine men in Mexico, Voodoo Mambos in Haiti, shamans in Siberia and in Indonesia, priests in the Vatican *(?!)*, rabbis in Jerusalem, fakirs in India, Imams in Egypt, kahunas in Hawaii . . . I was even abducted by aliens—which I spelled out in my book, "Chances of Having a Fifth Encounter," . . . but as everyone knows *(I didn't)* it was a friendly abduction *(what the hell?)*!"

"Hoo-hah!"

"But of all the places I've been to, I've come to one conclusion—the Universe is One!"

Everyone cheered. I turned to Dale. "I haven't been to any of those places and I could've told him that," I whispered.

"Shh!" he whispered back, and kept his eyes on Professor Wow.

"And of what I've learned, I'll give you a sample tonight. Tonight, we are going into trance to experience the bliss of the universe. And I've invited my outer space friends to join us—so perhaps we will see them on the way!"

"Hoo-hah!"

"I want everybody to get comfortable. Lie down if you feel so inclined." Many did feel so inclined. They pulled out blankets from somewhere and laid on them, covering themselves up with an available second. I remained seated on my Tush-Cush, but I felt like I was back in kindergarten during nap time. I just didn't have my bankee.

"And before we begin," Professor Wow was saying, "Eleonore Peace will lead us off with a song. Feel free to join in, if you know it."

Eleonore Peace stepped out in front and began to sing some tune I never heard of. She had a voice like a screen door hinge. We were supposed to close our eyes, but I kept opening mine to see how she was actually attaining those notes.

"The universe loves me . . . I love the universe . . ." she warbled, "I am at peace . . . Peace is me . . . I love everything around me . . . Everything loves me . . ." She went on and on. Some joined her, but it sure sounded like she was making this stuff up as she went. She finally stopped her parakeet screeching and Professor Wow stepped out again and began to speak slowly while tapping a little gong he had with him.

Gong. "Now I want you to feel relaxed *(this took some doing as Eleonore Peace's grating vibrations were still stuck in my nervous system)*." Gong. "And pretend you are floating on a cloud," Professor Wow intoned. Gong. "Breathe in the fresh air around you. Note that the clouds love you. Love them back." Actually, I was already tired of all this loving, but I stayed with it. "Now I want you to enjoy the wind." Gong.

I wasn't sure what "enjoying the wind" meant; but I tried to enjoy it. Professor Wow started going into this . . . "rrrrrrrrrrrr . . . rrrrrrrrrrr . . . rrrrrrrrrr" followed by a . . . "nnnnnnnn . . . nnnnnnn . . . nnnnnnnn." Was that supposed to be the wind? But then Eleonore joined in with a . . . "yyyeeeeeeeeeeee . . . yyeeeeeeeeee . . . yyeeeeeeeee." And somebody else (Dr. Tranquility?) followed with a . . . "woooooo . . . woooooo . . . woooooo."

And so it was all a kind of, "nnnnn . . . yeeeee . . . woooo," sort of experience. Gong.

Somebody else started reciting poetry. Walt Whitman, I think. Or Wordsworth. Somebody. I'm not up on poetry—it just had a familiar ring from some class I had way back when. Then Professor Wow began to incant some sort of Apache prayer that merged into a Biblical Psalm. Then he told us about floating and being the light, and more stuff people would hoo-hah to if they weren't floating in the stratosphere somewhere.

Then we were told to meet our guardian angel. I didn't. The Tush-Cush was starting to cramp me.

Then we were told to meet our friendly neighborhood space alien. I didn't, but I heard some people sobbing in the background. It sounded like someone was at a church confessional relieving himself of his sins. Another was muttering her life story. It sounded pretty boring and was far enough away so I could ignore it.

According to Professor Wow, the alien being watching over us from his armchair aboard his spaceship was named Flandu. A personal friend of Wow's it would seem. It sounded too much like fondue, so all I could think of was melted cheese and crackers. Flandu had a personal message for all of us, and we were supposed to listen. Flandu can speak telepathically to 50 different Earthling's on Tush-Cushes all at once. Someday when our civilization is advanced enough, we'll be able to do that as well.

We basked in this blissfulness for something going on an hour (or what seemed like an hour). We basked in something, anyway. Professor Wow finally stopped talking and let us "be". I could still hear some sobs and whispered confessionals in the background, but I started to nod off.

I did not get any personal message from Flandu at all, as far as I could tell. Although I did develop a craving for cheeseburgers. Gong. All too soon (supposedly) we were leaving Flandu's spaceship. Gong. We were descending through the atmosphere. Gong. We were coming back into our little Blissed room on our blissful Tush-Cushes. Gong. We were spent.

"And just think, more of this can be yours if you spend the weekend with us at the Bliss Retreat—for just $150 . . . for expenses." Professor Wow was finished. It was now time to share our experiences and our inner most secrets. I got up to pee, and on the way looked to see if the academy had any vending machines with packages of cheesy crackers in them. No such luck.

I came back and everyone was drinking water. Everyone was sharing. Everyone was caring. Hugs and tears were going all around. I wanted to go home.

"What did you think?" Dale asked me.

"Interesting," I told him, straight-faced. That was no lie, it was interesting. I just doubt I will be back.

"I told you. Worth the twenty dollars you paid in, wasn't it!"

"Can't say I experienced such before."

"Did you talk to Flandu? I didn't think he was going to do Flandu tonight. Did you talk to Flandu?"

"No. Just his landlady. She put me on hold."

"Aw. Too bad."

I like Dale. He's a nice guy. But sometimes he's just too . . . Actually, I liked these people too. There are worse things in this world than people sitting around on Tush-Cushes talking to space aliens and emanating love to rain clouds. Nazi Germany could've used a few groups like this.

Still . . . for me . . .

"Bliss you," said the thin, homely gal I met on the way in as she collected my cushion.

"Bliss to everyone," Dale answered her.

"To everyone!" she seemed enraptured by the blessing.

"And no mess," I added. I walked out the door. End of story.

Bliss you.

Hoo-hah.

MARCA'S UTERUS

They woke me up with their hammering while I was still trying to get some shut-eye. Marca was our next-door neighbor. It seems she had some lady's problem. Something about her uterus. It was upside down or inside out, or whatever happens to a uterus when it gets all cranky and bent out of shape. So they decided to fix it and fix it at home. The workmen must've come in at 6 am. The sun had barely risen. They were constructing a tent in the backyard. Clang clang, bang bang. I have no idea what they were doing. I got up—bleary-eyed and yawning—to look out the window. It seemed to be a beautiful day and from my second floor bedroom I could peer down into the neighbor's yard. Guys were bringing in big sheets of plywood and roofing tile. Flump! Onto the lawn and rose bushes. Nobody cared. At least they weren't my rose bushes.

I got up to make coffee. I'm not good at making coffee. I can barely see in the morning. I tried to go back to sleep, but all the drilling and sawing noises kept waking me. And then there was the loud talking among the crew outside my walls. A lot of, "fuck this!" and "fuck that!" stuff. Workmen are required by their unions to say, "fuck" fifty times an hour. Most go gleefully well beyond that.

So I made coffee. I was still yawning when Harvey, the cat, came by looking puzzled. It seems he didn't care for the workmen making all that noise either. Harvey by this time was, I dunno, 40 years old and 40 pounds. We had him forever. A big stupid Persian who liked to sleep. I bought him some toys years ago and he said, "fuck that!" He was apparently a union member himself at one time. Harvey would make a lot of hair and shed it all over the furniture. Then he would get up and eat, and then come back to one of his favorite nesting places—which is anywhere in the house—and make more hair to shed. He came to me all worried and grumpy, and I petted him and told him everything would be all right. Then he told me to fuck off and went back somewhere to sleep.

So I made coffee. It turned out like mud, but then I said I'm no good at making it, especially when I'm half-asleep. I stepped outside to collect the paper. Guys next door were unloading scaffolding off the truck. I didn't say anything to them and they didn't say anything to me. Every single one of them wore dirty striped dungarees splattered with paint. I watched for a moment then went back inside to listen to the weather report. I often do this though I can't justify it. I've already been outside to get the paper. Why do I need to turn on the radio to get some guy to tell me what the weather's like? I do it anyway. I sit to have a cup of mud and read the paper. After awhile the guy on the radio gets on my nerves, so I shut him off. He was covering up the noise next door, and now I became more aware of it. I was also starting to wake up.

The paper was filled with the usual mass murderers, so I went to the window. They were wheeling Marca (I assume she was somewhere in that cart thing) out of the house and into the tent. The tent was lit up like a movie studio. She was lying on some sort of wheeled stretcher covered head to foot in some shroud. I can only guess where she was under there. In a snap she disappeared into the tent. Two guys with mirrored sunglasses holding shotguns stood guard at the tent flap. I don't know where they came from.

I ate ham and eggs. I consider ham and eggs first thing in the morning something of a treat. I was treating myself to that for having been rousted out of my bed so early. I didn't have to go into work until much later that particular day, so I ate leisurely, even adding a frozen cinnamon roll into the mix.

Next door, there were more drilling noises and something that sounded like a theremin—or an electric winch with a very peculiar whine to it. I kept the windows closed—at least on that side of the house—but as it was going to prove to be a warm if not unpleasant day, opened the windows on the opposite side to let the breeze come through. Actually, it just stirred up a lot of hair on the carpet, but I kept them open anyway, despite the noise (I could still hear the stuff next door) because the air felt good. I had a second cup of mud and was starting to feel revived after my ham and eggs. Even a bit cheery, so the noise next door wasn't getting on my nerves as much.

I showered and shaved, and had some extra time, since it was still pretty early, to do some research for my work left over from last night. Where I work, every day is more or less casual Friday, and as I am a technical writer on assignment and therefore contracted out, to a certain extent I can come and go as I please. So I dressed comfortably, but not as a slob, and stepped outside to enjoy the sun for a moment and finish off my cup of mud. It must have been break time, as all the workmen were hanging around smoking cigarettes and drinking beer. Apparently these guys drink beer on their breaks, as opposed to coffee, even if it's only 8 o'clock in the morning.

"You working on Marca?" I said to one of them, just to start a conversation, and because I was curious as to the fuss.

One of the dungareed workers with a graying, unshaven look, calloused hands, and a face like the back end of a bus came over to talk. "Yeah," he said, puffing on a cigar and taking a swig from his can of beer.

"How's she doing?" I asked. I noticed that the guy smelled like Dalox.

"Oh, she's doin' alright," he answered, "Just a tougher job than we expected 's'all."

"How so?"

"It's the damn clitoris," he continued, scratching his nose, "Clitoris is often the problem in a case like this. Had to get the winch out."

"I thought I heard something like—"

"Yeah . . . you never know what yer gonna run into in these situations," he started to pick his nose and check his finger for boogers. A young, skinny, gawky colleague of his with a face like a horse came up beside him, taking a chaw of tobacco between his teeth and spitting on my lawn, killing the crab grass.

"We had to use the vise grips!" the young guy was saying in a rather slurpy manner.

"Those bar vises can take a lot of tension as long as you don't torque 'em," the older man added having finished his nose inspection.

"I had heard she was suffering from something—"

"Ah! Women and their fuckin' problems!" the older guy said, blowing out a cloud of smoke.

"What exactly is the issue anyway?" I don't know why I kept asking this guy questions.

"Beats the shit outta me. I just work here," the old guy sucked on his beer can. "You have to ask the doc."

"Somethin's wrong with the u-tye-russ," the younger guy explained and spit.

"Those things go haywire more than a goddamn car transmission," the older one added. "If you ask me, the damn thing's due for a re-designment."

I agreed, even though I wasn't exactly sure what he meant by "re-designment." By now these two were starting to annoy me, so I decided to head back into the house. But the doctor (I guess that's what you'd call him) was leaving the tent and heading to the house. His head looked like some kind of shrub. He had a band around his forehead that had various assorted goggles, spectacles, monocles, lights, and something like a radar antenna. He was wearing rubber gloves that looked like he had been dealing with liquid nitrogen, and was dressed in a full length white smock. He feet betrayed a pair of pink flip-flops. As he was heading into the house, one of the workmen handed him a can of beer. He didn't remove his gloves, he just grabbed the can and headed towards the door, taking a swig on the way.

"How's she doing?" I yelled. Again, I don't know what compelled me to start up a conversation. Curiosity I guess. Besides, I really didn't feel like going into work yet.

"Who are you?" he asked, not impolitely.

"I'm Marca's neighbor. I live here next door."

"Ah," he said wiping the sweat from his many tentacled brow while sucking down more beer as we approached each other. "She'll be fine," he nodded to me. "It's just a bigger job than I thought. May take hours."

"What exactly is wrong with her?"

"Oh, it's the damn u-tye-russ," the doctor complained. What, everybody pronounces it that way? "We're going to have to bang it back into shape," he continued. "I'll need more tools."

"How exactly did it get out of shape?" I asked, again why, I don't know.

"Oh, they get that way sometimes," the doctor answered. "She'll be fine, though. She's a trooper."

"Good." I answered, not knowing what else to say.

"Sent away for a new power jack. Should be here any minute."

Sure enough, a few minutes later, another truck pulled up in front—parking in my space along the front yard—and out stepped two guys who pulled something on wheels out of the trailer end with CATERPILLAR written on the back of it. They kept the tarpaulin on it, so all I could see was the bottom half of it; but they wheeled it into the back yard and into the tent on its own power utilizing just a control box with a joystick on the top of it.

Well, that's when the noise really started. And I decided I'd had enough and packed myself up to go to work. As I was heading to my car I saw Clarence—Mister Marca, that is—leaning on the fence and looking very worried. I went over to him and he gave me a slight nod as I approached.

"Don't worry," I told him, "she'll come through it. She's a strong girl."

"I know that," Clarence said, scratching his cheek, "You just hate to see it happen. But you know those damn u-tye-russes. Every now and then you just have to take care of them like this."

"How much is this all costing you?" I asked, somehow trying to make it sound comforting.

"Enough," he said glumly. "But I only have to deal with the deductible. Luckily I've got insurance."

I just gave a grunt in agreement and gave him a pat on the shoulder before I headed to my car. From the tent came the grinding, whirring noise of what sounded like a roto-rooter. It was louder than a chain-saw. I drove away thanking God I didn't have a u-tye-russ.

In the . . . excitement? . . . of the morning, I left without some important papers I was supposed to take along—and my mail. Dreading going back there, I tried to talk myself into believing I would be fine without those items. Having driven an extra mile or two, I realized I couldn't get along without them, so I turned the car around and headed back. I wondered if I would regret my return. I did—and within seconds. As I pulled up into the driveway and headed to the house, I could see over the fence and into my neighbor's yard a commotion going on. There was some little pink something-or-other bouncing up and down and running around the yard going, "*Skree! Skree! Skree!*" And all the workmen were chasing after it with hammers and pipes and baseball bats in their hands trying to whack at it. There was the usual and obligatory swearing that went along with the whole measure. Somebody dug up a bass fish-net and was going after the little thing with that. I quickly hurried into the house, got what I needed and dashed back into my car with the "*Skree! Skree! Skree!*" still ringing in my ears. I stepped on the gas and got to work as fast as I could.

Later that evening when I got home, the workmen were gone, although the yard was a mess. Clarence's lawn was all torn up with footprints and treadmarks of all shapes and sizes. I got busy with a late night phone call, and forgot to check on my neighbor to see how things went. Oh, and Harvey the cat threw up on the rug.

The next day the neighbor's house was quiet with no sight or sound of anyone or any activity. And then came the weekend and Clarence was out there fixing his lawn with a rake. Marca was up and out too, standing there in a simple smock, hanging up wash on a clothesline. She waved to me pleasantly as if nothing happened. I was tempted to ask her how she was, but I could actually see for myself, and I didn't really want to know what all had gone on. I was afraid she'd tell me. It would seem modern medical science can do some amazing things with enough help and power tools.

SUPERHEROES NEED LOVE TOO

He picked nervously at the threads of his fire engine red unitard, having discovered one of his seams was coming undone. "Y'know, sometimes when I'm in a burning building," he was saying, "and I'm trying to save the lives of twenty or thirty people at once . . . and it draws a crowd—as it usually does—I sometimes want to stop and say, 'Wow, you people really can't manage all by yourselves, can you!' I know it would be wrong. It's kind of a catty thing to say, especially at a moment like that . . . but it does cross my mind."

"Go on," the therapist said, trying to look as interested as possible.

"And then I might see this chick—sorry, this young lady . . ."

The therapist waved it off.

"I'll see this young woman, and she's really hot . . . I don't mean because of the fire . . . it doesn't have to be a burning building, y'know . . ."

"I'm following."

"And I think . . . why can't I have her?"

"Why can't you?"

"Well, you know . . . super-powers and all." He leaned over and tried to whisper secretively, "I could do some real damage, if you know what I mean!"

"I think I get the picture," the therapist responded, trying to look unimpressed—or at least unshockable.

"And it's kind of a distraction, what, with saving thirty people's lives on the top floor and all!" the Flaming Hammer complained. He was still picking at his threads, but now he forced himself to stop.

"What is it you want?" the therapist studied his thread pre-occupation, as well as his sudden retreat from that activity.

"I don't know. I guess I want to be thought of as normal. Just another guy. Y'know what I mean?"

"But you're not normal. Nobody else can fly or throw balls of fire conjured out of their hands, or melt steel with the light-rays from their eyes. You're the Flaming Hammer. You fight crime and save lives. Nobody else does that. People treat you differently because you are different. They expect more from you. You expect more from you. Don't you?"

"Yeah. But that doesn't make it easy."

"I didn't say it was easy."

"Yeah, but underneath . . . when I take off the cape and the mask and the flame retardant suit . . ."

"Why do you wear a mask, anyway?"

"It's kind of expected of me, y'know? Anyway, when I take off the suit and lounge around the penthouse in my underwear, I'm just like everybody else. I drink beer, watch a game on tv, grab a burger every now and then—'course, I can cook it in my bare hand, which not everybody does . . ."

"No one does."

"Right, no one does . . . Sometimes . . . I dunno . . . I could go for a little female companionship."

"Do you want companionship or love?"

"Well . . ."

"And do you want love or sex?"

"Actually, all of the above sounds pretty good. But in the absence of all as a package, I'll take sex."

"A mate?"

"Is that what I'm talking about?"

"You tell me."

"But where would I find such a woman?"

"Have you tried the internet?"

"No."

"I wouldn't recommend it either, especially in your case. It just seems to be what everybody is doing these days, which is why I asked." The therapist leaned back in his chair that squeaked with the slightest breath. The Flaming Hammer adjusted the little golden wings on his mask and head cover, clearing his throat. He felt uncomfortable talking about all this.

"Do you date at all?" the therapist continued.

"No. For one thing, when do I have time? There's always some type of crime going on in a city this size . . ."

"So then, we may also be speaking of a down-time issue."

"Tell me about it."

"Is there anyway you can schedule in some private time for yourself?

"Great idea, but when? Can I put on the calendar a quiet moment? Can I announce in the papers that no crimes should be committed at such-and-such day and time because I want a few private moments—and expect people to respect those demands?"

"You may be putting too much on yourself. You can't expect to stop every crime from happening, save every person from peril."

"Well, of course I can't, but people expect me to try. Hell, I'm the Flaming Hammer! I'm suppose to come to everyone's rescue! And if I don't—well, why didn't I? What was so important that I couldn't prevent this shootout, this bank robbery, this carjacking from happening? What good is a superhero if he's not around?"

"Is that you talking or what you believe to be the general public?"

"The public, of course. Maybe it's both, I dunno."

"So you may have feelings of guilt associated with this profession you've chosen."

"I guess. And it wasn't a profession I chose. It sort of chose me. What else are you gonna do with all the abilities I have?"

"You could've gone away. Lived in a peaceful location far from the city and crime. You could've become a recluse instead of donning that suit."

"Whose side are you on?"

"I'm not on any side. I'm merely stating what a person in your situation might have done. I'm not advocating it as a good or bad idea anymore than I am approving or disapproving of the lifestyle you've chosen to live. I can see, however, that the choice you did make is causing you some distress."

"Yeah. Anyway, that's not me. I'm a natural born crime-fighter. Even if I didn't have these powers."

"And if you didn't, are you saying you might have become a member of the police force?"

"Maybe. Something like that."

"Are you sure it's not the attention you get? After all, you're always in the papers and on television for one reason or another. The public loves you."

"No. Yeah. I dunno. You think it's wrong if I kinda like the attention?"

"I'm not here to say what's right and wrong about you. The attention does seem to be positive, and if I may say, mostly deserved. It's probably not something too disgraceful if you enjoy it a little. I'm just asking if you find yourself glorying in the media coverage. You do walk around in a gold-trimmed, bright red unitard and cape a lot. That's not something other people do."

"I guess there's a certain amount of show-biz in what I do. I want the crooks to see me comin' and let other people know I'm on patrol. And I do need to be able to move freely."

"Doesn't the cape get in the way?"

"On occasion. But it makes a helluva picture when I'm up in the air with the sky as a backdrop. Besides, would it be as effective if I did everything I do now in a business suit?"

"More modest, perhaps; but maybe not as effective."

"You think I'm not modest? You think this is too gaudy?"

"I don't think anything. I was asking you if you feel you do what you do to indulge in the attention, or is that just a by-product. Is all this a substitute for a woman—a close relationship—in other words?"

"Oh. I hadn't thought of it like that."

"Is that what you are coming to me about?"

"What else would I do?"

"I don't know. It seems to me you're feeling lonely, and would like, perhaps, a mate, or at least a more active, and anonymous, social life. And . . . you don't seem to be able to get that for yourself because of who you are, doing what you do. Is that correct? And if so . . . are you substituting your crime fighting posture as a compensation for the other. And if THAT is true, can you live with that, can you reconcile yourself with that—or do you need to make a change in order to find the happiness you seek?"

"Wow. That was a mouthful."

"I suppose it was, but aren't those the questions you came here to solve?"

"I guess maybe I did."

"Something to think about over the next few days. That's all the time we have today, Flaming Hammer," the therapist started scribbling in his day-planner. "Same time next week?"

"Yes. That'll be fine. Of course allowing for the usual unforeseen circumstances."

"Agreed. But just to remind you, as this seems to speak to your time scheduling issues we just covered, your therapy is going to be much more effective if we stick to a regular, steady, progressive schedule."

"I understand. Well then, same time next week. If you'll excuse me . . ."

The Flaming Hammer got up and headed towards one of the office windows.

"Oh. Use the one at the far end," the therapist cautioned, "it's much bigger and it's easier to close once you're gone."

The Flaming Hammer tossed the man a salute, went to the appropriate window, opened it, gathered up his cape, and jumped through the opening and out in to the empty air above the traffic noise, to wend his way through the wild blue yonder.

The therapist finished dotting his appointment book and went to the window. He shooed a pigeon away from the window ledge and closed the window. He returned to his desk, sat, straightened his suit, vest, and tie, and started make notes in a folder marked, "Flaming Hammer." Then he clicked on the phone console on his desk.

"Marion? Would you send the next one in please? Thank you."

LICHENS

Marie was a lichen specialist. There are big names for such things (and little pay) but take it for granted she specialized in the study of lichens. She was raised in Scotland before her wedding took her to America to live. Scotland itself specializes in lichens. She had actually been born in the Orkneys, which have nothing but lichens. The family moved to Edinburgh when she was about nine, and found herself a husband when she was twenty-two—coming right out of school . . . college, that is.

Marie was a lonely but peaceful child, having spent lots of time chipping off and poking around on the stuff that seemed painted on rocks or on the occasional tree she encountered. This led to her major in school where she met a man from the states who came to Scotland to study geology. She went back with him to northern Michigan where she spent her time picking around on rocks and trees in the U.P., and preparing for a master's degree in lichens. She completed her first year, but did most of her second through extension courses—the newlyweds were strapped for funds.

It happened when Trevor, the new husband, was away. Marie was out in the middle of some wilderness or other, not far from their home; within, say a thirty mile radius, that she discovered an itching on the back of her hand. Since she usually wore gloves when she was out in the field, it felt as if a burr or some kind of thorn had gotten stuck between it and her skin. She pulled off her glove and shook it out. Nothing came. She felt around inside of it and found nothing. There was a little red mark on the back of her hand where she had been scratching, but nothing out of the ordinary. She found a good sized rock to sit on and planted herself there studying her hand. As it was late March, and cloudy, and damp, as late March in northern Michigan tends to be, she felt like lounging around on a cold, clammy rock. She wanted to finish taking her sample and head out. She put the glove back on, and resumed her work.

But the itching started again. This time she scratched through the glove with more energy than previously. Still nothing when she checked her hand again. She finished her work despite a bothersome, repeated itch, even dowsing her hand with water from her canteen and applying a little camper's soap and moisturizer to it. The twenty some mile drive home was punctuated with the occasional itching spell as well. She turned the radio on to keep her mind off it.

Once home, she washed her hands thoroughly, stored her gear and samples, then made sure she showered completely before heating herself some canned soup and bread for an impromptu supper. She lit a fire in the fireplace and watched some television as she ate. It was mostly the same old news about how the world was going to hell, and she didn't feel like listening to all the pundit commentary, so she shut off the set and tried reading from a magazine as she set aside her dishes and curled up on the couch in her flouncy white bathrobe.

She awakened with a start and found that she had been asleep for hours. The house was now quite dark, and she was unsure of what time it was. It made no sense to stay cramped up on the couch, so she trundled off to the bathroom, unconcernedly scratching her hand on the way. She turned on a light, went to the medicine cabinet, and pulled out a toothbrush and toothpaste. She stared bleary-eyed at herself in the mirror while unscrewing the cap on the toothpaste tube. As she started applying paste to brush she noticed a brown spot on the back of her hand where all the itching had come from. She let out a short, perplexed gasp as the appearance of such a spot, not much bigger than a nickel, but big enough, surprised her. Also surprising was that, at the moment, it didn't itch. But it did feel sore, like a bruise.

She found some medicinal cream in the cabinet and swathed the brown spot in goop before finishing up her teeth and going to bed. That night she dreamt of strange worlds completely unpopulated by people. It was as if she were a tourist on another planet. Unusual vistas stood before her—mostly of barren rock and wind-carved hills with little or no vegetation and no animal life. The sky was sometimes light brown, sometimes purple, sometimes a variable spectrum of pale to navy blue. She would reach a hilltop and look beyond and some other kind of terrain would pop up covered in sand or freshly spewed igneous rock. When she took the trouble to look at herself, she was barefoot and wearing her white flouncy bathrobe. High cirrus clouds drifted over head and she thought she heard distant thunder, but nothing that would indicate a storm was coming.

When she awoke, she found herself rumpled up in her bedclothes and covered in sweat. She was a bit stiff and headachy. She put on her robe and shuffled to the bathroom. She had a repugnant taste in her mouth and an odd smell in her nose from what source she couldn't locate. When she looked in the mirror she was awakened from her stupor to discover a brown spot on her face—about the size of a nickel. She studied it. Poked it. And then took a look at the hand doing the poking—which in the mirror seemed to have gotten worse. Surely, the entire back of her hand was now a grayish brown and flaky. It looked sort of like it was covered in lichen.

She ran her hand under water and tried scrubbing it off. It just peeled to reveal more layers. She ran to her study to look at all her samples of the stuff she had been collecting for her field work. She had been scrupulous about putting things into sealed containers. Of all her samples, nothing looked like the stuff she had on her hand.

She decided to call in to the field hospital and ask somebody if anyone there knew of what sort of infection she had picked up. They told her to come in to the outpatient clinic and they'd check it out right away. She got herself dressed, being careful how she held her hand and what it rubbed against, got in her car, and headed down the highway.

While still on the rather remote road the couple used to get to their home, Marie's car developed a flat, and she found herself pulling over to the side of the road, parking it in among weeds and brush that were just sprouting up with the season next to the pavement.

She knew that there might be no traffic along the way for hours, so she did her best to repair the tire herself.

Things became more complicated when the car fell off the jack. It must've been something about the way she placed it. It must have been something about the soft spring mud that the car found itself parked in as it fumbled along off the asphalt and into the newly sprouting weeds—for the road had no real shoulder. Whatever the cause, as she was trying to change the tire, the car slid off the jack and into the mud, stranding her. She was luckily away far enough from the vehicle at the time not to be injured; but not far enough away to send a plethora of shouted obscenities to her ride and not create an echo effect.

It was too far to go anywhere else but home. So she spent the rest of the morning hours walking back. When she reached home, she spent a little while resting in a chair, then called the hospital. It seems her needs were not serious enough for them to send an ambulance for her, so she spent some time cruising through her phone listings to see who she could call that might be near by that could play temporary taxi service for her.

She finally left a message on the machine of her friend Lillian who usually was home by 3pm. Then she visited the bathroom. She now found another brown patch on the other side of her face, and the first facial patch was starting to gray and flake like her hand. She had had gloves on the entire time she'd been outside and hadn't bothered to remove them. When she did she found that most of her hand had now browned out. And, to her horror, her other hand had spots on it as well. As soon as she became aware of the infection, all of them started to itch. As she scratched she found big hunks of what must have once been flesh pepper off of her and into the sink. She screamed and forced herself to stop scratching.

She put cream on her hands and face again, gauzed up her hands, and put new gloves on them. Then she tried Lillian again—just the answering machine—again. She tried to calmly state her problem to Lillian's little voice recorder, but she was clearly frustrated by not being able to reach anybody, and by the speed with which whatever skin illness she had was progressing. She was now very worried and some of that shakiness resounded in her voice as she spoke into the phone at nobody.

She made herself some tea, and tried to keep her mind off of her ills by watching television, but kept coming back to her condition as it seemed to be getting worse by the hour. Finally the phone rang. She ran to answer, expecting Lillian. It was not, it was somebody else. Her neighbor . . . her neighbor of about five miles down the road.

"I found your car in a ditch not far from our farm," the man was saying. He was 60 something, perhaps 66. His name was Greeley. Marie had barely spoken to him since they moved in—but that was only months ago, and they really hadn't had time to socialize a lot with the other people in the county. Typical of rural U.P., things were spread out and the area was hardly densely populated. Greeley remembered her, and her car, from a couple of chance meetings in town.

"I'll see what I can do to get the tractor to pull it out," Greeley was saying, "I'll do what I can to help with that tire . . . but I may have to wait until my son comes home for that."

"Please, if you could, the car can wait. I was on my way to hospital. I was wondering if you could take me there instead."

"Why? What's wrong?"

"I'm . . . not sure," she thought better of explaining the situation, "I just think I need to see a doctor."

"Well . . . I don't know," he answered, "The wife's gone into town and took the truck with her. All I got is the tractor. Can it wait? Either she or my son should be back within the hour—I would think."

"Uh . . . yes . . . yes, I suppose I can wait that long. But let me know the minute either of them comes home."

She hung up unsure of what to do. Was she to convince the old man that he should place her on his lap for the 17 mile ride into town on a tractor that chugs along at 10 m.p.h. in 40 degree weather? She took some more headache tablets and tried to lay down to rest—though resting was the last thing she felt like doing.

The phone rang. She wasn't sure where she was at first. The room was dark. What had happened? She'd fallen asleep again, though she didn't remember nodding off, and she certainly didn't remember dreaming this time. Where was she? She had apparently sauntered off to the bedroom, though she didn't remember doing that. She stepped into the living room. Her headache came back. The phone kept on ringing. The answering machine clicked on before she could get there. It was Lillian, asking how she was and what she wanted. Lillian hung up before Marie could pick up the phone. The living room was a kind of fuzzy gray. The sun had set maybe 20 minutes ago. The room was darkening by the minute, but it wasn't the pitch black darkness that marks the middle of the night.

She checked the answering machine. Just Lillian's message. Nothing from the neighbors about the car or the trip to the hospital. She called Lillian right back and got another voice mail. Does that bitch spend her entire life on the phone? She tried to reach the neighbor and the phone kept ringing. These people don't even believe in answering machines. She hung up and wandered into the bathroom searching for more headache tablets. She turned on the light, and reaching for the medicine cabinet saw herself in the mirror. She screamed. Her entire face was gray.

She dressed in whatever fashion she could muster. She kept the lights off, she didn't want to see herself, but in the dim light, she could tell both her arms were flaky and scratchy like a lichen covered tree. She could no longer wait for the Lillians or next door neighbor farmers. She put on hat and coat and hiking boots and headed out the door.

A 17 mile walk was in store for her through the night. And it would take all night.

*   *   *

When Trevor arrived home, he found the place a mess. And no sign of Marie. He checked the mail, checked the answering machine. There was Lillian's message. And there was a message left by the neighbor asking him to stop by as soon as possible. It sounded urgent. Trevor didn't know the neighbors any better than Marie did. It was unusual to be invited over to their home on such short notice and for something that seemed to be important.

He drove over to the place, not knowing what to expect. The old man greeted him at the door. "I've got something to show you," he said cryptically. Then he led Trevor out behind the house and out into the field somewhere.

"Isn't that Marie's car?" Trevor asked, noticing it parked in the driveway.

The old man nodded, "Broke an axle pulling it into the driveway with the tractor. Your wife called and said she had a flat down the road. Right fender was buried in the mud when I arrived. Took me all afternoon to chain it to the tractor and pull it out of there. Right about that time my son came home. I immediately sent him out to your place to pick up your wife. Said she had been feelin' poorly and wanted somebody to take her into town to see the doctor. When he got there she was gone."

"You know where she is?"

"Hasn't come back yet?"

"Not that I'm aware. I just got home myself. I've been on a business trip for a few days."

"Well . . . maybe she's safe. I don't know if I have good news for ya."

"What did you want to show me?"

"Y'know, there's all kinds of legends about creatures in the forest around here. Number of people seen bigfoot. I haven't. Thought it was all talk.

Never any proof. Up until this morning." They stepped passed a small grove of trees and onto another field where some type of sooty shape lay on the ground in the mud. "My son saw it first. Wandering around yesterday morning. Didn't know what it was. Some kind of critter. Awfully big. It came back and started spookin' the dogs. He saw it creepin' around just before sunset. Took out his rifle plugged a couple of holes in that thing. It's right over here. Thought of calling the sheriff first thing this morning, then I noticed the cover on its back. Decided to call you first."

They stopped before a crumpled body, hard to discern what it was. It was all gray and flaky and twisted up in a ball. It also smelled of pungent mold.

"It's decayin' mighty fast," the old man said. Trevor knelt down for a closer look. Dusty patches of it were blowing off in the wind the way the ashes of a flaming newspaper waft into the air. It did resemble something human. Bigfoot?

"That thing on its back . . . ain't that yer wife's jacket?"

The jacket was all torn and muddy, but it was indeed Marie's winter jacket. The figure was like some kind of abstract sculpture in moldy ash of a human. It had no other garments on it except the jacket. Something that resembled a hand seemed to have atrophied in position of raking itself across its own flesh. Through the dried mud could be seen bullet holes in the jacket.

"I hate to say this, but I think that thing may have killed your wife and taken her jacket. I don't know what it is, but it may have . . . well . . . I can't say what a thing like that feeds on."

Something about the face—what was left of it . . . Trevor stood up in horror. "It's not bigfoot," he said.

THE FLIES

He had collapsed in the alley. Old man. Night. Dirty part of town. Streetlights withering. No traffic. No people. But you could hear the rumble of a metropolis in the distance. This is the part of town everyone forgets about. Only criminals. When they bother. But they usually don't. Criminals robbing from criminals. Makes no sense. So nearly everyone stays away. Except the rats. And those who are the most unfortunate. The homeless. The sick. The needy. The mentally deranged. Like this guy. Around the corner was the church. Still occupied. The priest must have been sent here because the bishop hates him. He's a wilderness missionary, just like those who go off to the jungles of New Guinea to convert the natives. Only here, his mission is in town. The church was old—by American standards anyway. Nearly 300 years old, and ill-kept. At one time it must have been beautiful. Black brick. Old world style. Tall, tall steeple. Inside some of the walls covered with patchy broken marble slabs. Gargoyles on the roof. Statues of water-stained saints and angels inside and out—weathered wood as if they had been at the front of sailing ships. It even had a little garden courtyard surrounded by overgrown vines and rusting wrought iron fences. A broken fountain and a bird bath coated with lime from water two centuries ago.

Nobody comes here. Except the wretched. Mass is still held on Sundays—to no more than a dozen. The organ wheezes through hymns like an old hotel heat radiator. The priest is in his 50s, perhaps the youngest priest to ever serve here. The organist and the ground's keeper are still leftovers from the Civil War. They should have died generations ago, and perhaps did, but nobody told them. Something animates them, so they keep on going.

Then there was the old guy in the alley. After midnight. They called me to deal with him. Why they didn't use common sense and call 9-1-1 I don't know. I had some field experience with this. I said some. And I knew the priest . . . from an old case I had worked on before; a case that was similar to this—before Father Grimes (that was his name, by the way) was banished here.

"William . . ." he always called me William, even though no one including my Mother calls me that. "William . . . remember that strange case you dealt with years ago? . . . I think I have another just like it . . ."

So I came. In the middle of the night. To this end-of-the-earth part of town. Like an idiot. To look at some old guy throwing up in an alley.

"What do you think?" Father Grimes asked.

I just stared down at the crumpled, but still living body of the nameless wreckage of a man that should have died before I was born. "I don't know," I answered. "Let's take him inside. And be careful how you touch him."

Father Grimes got an old blanket from somewhere that we placed on the ground next to the old fool. Then we shoved him with our feet until he rolled onto it, and dragged him into the courtyard via the blanket. We couldn't hoist him on the bench, light as his emaciated frame actually was. We just left him lie there.

"Well . . . you're the expert," Father asked, waiting for me to say anything. I just stood there and stared down at the poor beleaguered victim.

"First time I saw this was in the Orient," I finally told him. Which was true. One of those crummy little rivers that snake through the jungle and try to make it to the sea before being headed off at the pass by another bigger river, somewhere in the central stretch of Vietnam close to the Cambodian border. Then I saw it again many years later in San Francisco, in a cheap hotel in an undercover red-light district buried in Chinatown. Now here. Both previous times the incidents were hushed up. I often wondered if incidents in southeast Asia spurred it on—or if this is something old as the hills that never got much publicity. And somebody sees to it that it never does.

"You haven't called anybody in authority to handle it?"

"Just you. I thought I'd try you first."

"I'm hardly an authority to treat this kind of thing."

"But you do know as much about it as anybody. People around here wouldn't know what to do with him."

Father was right. He was there in San Francisco the first time we saw this breakout. Somebody in his parish. An old whore, if I remember correctly. Now it's just a homeless guy who stopped into the church on occasion to get out of the rain. This is the first Caucasian type I've seen to be afflicted. So race has no boundary like some strains of certain afflictions.

"What do we do?"

"Get me a glass of water." Father turned to go. "And some rubber gloves if you've got any."

"The janitor has some." Off he went.

I continued to stare down at the poor old bastard. "Hey there, old man; what's your name?"

The man could barely respond. I could see he was in the grip of some intense pain. He was probably scarcely conscious of my presence. His head rose slowly up to look at me, but his eyes were very foggy. As far as I knew, he was looking at giant daffodils swaying in a pink sky. He tried to speak, but the only thing he could utter was something like, "Agggh . . . ugggccchhkk!" And even then it came across almost as a whisper.

Father returned with water and gloves.

"Do you know who he is?"

"No. No idea where he came from either. Just shows up from time to time."

"How long ago did you detect this in him?"

"Just when I found him in the alley. And I called you. I brought a flashlight. Thought we'd need it."

"Good thinking." I put on the gloves and took the flashlight from the priest, and shown the light down on the old guy. His face was breaking out in purple blotches. I waved my hand in front of the guy's face. No reaction. He was doubled up and contorted in suffering. Waves of pain shocked him in spasms.

"Your man was doing some cleaning in the rectory, wasn't he?"

"Yes."

"Does he have any dust masks?"

"Yes, he does."

"Bring them. Put one on yourself."

The Father left. I tried to help the old man take a sip of water. It took several attempts but I finally succeeded. I could tell the man was actually very thirsty, but he howled in agony with the one and only sip. By the time I was able to let the old man lie comfortably down, the priest was back with the masks. He handed me one and I put it on right away.

"Did you see his reaction to the water?"

"Saw it from the window."

"I'm afraid there's nothing much we can do for him." I clicked the flashlight back on and used it as a pointer. "See there? Swollen patches on his temples. It's got his brain as well as his guts. It's just a matter of time. All you can do now is wait for the results of the autopsy."

"Dear God," Father Grimes mumbled. "I should give him his last rights. Of course, I don't know his name."

I'm an atheist. I don't care for all this God stuff. But I know it comforts people, and right now that crumpled up once-a-human-being needed comfort. "I don't think it matters, Father. God knows his name."

Father Grimes knelt down and began giving the man absolution on the spot. The old fellow seemed oblivious to what the Father was doing. Hopefully he somehow understood.

"Oh dear Jesus!" the priest said, standing up suddenly.

Little maggots were seen crawling over the old guy. They seemed to be popping out of his skin.

"Stand back," I told the priest.

"I haven't finished absolution!"

"Finish it quick! We've got to go."

Father Grimes went through the remaining motions and the gibberish and the Hail Marys or whatever the Hell he does at times like this, and then I quickly pulled him out of the line of fire. We stood behind a tree nearby to watch, like gawking tourists staring at the remains of a train wreck.

The old man let out a few more grunts and groans and settled back, eyes glossed over, opened mouthed. Out of his mouth came flying dozens and dozens of little flies. They swarmed over head in the middle of the garden. I looked them over with the flashlight, but the light seemed to attract them, so I switched it off before the Father and I were enveloped by them.

Nor was this enough to kill the old man. He continued to grunt and groan in agony as more flies came spilling out of his mouth, more little white maggots shorter than my fingernail came worming their way out of the pores of his skin.

"Got any paint thinner, alcohol, something combustible?"

"I suppose. Why?"

"I don't think we should wait for an autopsy."

The Father stared at me for several moments—horrified.

"He's not going to die, you know. Not for awhile. In the meantime he's going to be manufacturing more of those little things. And they can infect others. You've seen the results. Do you want that?"

Father Grimes said nothing. He reluctantly headed back into the rectory to get what we needed. "And bring some bug spray!" I hollered after him.

The flies continued to swarm over their groaning victim. For all I knew, it was their mating dance. Sex in flight over a still living, rotting corpse. The flies were little enough that they could find a way inside—where they were dangerous. Ears, nose, mouth, sometimes they even aim for the eyes, but that's a too narrow gap for them. It's just irritating to have them crash into you wherever you look. Crush enough of them against your skin and their combined bodily fluids leave a kind of poison behind that can leave a bad rash on your skin for days.

I stayed where I was and did nothing but watch as the old man suffered and moaned with thousands of bugs crawling or flying out of him.

When the Father returned with supplies in hand, I gave him the job of supplying cover with the can of insecticide. Thankfully normal bug spray is enough to kill them. They survive by sheer numbers.

"When we go, pay no attention to what I'm doing. Do your best to blast all of the little buggers out of the sky. Use the whole can."

"And you're doing what?" I didn't answer, I just glared at him. "This is brutal!"

"You want the infection to spread?"

Father Grimes may have been a man of God, but he was also clearly terrified of the implications. He said nothing. I pulled my coat over my head, so did he, so that we looked like we were somehow playing "ghost". An eerie analogy I admit. With that we charged into the middle of the garden. Father led the way, spraying and spraying with a kind of righteous fury. The bugs scattered through the poisonous cloud Father was conjuring. I could see clumps of the little critters falling out of the sky like raindrops. Good thing they were easily effected.

I went over to the old man and kicked him in the head. Several times.

"What are you doing?!"

"Pay attention to what you're doing!"

"This is murder!"

"The man's dead already, he just doesn't know it. Besides, I'm not going to do this to a living person!" I said as I started pouring wood alcohol over the old man's body. I kicked his head once more, just to be sure. His head squirted like it was jelly surrounded by the soft-shell of a pumpkin. And I found my pants leg covered with lots of little maggots in the process. Not thinking, I quickly squirted alcohol on my leg, which drove them off, but made me vulnerable.

"You fool!" he hollered. He pulled something out of his pocket—a pocket-knife? How fortuitous. And then tore off my pants leg with it. Then quickly hosed down my leg with the spray from the insecticide. "You need to wash that off right away!" Having doused my leg in alcohol and poison in the middle of a panic, I was not about to argue over the obvious.

I pulled out my cigarette lighter (one of the few times I was thankful I hadn't quit the habit yet) and tossed it on the old man. He went up like a firecracker. Father and I dashed for the doorway to the garden and slammed ourselves inside the church.

"What happens if the fire spreads?" he asked.

"You won't have a garden."

The smell was of burning rotten meat—hardly that of an appetizing barbeque—and the burning alcohol left a stench of its own. Luckily the huge flame that erupted burned itself out rather quickly and the old garden was apparently too dank to fuel the flames.

What was left was a cinder in the form of a skeleton and some ashes. And a scorched garden bench that was luckily mostly wrought iron.

Some time later Father and I stood next to what was once a human being—a nameless, suffering human being—and the miniscule smoky bits that globbed together in a big gooey pile at its center that was the infestation that killed him.

"Did we get them all?" Father said hopefully, not knowing what else to say while staring at the ghastly sight in front of us.

"No," I answered trying not to sound too fatalistic. There were too many. Some always get away. Thing is, they can hibernate for years. Get any on you?"

"Not that I'm aware."

"In the morning we'll take a look at the trees and shrubs for traces."

"They hide there too?"

"I would assume so. Nobody knows enough about 'em."

We stared at the dead body like those at a camp-out stare at the firepit now cooled to ash. I looked over the mask I pulled off and found a few fly corpses stuck to it. "I suppose now is a good time to call the authorities."

THE MAN WITH THE BALONEY
SANDWICH FACE

There he was riding on the commuter train with me. I wasn't the only one who stared at him, but I stared the longest. The others soon ignored his presence after he got on. How does a man go through life with a face that looks like a baloney sandwich? I kept on thinking about it. I supposed it wasn't his fault. Maybe he had parents that looked like that. Who knows? But just exactly how does such a thing come about? Pushkin or Chekhov or somebody Russian once wrote a story about a guy who became a giant nose. Shostakovich even wrote an opera around the idea. It bombed. No kidding. And then there was Kafka and his famous human-transformed-into-a-bug story. But this is the stuff of fiction. You expect the unexpected in such a situation. But here, in real life?

Notice I said "baloney" as in "bah, humbug!" This, as opposed to Bologna, which is how the cold-cut is supposed to be spelled. Forgive me for not checking up on my history (as I really don't care anyway) but it would seem grinding up a batch of leftover pig parts and squishing them into a sausage in such a way must've taken place in the Italian city of Bologna—probably back in the Middle Ages—somewhere when meat was scarce. Perhaps a plague or something. They then started doing it everywhere else and somebody sold it with the line, "Look, just like they do in Bologna!"—as if that were a selling point. So the stuff became known as Bologna (pronounced in Italian: *bo-LONE-ya*—you know Italians). Then somewhere along the way *Bologna* became too difficult to pronounce—probably by Texans, the same people who couldn't find a good way to pronounce *Arkansas* (Texans by definition have a unique way of screwing up the language)—and it became *baloney*. And that became synonymous with bullshit. Perhaps because baloney is nobody's idea of a good meal.

Anyway, I don't know if there is a word of truth in that, I just made up the whole scenario. The point is, let's spell it the way it is pronounced; and that is a distraction from the real issue which is still my point: what's a guy doing with a baloney sandwich for a face? How does that even happen?

I tried to ignore him as I got off the train. Turns out he got off at the same stop I did but went into a different building. I didn't think about it much after that—or tried not to. I didn't see him on the commuter on the way home. But then, I took the 5:41. Maybe he took a different time slot. Didn't see him the next day either. But the following morning, there he was riding into town with me—or rather he was seated in the same car: all dressed up in a suit and tie . . . and a baloney sandwich head. He was going over some notes placed on the briefcase on his lap. I'm thinking he was a lawyer or an accountant. He also had a laptop, but didn't fuss much with it as he was more concerned with the papers. These days if you are concerned with papers, you are going to present them to somebody for official reasons.

I ignored him and went about my day, but often stopped to think about baloney (bologna), especially around lunchtime. In the employee's cafeteria they had an order of hot bologna in barbeque sauce. I couldn't pass it up.

I would only see him on the train from time to time. It wasn't a regular thing. Once an old lady with a little fluffy dog snapped at him (the dog, not the lady) and he found that unsettling; but otherwise he was a quiet sort that kept to himself.

Then came the day he actually entered my office. I was going over some reports on my computer screen when in walked my boss, Mr. Riley (there's all kinds of stories about him too, but never mind that now) and introduced me. "May I present Mr. Sanders of Carson, Carson, and Daly" Riley said pleasantly. And, of course, I did the old Freudian slip of saying, "Mr. Sandwich, how nice to meet you!"

I was reluctant to stick out my hand—I thought it might get all greasy. Well first, before that happened, I stood gawking at look-who-just-entered-my-office for a moment. Turns out it was an ordinary hand I shook. "Treat him well," said Riley on his departure, "he's got some good ideas I think we should look into."

Sanders wasn't a lawyer or accountant, he was a sales rep for an ad firm. I asked him to be seated, and he pulled out his papers (brochures, actually) from his trusty briefcase that he always carried with him.

"Ppppp I'm told you're the man I should talk to," he said pleasantly. He always began every sentence with a curious buzz from his . . . *lips?* "Ppppp as you know, we at Carson, Carson, and Daly are always looking for new advances in communications, so that are clients are always at the forefront of the best and bbbbbbrightest trends. Ppppp I have here some of the latest developments in the field, if you'll just take a minute to look over what we offer. And, if you are really interested, I have a disc here you can pop into your computer—or I can show you on mine—that goes into more detail."

"Thanks," I said, wondering just exactly where his eyes were, or for that matter, how he manages to speak out of all that baloney. I gave him some non-committal interest, more out of politeness and respect for my boss than for anything I was impressed by, and then led him towards the door. I shook his hand again seeing as how I hadn't gotten a disease yet from the guy in so far as a 15 minute meeting goes, and tried to lead him out.

Then he said to me, "Ppppp haven't I seen you before?"

"I don't know," I answered stupidly.

"Ppppp yes, yes! I think I've seen you on the commuter train."

"Now that you mention it."

"Ppppp I never forget a face."

"Me neither."

"Ppppp you come in from Hargrove?"

"Chancellor, just outside."

"Ppppp ah, yes!" he said, mustard dripping from the side of his . . . face. "Ppppp lovely little community. Almost moved there myself. Ppppp property taxes turned out to be a bit steep for us. And with a new wife and a baby on the way . . . had to think of counting pennies."

Oh God, he's got a wife and child?! "Yes, they are a bit stiff there."

"Ppppp you must be doing well for yourself here then."

"I do alright."

"Ppppp me? I just started. Ppppp hope to do well, though. Hey, you can help me on that path, eh? Hah-hah!" He remarked jovially, pointing to the brochure still in my other hand.

"Ah . . . yes . . . hah-hah," I returned with artificial politeness.

"Ppppp well, if you need me for anything else, or have some questions, just call," he handed me his card. "Ppppp I'm always at your service." And with that he left. I immediately threw the brochure and the computer disc away, and went home to have nightmares about the woman who would marry such a guy and the horrifying brood she must be nurturing in her womb. Who knows, perhaps she looks like a baloney sandwich too? Or maybe a pastrami on rye? And what about the child? Where are such people coming from?

I only saw him on the train a couple of more times. I always sat as far away from him as possible. He did call me on the phone a couple of weeks later, "Ppppp how are you doing? This is Mister Sanders from Carson, Carson, and Daly. Ppppp I wondered if you had a chance to look over the material I gave you, and if you had reached any decision?"

"Yes I did. No, no decision has been reached yet. I wanted to talk it over with the board, first." Why I told him that, I don't know. He'd just keep on bugging me.

"Ppppp well, if there's anything I can do, let me know."

Luckily my vacation was due, so I wouldn't have to talk to him again. I went sailing in a one-man skiff I rented just to go around the bay—something I hadn't done since college. When I got back to the club, there in yachting togs at the counter was a guy with a baloney sandwich head looking over the rental information. There really couldn't be two such people on the planet. Before I could pick up my club ID at the counter, and dash out, he flagged me down.

"Ppppp remember me? Sanders from Carson, Carson, and Daly! Ppppp fancy meeting you here. Small world, isn't it? Ppppp day trip or vacation for you?"

"Vacation."

"Ah, ppppp mine doesn't start yet for another two months. Ppppp but CCD offers me a good deal with the work. Ppppp how does your firm do?"

"Well enough for my purposes, I suppose."

"Ppppp been sailing? Thought I'd take it up myself. Ppppp must be fun out there on the water!"

"Fun, yes."

I couldn't get away from the guy. He just wanted to chat and chat, now that he was unhampered by the briefcase, suit, and tie. And I had been out on the water all morning, and was getting hungry. Enough so that I was willing to eat anything, even baloney. Somewhere in the middle of whatever he was talking about, I made a lunge for him and bit off some of the lettuce that was sticking out of his face. I don't know why I did it, I just did it. There was a stunned moment of silence from him, then he left. I never saw or heard from him again. I don't know what became of his wife and child, nor of Carson, Carson, and Daly.

I know what you're thinking. I'm prejudiced. One shouldn't judge a person entirely by his appearance. After all, he seemed to be a decent enough chap. But a baloney sandwich face . . . really? Okay, I'm not Buddha. I don't always see the goodness inside people. Sometimes I'm put off by the whole wheat and mayonnaise that makes up the part of them that should be their face. But I'd be willing to bet you have your own little peccadilloes that I would be shocked at too.

THE VERY WITCHING HOUR OF NIGHT

'Tis the very Witching Hour of night, and all the goblins that ever was was seen on such a sight. And lo, the very goblin Rancor, came to his mistress at the swelling of the Moon and stated, "What is it Mistress, that I should do that shall make the people swoon?"

"Dear Rancor," said the black and evil Mistress of the Night, for she was powerful, and loathsome to the sight, "I cannot upon me guide thee thus, for surely you do know that Rancor is as Rancor does; and so be off with you and raise the rancor that you may or might in conquering the night to make it unsafe for those of human born."

"I'm not so sure," did Rancor speak, "that I've the wiles to wend their ways, as they have rancor enough for themselves. What need they I for their distraught for naught shall come of it but idle whim—the which the while they'll blame on errant sin."

"'Tis your skills that make them so," the Crone did low to the impish menacing creature fixed below her regal throne. "Without your knack they won't attack each other in the ways that mortal flesh have come to emulate. To the gate and send your wicked schemes anonce the night and let the humans do each to each the frighting of themselves."

"As you wish, my Lady," Rancor stirred with resolution and bowed, and off he went into a crowd of unblessed acromones. Thus does Rancor rend himself to those about the scene where offer up their screams do they in chaos agitate. The humans done as yon simpletons do were through and through with fear, as rising clear above the turmoil, great Rancor now sits and stirs the pot of what humanity is capable of indefatigable atrocity. The night was young, the panic begun, great riots reeked their havoc on the streets as let loose by lamentable leach-like ghouls of garish horror.

And wars were unleashed, and crimes committed, and vengeance seek vengeance out every which and every where it beseems such souls to make. For the sake of nary a pleasure or measure of sanity, the humans on this night of nights, a night of woe for those who show the worst that mankind can create, plunged into that abyss of dread and reeking red with oblivion's curse drew much the worse for themselves—did they in rancor create.

Up spake Lady Bright upon whose sight many a wretch did wrath abate, whilst Rancor in his glee noticed not till we, then did stop and stare at she who beams a radiance that no one else may negate, "What have we here; why all in fear?! What lawless lice have loosed themselves on all about without a thought to what ways wide abides this angry throng?" Her voice a song, her hair a fair cloudlike array, her gown a white and silver spray. Yet now it seemed her throat had screamed an uncharacteristic bray.

"What has happened to the people of this hour? Why all this turmoil? What keeps all so sour? Is it you, blind dumb Rancor, that has worked your evil will among this most unhappy crowd? Be not you proud, for this is not a mission that befits their disposition; nor is it a thing forthwith to do. Although it is your nature to embroil each human figure in appalling acts of manner as befits such impish Rancor, let not it give you reign upon the world as one great unbound handler. Let Rancor now rescind his charge and bring things back to saner levels, and humans find their wits and ways as befits their days."

"Holy Lady!" Rancor spoke, "'Tis the Mistress of the Night, your blackened sister, in her gesture to the darkened time of year that bids me thus! So though I relish in the fuss, I could not do without her word at very high command!" Thus did Rancor cower 'neath the beam of Lady

Bright, whose rage was unmistakable, and whose power trumps the night when called upon to do so.

"Go thee thy ways," Lady Bright commanded to the imp, "and let no more Rancor be! I shall take up this plight and with my sister speed!" And lo, did Rancor limp along, his head in hands, his work is done; and thence he went into the night, and out of sight, the frighting by his handiwork beyond all measure won.

Ascending in a storm of righteous anger (as anger-filled as angels ever get) the Lady Bright sought out the night the lair of Mistress Black, and there she found the evil crone consumed in lurid knack.

"Aye! So 'tis my younger, brighter, sister dear, the one whom fear removes! How comes it you, upon this Moon have entered mine own abode?"

"It is the Moon by light and boon that I do represent, by which I can when trouble spans the night I enter here. For you, my dear, have made it clear you wish to pose a threat to those below, the people whose woe you seem so soon to set; by casting nets of poor fool Rancor on this night of nights in works of meaning menace."

"Poor Sister, do you not know I rule the night, and am free to conjure fury in whatever means I may?"

"And I was set upon the sky to send my silver rays to break the boundaries of the fears you send their way as protection for the simple folk who know no better what you be to them in all their misery. I charge you, on this night of nights to break your spells and wend your way worries back here to this Castle Corrupt until a time I've put upon to make your presence known. I've already charged simple Rancor to make his way back home!"

"Cheat you are, my rising star! You know this is my queendom! Unwelcome here you are, be clear, you never shall intrude!"

"Upon my word, though you blanket the world, I have more power than you. And by my force, we've each our course, but of humanity, you shall not pursue; not while I protector be. No, not while I, the Lady Bright, my brightness rain on thee!"

And with that Lady Bright did shine into the crypt that was the Mistress of the Dark's abode until she screamed to flee. "All right!" did Mistress Mayhem shriek, "your power put away! I'll fold myself into the night and let you have the day! But be Thou warned when next year charms its way into our view; again I'll reign from night to day, humanity's mine to use!" And so she cowered back into her box, the depths of Castle Corrupt to keep, until such time as a year and a day, when all her powers awake.

And if you view before the Moon arises on such a night, be forewarned the Mistress prowls, her minions abound, before ever the Moon doth rise and the Lady Silver intervenes.

HOWARD'S PICKLE

Howard had a magnificent pickle. Of course he knew that because everybody told him as much. People would stop by to see it from time to time. "That's one magnificent pickle!" people would say as they were going by. Kids on bicycles would whoosh by only to stop and stare. Yes, Howard had a mighty pickle, alright.

Actually, Howard had a whole yard full of terrific pickles. He grew other things like beans and tomatoes, but it was the pickles that everybody talked about. Every August he gathered them up and carted them off to the farmer's market in the village square. Women gathered from all over the county just to buy his pickles. You could cook 'em, can 'em, smoke 'em even, eat 'em raw. Nothing tasted like Howard's pickles. He claimed he had a secret ingredient mixed into the soil. He never revealed what it was. In reality, it was Hiram Peabody's ass.

Hiram Peabody had a strange looking creature in his barn. It turned out to be an ass. It was some sort of mixture of donkey and some other wild horse-like thing apparently bred from some circus animal brought over from Asia. It wasn't a mule, although it looked like it. And it was bigger than a donkey, but not by much. It was more correctly—an ass. An

Asian ass. Or maybe it was just a mutt—if such a term can be applied to donkeys.

Anyway, Hiram used his ass for all kinds of odd jobs around the farm. And the thing was cheap to feed because it had an appetite like a goat. It ate just about anything placed in front of it. It ate what the horses ate. It ate what the cows ate. It ate what the pigs ate. It even scrounged through what the dogs and cats scrounged through. And from its unorthodox part-asian digestive system, out came an equally unorthodox refuse in prodigious quantities—so much so that Hiram was looking for someone to take it off his hands (to use a phrase). And stink? Hiram's ass made such a stink even the cows wouldn't go near it.

So Hiram found a fool willing to take this stuff. That fool was Howard. Howard lived alone. He was a certified public accountant and worked out of his house. Howard was frugal and never spent money on anything so he never went anywhere. He was not much to look at and was reticent and uncomfortable around people, so he never attracted much notice from the opposite sex. He never attracted much attention from anybody—except his pickles. Howard was the perfect dumping ground for the remains from Hiram's ass. Hiram knew Howard had taken up gardening around his little house at the edge of town, so one day Hiram asked him if he had need of extra fertilizer. The arrangement was quickly and easily made, and one day Hiram drove up to Howard's house in his pickup with bushels and bushels of the smelly stuff. Ever since then, Howard's garden had bloomed beyond recognition. The biggest flowers you'd ever seen, the biggest squashes and peas. But the vegetables that loved the ass's discards the most were the pickles. In time, Howard planted 14 different varieties, and cleared as much space as his backyard garden would allow for them. Luckily the house he bought had a big enough yard to fulfill his needs, and he was near the edge of a woods so that there weren't a lot of nosy and competing neighbors around.

There were, however, competing animals in those woods: raccoons, opossums, squirrels, chipmunks, crows, and so on, that also loved his garden, and so he had to be ever vigilant and ever clever at devising ways to keep the critters out. This included everything from electronic fences, to muslin tarpaulins, to home-made gadgets that acted like burglar alarms to scare them off.

Now this particular year, Howard grew a really massive pickle—one you need not only both hands to hold, but both arms. Hiram's ass must have gotten into some really ripe pig slop that year, or the weather was extra kind, or the sun was extra focused on that one spot in the garden; but Howard grew a really immense pickle off of one vine wrapped around a tarpaulin post. It seemed to get bigger day by day. Suddenly Howard was popular. As he sold his pickles and other veggies each summer, Howard was becoming better known, more accepted, more spoken of in kind terms. Sure he was quiet and shy and kind of homely, and never did get himself married; but he's just the reserved type, that's all. He may not be much socially, but look at his pickles!

And they always did seem to come out perfect. With enough protection from the critters and bugs and blight (and Howard did dote lovingly on his pickles) there's not a one that was ever a throwaway. Talk about high yield. But then that year, that year alone would make him famous. That was the year he grew a really enormous pickle. They pulled out a tape measure to measure it—length-wise and girth. Each week they had to use more and more tape. There was talk of the Guinness Book of Records. Women began to faun over him for his monstrous pickle. They would flirt with him and tease him. Who would eventually end up with Howard's pickle? They began to talk among themselves. Rivalries started.

Meanwhile the rest of the county put forward the idea that Howard should auction it off. Whoever was to benefit from Howard's growth should be the one to pay the highest dollar. Maybe some of the proceeds could go to charity. Whenever it was ready, they planned to have a big celebration at the village square: bring in the high school marching band, have the mayor say a few words, have sack races and offer punch and ice cream—even have the local softball team play a special game. The Guinness Book people will be there for the final measurement making the town famous. Then at the height of the festivities, auction off the pickle. But when was that to be? The pickle kept growing.

Here's where the story takes an ugly turn.

It was Hiram's ass that grew Howard's pickle to its overwhelming size. Hiram wanted a cut of the action. He was willing to keep Howard's "secret ingredient" of the soil secret, provided he got something for all the newfound wealth Howard was creating with his pickle patch. So one day after some of the other amazed townsfolk had just left after yet another tape-measuring ceremony, followed by the customary and appropriate, "Oh Wows!" Hiram stepped up to see Howard.

Hiram offered Howard a deal, it actually sounded more like blackmail—revealing the secret of Howard's success—but Howard, the ever respectable CPA, told him no because it was more than just fertilizer that accounted for the success of the crop. It was also Howard's studious and meticulous care, his careful watering and timely weeding, and the fact that they had had a robust spring that year with an abundance of rainfall followed by bright, sunny, warm weather, that all contributed to it. Hiram was not satisfied, and when he threatened to bar Howard from anymore ass fertilizer, Howard excused himself, went into the house, and left Hiram to stew in his own envy.

If only the girls hadn't come along. If only those young ladies in their pretty sundresses riding those bicycles hadn't just then come along, riding by the house to view the pickle. They stopped just for a moment, called to the house, waited for Howard to appear at the window, then waved and winked coquettishly at him from the street with an appealing, "Hi, Howard!" before they rode off. Hiram was an old widower, and he liked female attention too. He had forgotten what it was like to receive it after all these years. All he had was livestock to talk to. Perhaps if he used his ass like Howard did, perhaps if he too had an enormous pickle, the girls would wink at him too. He went home furious. If he couldn't have a big pickle, then Howard wouldn't either.

That night by moonlight, Hiram slipped into Howard's yard. Avoiding as many of the booby-traps as he could see, Hiram crept up to the giant pickle and with a carving knife slashed the pickle violently. It turns out much of what made the pickle big was water. The pickle spouted juice from its end as it deflated, spewing Hiram with its contents all over his face and chest, seeds spraying everywhere. Hiram collapsed, his eyes burning with pickle juice. He knocked over wires and posts and set off more than one burglar alarm. He tried to get out, but tripped over barbed wire and other snares, and being so tangled simply wrapped himself up as if caught in a giant spider web so that he could barely move, and ended up lying there, snared, eyes blinded, weapon of the nefarious deed in hand when people came around to see what was the matter.

First out, of course, was Howard in his nightshirt (Howard was the type who would wear one). Lights up, sirens blaring. Neighbors began to appear. There was Hiram, pathetically moaning under the floodlights. A gasp went around as people realized the damage done to the great pickle. And there, in Hiram's hand, the weapon that did it. Howard was stunned and speechless. He stepped over Hiram in his well worn bedroom slippers and put his hand on his deflated pickle—it looking like a dripping, wounded animal, or perhaps a used balloon, struggling for life at the end of its vine.

Somebody contacted the mayor, and the mayor arrived, threatening Hiram with life imprisonment, or whatever he could concoct for the district attorney to hit him with. Everyone else remained silent as Howard hobbled his way silently back into his house.

Came the day of the great pickle auction when the marvelous magnificent pickle was to have been picked and placed up for sale to the highest bidder: the band played, the mayor gave speeches, and the softball team won the game. Howard's pickle had been dealt an ignoble fate, so it was cut up into healthy slices and auctioned off in bowls full of pickle chunks. A handful of wives won a bowl each to be cooked up into jars of slim-jims. It was not the same as if the pickle had been whole, but Howard's loss was the community's loss and people swore the action of one selfish individual was not going to steal their glory.

Howard had to be coaxed out of his home, but they managed to get him to the festivities eventually. As reparation to his crime, Hiram Peabody had to pay Howard whatever Howard demanded for the loss of his pickle. Howard chose Hiram's ass, which now became Howard's ass. The county sheriff made sure this transaction took place, and a special town ordinance was made to allow Howard to keep an ass on his property.

So then the pickle was gone as all good things inevitably must go. But then there were the photographs, the local newspaper articles; no Guinness Book record, but lots of jars of slim-jims. And there was a vow that next year there would again be another pickle. Howard promised them all he would grow the biggest pickle they had ever seen—with a little help from his ass, of course. And he could make that promise year after year—as long as his ass was alive, anyway. So they always looked forward to the next summer and the next pickle festival; for it seems that if you grow your pickle big enough, it somehow belongs to everyone. Everyone will want a piece of it.

BIGGER BOOGERS ARE BETTER BOOGERS

Billy had this theory about boogers. If you went out of your way to inhale a lot of dust and dirt and sand, and mushed your nose around a lot, you'd get really big boogers. The theory being: the bigger the better. For what purpose is debatable. Okay, Billy was a weird kid. The point is what was even weirder is that we were willing to listen to him. Even believe him. Even try it for ourselves.

"Hey, Billy! Is this how you do it?"

Yeah, none of us were too bright. So we would gather in the sandlot behind the quarry where there was a lot of dirt and mud and crabgrass, and kick up a big mess into the air. Then we'd stick our faces into that cloud of debris and take big sniffs. It was actually kind of fun. Whenever it hadn't rained for a while, you could gather up big clumps of dried dirt—some as big as your fist, some even the size of volleyballs. We could carry them up a little six-foot rise that looked like a mini-cliff and toss our dirt clumps in the air. *Boosh!* They'd hit the ground. A cloud of smoke would gush up into the air as a result. We could pretend we were throwing hand grenades at the enemy, or that meteors were falling from the sky. Our faces were all grimy from all the dried earth that landed on us. We thought that was *soooo* cool! Until one of the guys at the quarry came by to see what the heck we were doing and chased us off.

Anyway, we inhaled enough of that fabricated soot to make us sneeze, which meant our noses were working overtime—they were rebelling. Perfect. Then all you had to do was let your hand grind into your nose until your eyes watered—sort of stirring the pot, so to speak—and then exhale really hard and start blowing out big ones. We had contests. Billy always won. He not only had perfected all the skills first, he had the biggest nose. Contest over, we'd begin again, and we would do this until we got bored and went on to something else—or we were chased out of our encampment.

Once we had a contest for quarters—this was high-stakes gambling. Everybody saved up quarters from their allowances and then on Saturday we had a big booger contest. Billy won. Now you may ask, why would we participate in such a contest with Billy, if big-nose Billy always won the previous contests? Billy was one year older and three years smarter. And just like he was able to talk us into booger contests in the first place, it seems only natural that he should be able to talk us out of all our quarters by participating in a sure-lose situation such as this.

We went home complaining to our mothers, and they offered no sympathy—none, to any of us. "Stop playing with that Billy!" they told each and every one of us. "And stop sticking things up your nose!"

"But Mom! We don't stick things up our nose! Just dirt!"

"Same thing!" they yelled at us.

Hey! What a great idea! Instead of just inhaling clouds of dirt, we could actually just shove clumps of dirt up our noses! That would show that Billy! So next Saturday and next contest, we just shoved big hunks of mud from under the crabgrass in our noses. That was the best stuff. When Billy saw what we were doing, first he yelled, "Cheaters!" and then he did the same. Billy won this time too. He had the biggest nose.

"But Mom! Billy took all of our quarters!"

"I told you to stop playing with that Billy! If you keep doing this you won't get an allowance at all!"

"Hey guys! You ready for another contest?"

"Oh go away, Billy! You always beat us and you take away all our quarters!"

"Who knows? Maybe you'll beat me this time and win all your quarters back!"

"Okay."

We never beat Billy. And as we ran out of quarters, we ran out of friendship for Billy.

When no one wanted to play with him anymore—at least at booger contests—he started creating what he called "booger events" at school. He would surprise people with his boogers, sometimes leaving them on his face, sometimes placing them on people's desks when they weren't looking. The girls appreciated this the least and squealed the loudest, something that brought extreme satisfaction to Billy.

When he couldn't generate boogers by natural means (whatever that implies for Billy) he would bust open cheap plastic pens and pour the ink into his nose, thus creating blue boogers. He was on his way to creating a masterpiece of blue-booger sculpture when the teacher caught him and sent him to the Principal's office. She was so enraged at Billy's booger activities that he was suspended and his parents had to come to school. The Principal couldn't get over the fact that both his parents had big noses.

Billy and parents eventually moved to another school district, although I can't say for sure it was his booger activity that forced the situation. I believe his father had a managerial post for Kleenex tissues and they transferred him to a new plant. In time we grew up and forgot about Billy, and tired of our own booger exploits.

Billy works in Washington DC now (last I heard) as a lobbyist. He still has a big nose.

JESUS'S STUPID KID BROTHER

He was the black sheep of the family. He was born way after everybody else in the family made it into the world; he was kind of an accident—unplanned as they say: Jesus's kid brother, Shmuly. Jesus was already out in the world, fixing people's houses and wagons when Shmuly came along. Mary, nice and forgiving as she was, always felt somehow imposed upon when Shmuly appeared.

"Honestly, Joseph, I told you I had a headache that night. It wasn't one of those fake headaches I sometimes get when . . . you know—it was a real one. And I'm starting to get a little old for children," she would say to him whenever Shmuly did something horribly wrong . . . which he did quite frequently.

"You think you're too old for children?" Joseph would respond, "how do you think I feel? I'm way older than you!"

"Well then, we shouldn't have had him," she would say petulantly.

"We shouldn't have had him then?" he would protest, "Why didn't you talk to that God of yours, since you seem to be on speaking terms?"

"Oh, and I suppose you couldn't control yourself for a night or two! Sure, blame God. Everything's God's fault. It always is!"

Be that as it may, they had Shmuly—God blessed or not.

Shmuly was a strange kid. He grew up practicing farting noises in the stables. While Jesus was out satisfying his curiosity by talking with Rabbis, Shmuly was trying to find out how far he could shove a rock in his ear, or see if he could set fire to dried camel turds. It turned out he could, and set fire to one of the neighbor's stables. It took Joseph nearly a year to pay it off. Jesus helped the family business from time to time, but he was often gone traveling and learning, and as this was before he started performing miracles, he wasn't able at this particular time to heal his neighbor's stable—much to Joseph's chagrin.

School was not much of an option for peasants of carpentry rank in a place like Judea. Still, Jesus somehow managed to acquire some learning on his own. But Shmuly was not so ambitious. He stayed around home to help his parents, but his help tended to be no help at all. He also showed no interest in learning anything anyway.

One day, on the way to pay the tax collector, Shmuly discovered a really big spider near the collector's station. When it came time for Joseph to pay, Shmuly handed the man his spider. Joseph got in trouble for that but was able to talk his way out of it. Shmuly wasn't doing it in spite or as some form of protest, he actually thought the collector would like a spider for a present.

When Shmuly became old enough, there was a discussion as to just exactly what he should do. In those days, it was standard practice for a son to follow in his father's footsteps and take up the same craft. Joseph was a carpenter, ergo Shmuly should be one as was Jesus as would be any other siblings before him. However, Jesus was weird. He started going around preaching to people. Well, that didn't bring in any cash. And his mother and the rest of the family supported him. Jesus was always Mary's favorite.

This left Joseph at home stuck with the family business and without much help. It became Shmuly's task to take up the carpentry mantel. Only Shmuly was so incompetent that Joseph wanted to get rid of him. He finally was able to get Shmuly a job fixing and cleaning public pits—we refer to them more politely as outhouses. They tended to wear out and fall apart, and somebody had to fix them. And it was extra income that helped pay for Shmuly's room and board. And, according to Joseph's thinking, even if Shmuly messed up the job—well, it's a job that's already messed up to begin with.

Shmuly became known around Nazareth as the public pit boy. He always smelled like it. Furiously, Mary made him go out and wash before supper. Hygiene was never one of Shmuly's strong points and he never seemed to mind (or notice) the smell. Meanwhile, big brother Jesus had gone off and left the carpentry business to go on his excursions and was becoming famous—as well as stirring up trouble. Well, now the family had two black sheep, according to the villagers; however, the kind of trouble Jesus got into and the kind of trouble Shmuly got into seemed world's apart. The trouble Jesus stirred up seemed somehow important. The trouble Shmuly stirred up seemed annoying. In time, Shmuly was known as the annoying public pit boy while Jesus was taking on the allure of some kind of messiah. There was even a debate in town, who was the better son: the messiah, or the toilet washer? Joseph wanted no part of the discussion and went about his carpentry business trying to hide his head in shame.

Mary got it into her head that maybe it was time for Shmuly to marry. "But who would have him, Mary?" Joseph complained. "He smells all the time and he's awfully stupid. Does he look like he could support a wife and family?" Mary had to agree that his prospects were not good, especially for a young man who insisted on licking his toes clean. But after all, she had to admit Jesus was all wrapped up in his preaching and was probably a washout in the matrimony department, other siblings had come along but they were either busy following along wherever Jesus led, or were developing lives of their own. The girls in particular were eager to find a different family to get out of this one—preferably a family that would take them without a dowry of any sort. That left Shmuly.

So Mary went on a hunt for a nice Jewish girl—hopefully a forgiving, gullible one—to see if she could put Shmuly up on the market. At the public fountain she would wait around until the girls came by to do their laundry, and in an off-handed way, would try to proclaim Shmuly's better qualities. Mary didn't lie—exactly—she just had a certain feel for promotion—much like modern television executives who advertise a show you are quite sure you really don't want to see. It did not take, however, as the package she was selling was still Shmuly underneath all the finely phrased wrapping.

Months went by, and finally a girl at the edge of the village, one named Kreppelhoch, decided to give Shmuly a try. Well, as Kreppelhoch looked a lot like a camel and was as bright as bad rain, one would have thought they would have matched. They were rather alike in many ways. And for a time, it looked like Shmuly might make something of this, as Kreppelhoch was the first friend outside the family he had ever had.

The trouble started when Kreppelhoch, feeling a stirring of emotion (or hormone), wanted Shmuly to become romantic. She forced him to steal away to a shadow behind someone's stable at sunset and tried to get Shmuly to kiss her and say nice things. First of all, Shmuly hadn't a clue what nice things were, so he couldn't say any. Second, he didn't know what kissing was either. Kreppelhoch had to instruct him. When the instruction went sour, as Shmuly sort of slobbered all over her, his perpetual stench finally overcame her and filled her with disgust. She vowed never to see him again, and had her father throw the boy out whenever he came by. Kreppelhoch's father even prevented him from cleaning their own pit—thereby losing another job for Shmuly.

In their frustration with him, people would sometimes tell him, "Why don't you perform miracles like your older brother?" Not knowing how to go about making miracles—or what they were exactly—Shmuly conceived of the idea of flying. He climbed on top of a roof and threw himself off—injuring himself. He then tried to say magic words to magically clean a pit. To his amazement and no one else's, the pit stayed magically dirty. They just turned away from him and shook their heads.

While all this was going on, famous brother Jesus was thrown in jail and the family was wrapped up in all of his trouble. Shmuly was somehow forgotten by the family, as the big show was in Jerusalem. Since nobody could find him and they had to leave in a hurry, a note was left for him when he came home from the pits which said: "Gone to Jerusalem to save your brother. Please bathe." He had to have a neighbor read it to him.

Shmuly had never left home in his life (to Joseph's consternation) and didn't know how to get there. He hopped a ride on a donkey cart and ended up in Jofra. Then hopped another cart and finally made it to Jerusalem. He actually had to surreptitiously jump on a series of carts because each time he did so the cart owner wondered why his cart full of hay was attracting so many flies.

When he did get to Jerusalem he was sidetracked by the glamour of the city. He was accosted by robbers twice, because they felt he was an easy target; but having ganged up on him, not only did they find out he had no money, but they discovered Shmuly's smell rubbed off on them, and they went scurrying into the night trying to scrub the stench off of themselves.

Shmuly found out there was big talk all around town about an execution. Well that was another thing Shmuly had never been to so he decided to check it out. Along the way he found some guy selling peanuts. He wanted to buy some but couldn't pay, so the vendor shooed him away. As this was happening, a Roman guard nabbed the vendor and hauled him away for selling peanuts without a permit. Shmuly saw his chance for snatching peanuts and as he was doing so, somebody paid him for a bag. Shmuly saw this as a nice way to make some extra cash, so he took over for the vendor and began selling peanuts to the execution.

He asked who was being executed and somebody told him, Jesus. At the time, Shmuly knew of his brother as Yeshua Bar Yousef, or Yeshi, as he was known in the village. As Yeshi became famous and his name circulated in society where they spoke either Greek or Latin, Yeshi became known as Iesos Kristos or Jesus Christ. Shmuly didn't recognize the language change on the name, so he took his peanuts to Calvary and started selling what he called, "Jesus Nuts," because he felt they would sell better with a catchy name.

"Jesus Nuts! Get your Jesus Nuts here!" he cried going through the crowd. He turned a pretty good profit too, as people seemed to be hungry for peanuts. But while watching the execution, he had a spark of recognition and pointed to one of the convicts and said, "Hey, I know that guy!" Jesus was a bit beat up, so Shmuly didn't realize it was his brother. He just knew he had seen him before. Finally Mary spotted him and yelled, "You fool, that's your brother up there!"

"Really? Wow!" was all Shmuly could say while munching peanuts. "He must've really pissed off somebody." Mary broke down, and all Shmuly could do was offer her peanuts. He offered Jesus some peanuts too, but Jesus wanted water instead.

After Jesus died, they carted him off into a tomb. Everybody felt really crappy, and Shmuly was no exception. A few days later somebody said Jesus got up, alive and well, and walked out of the tomb. Suddenly everybody was out spreading the word about a miracle, and the rest of his family went off to be pious doing whatever kinds of things pious people do. The carpentry business back home was done for, and Shmuly didn't know what else to do but clean pits.

Then Shmuly became inspired and figured that if big brother Jesus could do it, so could he. He went around spreading the word that he was Jesus's kid brother, and when that knowledge didn't fly with anyone, he began promoting himself as the secondary or assistant messiah: Shmuly Christ. He even had somebody print up banners for him that said, "Shmuly Christ, Tell Your Fortune, Buy Peanuts" But since Shmuly couldn't read (and most people couldn't anyway) a number of the signs made up for him said, "I stink!" and "Big Fool." The sign-makers went away chuckling and pocketing peanut money.

Shmuly tried to do the traveling thing his brother did, but couldn't find disciples like Jesus had been able to. Many people just thought of him as an idiot and stayed away. Shmuly tried to preach but didn't know anything and ended up talking about public pits. What kind of inspirational things does a prophet say, anyway? He tried again in different towns and talked about "great things that are going to happen," although he didn't elaborate on the statement. Then he was asked when he was going to get rid of the

Romans and the line of King Herod. After all, Jesus had raised their hopes that he would do that and just got himself killed. Now along comes his kid brother and talks only of "great things" then goes into diatribes about peanuts and public pits. He was shunned.

Using another tack, he learned that what Jesus talked about most and seemed to draw the most crowds for was something about peas on earth. People seemed to want Peas on Earth more than anything. Jesus apparently promised them peas on earth. He would try to fulfill that promise. He didn't know why peas would be of much interest to anybody, although there were plenty of folks who were hungry. He also didn't know where to get bushels of peas from; but if Jesus could make fish and bread appear, he could bring peas to the people. He grunted and groaned and nearly busted a blood-vessel in his neck, but he couldn't make any peas. He soon gave up.

Town after town he visited and just got on people's nerves. He became known as Shmuly the Annoying Messiah, as all he could do was annoy passers-by. He was eventually robbed on his travels by the same robbers who tried to do so to him before. Only this time he actually had something to steal—his peanut money—and the robbers were willing to put up with the stench in exchange.

Shmuly came to give up the Christ business and tried to go back to cleaning public pits, but no one would have him. Struggling, starving, too poor to survive, he fell into a public pit and died of asphyxiation. It was actually amazing he lived as long as he did, seeing as how he was so ill equipped to accomplish anything.

All historical records of Shmuly Christ disappeared, and he was written out of the Bible during the council of Nicaea. No one remembered him at all until a lost record at an archaeological dig in the Holy Land in the late 20th century revealed his name and some of his doings. The group, "Jews For Jesus" picked him up from the rubble of history and began emulating him. A group was even formed called "Jews For Shmuly" some time later. Their symbol is a peapod. You'll find his name inscribed on the walls of certain public rest facilities in New York City. Sometimes under toilet seats you'll see the inscription: "Shmuly Was Here."

THE NIGHT TRAIN STOPS HERE

"The night train stops here," the Station-Master said as he passed by on the platform. He was stating the obvious. That's why I was there, along with two other poor souls. You don't hang around at the station of a little whistle-stop like this at midnight if it doesn't. He clumped around in his creaky shoes, examining his pocket watch, and making sure the lanterns were burning before he headed back inside. I sat on the bench under the window, waiting.

There was the pretty young brunette, hair all dolled up, lots of feathers and frills, lace and volumes of skirt, standing near the edge—parasol in hand. The parasol was folded, it was only needed when the sun was out. I was beginning to think myself rude, having not offered her my seat, but it didn't look like she wanted it anyway. And besides, I was covered with dust from the prairie, my horse having given out over the trail, and me having to hike through the sagebrush carrying the saddle on my shoulder.

Then there was the older gentleman: banker type. Brocaded vest under that fancy dark suit, brand new black Stetson, pocket watch on a gold chain, lots of curly gray hair in that beard arranged around his face just so—carpet-bag beside him. He probably had half the bank's profits hidden in that bag, yet pretended not to. He didn't want a seat either. He just kept looking at his watch. Probably had to get to Chicago before dawn to pay off his new properties.

Do I sound cynical? I don't like bankers. They never did me a good turn. He may be just an ordinary gent. An okay Joe. I just hate the smell of bankers. I turned my attention back to the sweet young thing standing before me. Alone? In a crummy, isolated train-stop in the middle of nowhere? How does that happen? Never saw her in town, but then I don't hang around town much anymore. Why would a girl like this spend time in a town like that anyway? Bet she smells nice too. Like roses or something. White gloves, white veil partially obscuring her face. Perfect makeup, little beauty mark under the mouth, shiny red lips, all dressed up in a powder blue-gray with lots of white lacey frills around her. A regular flower. Just a beautiful flower. I almost felt like thanking her for allowing me to look at her. I kept my mouth shut, of course. You never want to spoil what's perfect.

Black sky. Can't really see past the flickering shadows from the oil lamps. Not even a breeze to stir up trouble, make some noise. The night train stops here. That's all I knew. That's all that was important. The banker type pulled out a cigar, spit off the end. The girl made a sighing noise, impatient for the train to get here. Now I felt the need to be gallant even though I was probably no good at it.

"Excuse me, Miss," I finally got up the courage to speak, "Would you like a seat? It's the only bench out here." She turned and looked at me as if seeing me for the first time, as if I had pulled her out of her world, wherever that was, of deep thought. She smiled sweetly, perhaps the only way she knew how to smile.

"No thank you," she said, a feathery voice to go with the feathery hat, "I'm fine. If I want to sit, I'll go back inside. But that was very kind of you." What is a rose like this doing out here all alone?! She went back to staring down the track, searching the darkness for the arriving train. The women I knew had all been bawds in saloons. This was an ornament fallen from a different world.

I sat back, my good deed done, and decided on a chaw of tobacco. As long as I wasn't trading places with the young gal, it didn't matter to me what I smelled like. I did shake a little of the dust off my boots. Even in this light I supposed I looked a little dirty. The Station-Master came back out again, his creaky shoes shuffling along the floor-boards. He checked his watch.

"She's late," he said, and adjusted one of the dying oil lamps. The flame leapt up, brighter than before. He turned and went back inside, shutting the door with a rattle behind him.

"These trains are never on time," the banker type said after the Station-Master was gone. He went back to puffing on his cigar. Neither I, nor the girl, had anything to add to that. He was right. The trains out this way were seldom on time. What can you do? Modern conveniences. Give me a good horse anyday. The banker type shuffled his feet. The girl gave a sigh. I just kept on chewing—although there was no place to spit. I didn't want to seem crude in front of the lady, so I discreetly went over to the side and spit on the dirt near the steps. A shooting star shot through the night, and the hoot of an owl broke out somewhere nearby. I thought that might unnerve the girl, but she seemed immune to such mysteries. Plucky gal. She obviously had the gumption to stay out here alone until the train came.

Bats. Must be a hangout nearby. Doesn't matter where you go you can always see bats cruising around after dark—especially around dusk when the bugs are at their best. But this is the desert. Yeah, I know it has bugs—but not so you could make a feast out of 'em, even for something as small as a bat.

"Seems to me," the banker type spoke up, but he was apparently addressing no one, "that sooner or later they'll invent a train that makes it on time." That disgruntled platitude mentioned, the banker type shut up. Neither the young lady nor I had anything to add, so again, we didn't say anything.

Off in the distance we heard the eerie cry of a train whistle trying to make its presence known by splitting the silence of the dark. "'Bout time," the banker type mumbled to himself, barely audible. *Woo-woooo!!* You could hear that unmistakable sound so very faintly coming from wherever the horizon was supposed to be. A few moments later, you could even hear the *chh-chh-chh-chh-chh* of that pumping steam engine. Almost a kind of hissing whisper in the night. The bats ignored all of that. The Station-Master stepped out again and checked his watch, looking as far down the tracks as he could. Way out there somewhere was a tiny match of a lamp burning in the distance, lighting the way for the locomotive, the eye of the cyclops on a big metal monster yet to reveal itself to us as the stretch to the horizon dwarfed it to minuscule proportions. The Station-Master harrumphed at it all and went back inside. He soon came out again to hang a mailbag up on a hook and change the time listed for the train on a blackboard hung next to the exterior ticket window.

I continued to chew. The banker type continued to smoke. The young lady continued to look gorgeous. And we waited for the arrival of the fabled iron horse. The Night Train, chugging its way through the depths of the desert night in search of destinations ultimately unknown to us . . . we were only interested in our own tickets. We were only interested in our own lives. The train had a life and purpose and destination all its own. We were only going to share it for a little while. And yet here it came, in thunder and smoke, and we were trusting ourselves to let it take us where we thought we wanted to go. Lighting its way with a single eye, it was poking through the blanket of darkness in the less than friendly land of the desert, grumbling over the mileage like a dutiful but thankless monster. And with each arrival and departure, it was going to change the course of people's lives no matter how slightly, just by transporting them to a new place and time. The banker would be mingling with his high-hat colleagues somewhere, the girl perhaps back with her family or maybe meeting her beau; and me, I'd be out looking for a job someplace where there are more people, less dust, and less hostile temperatures. Hopefully. I guess that's what that big beast brought to us all—hope. Or maybe escape. Whatever it was we were seeking, the method to get there was now approaching fast.

Woo-Wooooo!! It let out again. Now it was within plain sight, barreling down on us in the size and shape that a proper train should be—night or day. *Tssssssssssst!!* It said as it started to slow in the approach of the station. The Station-Master stepped out on the platform one last time. The girl refolded her already folded parasol (an unnecessary accoutrement at night anyway, but the twirl she gave it showed force of habit). The banker type picked up his carpet-bag. I spit out the last bit of tobacco and headed for the platform's edge.

Then in it came, with a whooshing and a screeching and a belching of noise and steam and vibration and rumble. Heavy rumble, like tons and tons of steel rolling beneath our meek wooden platform. And with a final unearthly squeal, belch of smoke, and spray of steam, it came to a stop right where it was supposed to.

A mail car opened up and some uniformed jacks hoisted the mailbag off the post. The banker type wasted no time in getting on. I offered the young lady my hand. "Thank you," she responded politely and with a smile that would melt butter, as she made the step up to the passenger car. My hand smelled like a flower garden when it was returned. I watched her disappear into the railroad car then stood on the step of the train to take one last look at the station, its master, and the inky black desert that engulfed the place. Then with a huge grunt and groan, an elephantine hiss of steam, and a squeal of metal against metal, the train lurched forward and began to move its great bulk into the night. I stayed on the step for awhile as the great locomotive chug-chugged itself, almost begrudgingly, into the start of another journey, and watched the station and its little oil lamps shrink into obscurity as it was lost in the night, a vague memory now eaten by the distance of the train.

HEADS

Simon Bartholomew Wexton had always wanted to visit Dr. Pressbauer's lab. Dr. Pressbauer had experimented with cryonics long before it became fashionable among the elite. There is this idea that if you freeze yourself at the moment of death, somebody in some future time can bring you back to life and cure you of whatever killed you in the first place. While this is just a theory, mind you, and to be sure, there are a lot of questions of the practical side of doing this, not to mention the ethical ones, it doesn't stop people from wanting to try it. The idea of immortality, ageless beauty, and endless youth is a powerful one to overcome. It is a lucrative enough field to sponsor an industry that would seem to be a growing one.

At any rate, before cryogenics became a business and something of a household word, there was Dr. Pressbauer back in the 1950s, experimenting away with freezing things. He worked for the university, of which Simon Bartholomew Wexton was initially a student, later a graduate, and then got himself established as a would-be assistant professor, in the upcoming spring.

Dr. Pressbauer applied three times to have his work funded, but each time the committee turned him down. The official word was that he had not supplied enough evidence to ensure that his venture was either possible or practical—or, for that matter, lucrative. Universities like to pretend they are willing to fund pure research, but in fact, they are victim to the same capitalist mentality that keeps the rest of society afloat, thereby making such committees concern themselves as to whether such research has a payoff down the road. Freezing dead bodies didn't sound like something that would turn out big buckos, so Pressbauer's work was always given a pass. Privately, however, the members of the committee thought Pressbauer and his freezing business was just flat-out creepy and they didn't want anything to do with him.

So Pressbauer froze things on his own, in his spare time, in his lab, in his basement. Well, Simon Bartholomew Wexton, dateless nerd and charismatically challenged as he was (much like Dr. Pressbauer, in fact), heard about the good Doctor's experiments and wanted a chance to see—even participate. Birds of a feather, apparently.

Simon begged and pleaded with Pressbauer to take him on as an assistant, once he had a fuller understanding of what his senior was doing. Simon followed Pressbauer around from class to class until the Doctor gave in, and told him to meet him at his house that evening after six. Simon would then be let into the Holy of Holies, and be rewarded with a chance to see how to freeze dead things for himself.

That evening, Simon showed up at Pressbauer's door in his usual rumpled trenchcoat which he seemed to wear everywhere, whether or not it was cold and rainy, and had his books and ring-binders in hand—which he also carried everywhere, whether or not he needed them. An onion-faced maid answered the door and let Simon in. While the maid curtly offered him a bench to sit on in the foyer, Simon chose to stand, clutching his books and binders as she left.

The foyer exhibited a glass case, much like that of a jewelry store, which encased the carcasses of several small dead animals: moles, voles, blackbirds, and whatnot. They didn't look stuffed (as in a taxidermist's shop) so much as freeze-dried. They were not elegantly mounted; in fact, not mounted at all, merely placed. Nor were they particularly attractive specimens. They were just there, in a case, lit as if on display, but not anything you'd want to look at.

The grandfather clock chimed in and startled Simon, almost enough to make him drop his books. He looked around at some of the other objects in the foyer: a copy of a Currier & Ives painting, branches from a tree hung up like sculpture on one of the walls, a marble pedestal with an otter's skull placed on it. An odd grouping to put at the front of one's house, to be sure; but Pressbauer was an odd man. Simon was about to become his odd assistant.

"Mr. Wexton," Pressbauer stated rather formally at his entrance. "How nice of you to be right on time," he added without a smile, or any indication of genuine civility. "May I take your coat?"

"No . . . I-I-I'm willing to keep it," Simon spoke through a nasal whine in his nose.

"But surely you don't need your books," the doctor returned.

"That's all right," Simon stated, "I don't mind hanging on to them." And hang on to them he did, almost as if they were a teddy bear.

"Very well, then; this way," Pressbauer added officiously, and turned and headed toward the basement door. Simon stumbled after, and passing through a creaky door, wound down a small, narrow, spiral staircase into Pressbauer's den of iniquity. Pressbauer flicked some switches, opened up a metal box with a key, pulled up on a large handle that buzzed a bunch of electronic gears into motion—and voila—a fully illumined laboratory came into view . . . fluorescent tubes flickering into brightness with a snapping, and a crackling.

"This way," Pressbauer said, the light making him look somehow more cadaverous than he usually did in daylight at the university. Simon shuffled behind, in awe of the makeshift lab revealing its unholy secrets to him as he went ever deeper into the void. "There's a lab coat over there if you need it," Pressbauer said, pointing to some hooks on a wall. Pressbauer got a smock out of narrow locker and dressed himself in it. Simon went to the wall, and, dumping his books on the nearest available stool, replaced his seedy raincoat with the lab whites Pressbauer expected him to wear. He could hear things bubbling and boiling and hissing throughout the lab, but as he was near-sighted he didn't get a good look at anything until he was done fastening his coat. That's when he got his big shock.

Sure, there were vats, and flasks, and tubes, and instruments of all sorts. There were glass tanks and small ovens and Bunsen burners and shelves on shelves of chemicals. That's kind of what one would expect in a lab. But as Pressbauer was funding himself with no outside help, it must have taken quite a while to stock up on all this equipment. And who knows exactly how long he'd been working down here and what he started with so long ago. None of that stuff was shocking.

There was also a long set of shelves loaded down with glass jars of every shape and size—little ones, and great big ones. Inside those jars, floating in various kinds of solutions, were critters of every variety one could think of: beetles, spiders, snails, clams, fish, squirrels, monkeys, even a couple of cats and a small dog or two. A bit creepy perhaps, but to a biologist—a scientist—no, that wasn't all that shocking either.

No, what was shocking was the long shelf of human heads—all of them in jars, all of them staring out through dead eyes from within a solution of Pressbauer's own recipe. And each head-jar was connected to a tube connected to a pipe that was either circulating a solution within the jars, or just pumping in cold air, perhaps even liquid nitrogen or something, as the pipes connecting all this junk together seemed encrusted with frost. Simon had been concentrating on whatever was lying on the counter-top, when he happened to look up and found a dead woman staring back at him from only inches away. And then he looked down the row to see the rest of them; perhaps as many as two dozen, all jarred up and lifeless. And therein lied his shock.

"Let us begin with experiment number 16-28-X," Pressbauer stated flatly. "Would you get me the file from the drawer, please." Pressbauer went right to work and was busy looking through his notes when he realized he hadn't heard anything in Simon's direction. He discovered Simon motionless, gawking at the heads. "Well . . . what are you waiting for? The file cabinet is over there."

"H-H-Heads!" Simon stuttered.

"Yes. Of course they're heads. What did you expect?"

"W-W-Where'd they come from?"

"From off of dead humans. Are you simply going to stand there and state the obvious? If you want to work here, my boy, you have to snap to and not be overwhelmed with the presence of dead figures. We do work with death, you know, on a daily basis. We are actually trying to find a way to overcome it, as a matter of fact. I hope this isn't going to impede your performance any."

"N-N-No," Simon answered, unconvincingly . . . trying to convince himself.

"The file, Mr. Weston, the file," Pressbauer had some impatience seeping into his voice.

Simon forced his feet to move from what seemed a bucket of glue that held him to the floor, and shuffled over to the file cabinet. He mumbled to himself, but couldn't remember what he was looking for; and of course, he was humiliating himself in front of his idol due to his display of apparent stupidity.

"16-28-X," Pressbauer reminded him from across the room, the impatience sounding more noticeable this time.

"16-28-X," Simon mumbled to himself. For some reason, he only saw heads floating in front of him instead of the tabs from the manila files; but somehow he managed to pull himself together enough to locate the appropriate one. He closed the drawer and shuffled back over towards Pressbauer, almost knocking the woman's head on the end onto the floor.

"Careful, you fool! I went to great lengths to obtain that. I don't need you wrecking hours of research with pure carelessness."

"Sorry," was all Simon got to say. He handed the file to Pressbauer and after a few moments, finally got up the gumption to ask, "Where are the bodies?"

"Hmm?" Pressbauer turned from his notes, "Oh, they're in there."

"Where?"

Pressbauer pushed back a sliding door, revealing a second room. In it were refrigerators. He opened up one. In it was a headless body, naked, blue, steam swirling up before it where the room temperature met the cold contained air.

"H-H-How come . . . they're like that?"

"What . . . stored upright?"

"H-H-Headless."

"I've got the heads out here, can't you see?"

"W-W-Why were their heads . . . removed."

"Well, I do plan to put them back someday."

"W-W-Why . . ."

"Remove them in the first place? It seems when head and body want to freeze properly they do so at different temperatures. I don't know why yet. You can actually get away with keeping the body at a higher temperature, for some reason. I guess because it's nothing more than a large piece of beef. But the head wants to be fast frozen, and deep. And it wants a completely different solution to keep it functioning than whatever lies below it."

"They're still f-f-functioning?"

"No, of course not. But they will want to when they are brought back. Much more so than the rest of the form. Heads are rather finicky. They require special attention. That's why I have extra."

"Extra?"

"Yes. I don't have a body for all of them. How much do you think refrigerators cost? If I'm lucky, I can get two into a single unit. But I don't have the space for dozens of refrigerators. And besides, a head can spoil so easily, you may have to throw it out anyway."

"Where do you get them from? The bodies . . . the . . . heads?"

"Oh, here and there. You never know where a body will pop up. Or even just a head. My boy, that's going to be your department from now on."

"My what? . . ."

"You're the one who's going to be obtaining the bodies for our future use. It's easy enough, I'll show you how." Simon heard himself gulp. "Now 16-28-X is our experiment with a bat brain," Pressbauer continued, "That's over here. What you need is a pair of those gloves hanging on that chain over there. We'll be dealing with liquid helium, and that can produce a nasty burn if it spills on you—not to mention freezing a chunk of you off."

Simon stuttered and stammered his way over to the file cabinet without actually saying anything. He found the gloves and put them on slowly without being conscious he was doing so. He just kept staring at the heads.

"Well now, don't dawdle, Mister Wexton, we have lots of work to do." Simon shuffled back to the Doctor and waited for the next command. "In cooler number 3, we will be wanting 14/btc-6 from the containers on the middle shelf."

Again Simon shuffled to the room full of freezers and refrigerators, all humming with their generated cold air. He opened the wrong one and found another naked, blue, headless body hanging in it, and closed it quickly. He then found the appropriately labeled appliance and opened it. He found a huge opaque jar labeled: 14/btc-6, and pulled it out. He fumbled with it a bit, then shuffled back to the counter where Pressbauer was still thumbing through his notes.

"Over in box 12, you'll find vessel 13-22-10. Please extract its feeder tube from it and bring it over here. But be careful, that vessel is bathed in liquid helium."

Simon went over to where "box 12" was indicated by Pressbauer and opened it up. At first it seemed to be nothing more than a beer cooler; but at its opening found a bunch of metal flasks, about the size of beer bottles, arranged together and all connected by a series of tubes to some machine hiding behind some closed area that was emitting a soft throbbing noise as if it were some kind of generator. He disconnected the tube on the vessel marked: 13-22-10, and watched steam pour out in clouds from both tube and vessel. He closed the box and brought the vessel over to the counter.

Pressbauer said nothing, but put on a pair of rubber gloves. He opened up 14/btc-6 and with a pair of tongs placed what appeared to be a large ball of snot onto a metal tray. He then examined the snot ball with a magnifying glass. "Good! Excellent!" he said. He then placed the snot ball back into 14/btc-6, opened up vessel 13-22-10, and poured a smidgen of its smoky contents into the jar. He shoved a chart at Simon. "Record the date and time here," he ordered, pointing to a line on the chart. Simon fumbled for a pen with his big gloves, then realized a pen was already attached to the chart, which was on its own clipboard. Pressbauer put 14/btc-6 away in its refrigerator, meanwhile, then did likewise with 13-22-10.

"Give me A-11-8216," Pressbauer stated when back at the counter and picking up his notes.

"A-11 . . . . ?" Simon was looking around the room.

"That one," said Pressbauer, looking up at Simon's confusion. Simon followed the direction of the point. It was one of the heads. It was a big ugly head: eyes going in opposite directions, black hair and a beard, broken nose, lots of moles or warts, tongue hanging out. Sure enough, underneath it was a sign that read: A-11-8216. All the heads had little numbered signs under them. He hadn't noticed it before because he never got beyond the heads themselves.

"What do you want?" Simon said, stupidly.

"Hand it to me, please," sighed Pressbauer, once again displaying a whiff of impatience. "And don't forget to disconnect the hose."

Simon reached over to grab the ugly head and noticed that his hands were shaking. Luckily he still had the gloves on so it was less noticeable. Much as he was queasy about his surroundings, he still didn't want to embarrass himself in front of the doctor who was nonetheless his mentor and idol.

Pressbauer pulled out another tray and some surgical types of instruments, and placed a few jars of chemicals labeled with numbers on the counter in front of him. Meanwhile, Simon turned a valve that shut off the jar-hose, and with another click unhooked it from the system. It made a small *pook!* noise. Then he shakily pulled the head-jar off the shelf.

"Remove it, please," Pressbauer said without looking up.

Simon set the heavy jar on the counter and dug into the solution, pulling out the head, which, through the gloves, felt like a bowling ball with a thick layer of squishy mud covering it, and pulled it towards him. The face on the specimen looked more revolting the closer it got, and one eye even shifted in its socket and swung to the other side. Startled, it was all Simon could do to hang on to it without dropping it. He carried it over to the doctor's portion of the counter as if he were holding a time-bomb. The doctor was busy opening up this jar and that, and placing siphons and syringes in them. He pulled his microscope closer and switched on a lamp that lit the microscope's tray. He then looked up to see Simon, holding onto A-11-8216, and looking as lifeless as the head.

"Well?" Pressbauer studied Simon, "Put it down." Pressbauer offered the tray by shoving it closer to Simon. Simon didn't move. He was getting paler and paler. "Are you all right, my boy" Pressbauer asked, removing his glasses.

Maybe it was the smell of the chemicals, maybe it was the hard yet squishy head between his hands, maybe it was the flickering of some of the old fluorescent lights, or the disturbingly constant hum of the many machines that kept things cold. Maybe it was the fact that Simon had fish for lunch. Or just maybe, it was the overall creepiness of the lab and the work the good professor was doing. And maybe it was Simon realizing that he didn't really want to continue to explore this line of work for a career. Whatever the reason, it all finally got to Simon Bartholomew Wexton, and in one great spasmodic eruption, not unlike the explosion of a pent up volcano, Simon Bartholomew Wexton vomited all over A-11-8216, his gloves, his smock, and the counter top—in fact everything in front of him—including a Doctor Pressbauer who tried to dive out of the line of fire.

Simon stood there, stupidly covered in his own filth, still holding onto that grotesquerie in his gloved hands. There was a moment of silence as Pressbauer, having thrown himself on the floor, stared up at his would-be protégé in awe at the coverage of the young man's spray. Finally, Pressbauer stood and tried to shake himself off.

"You . . . *IDIOT!!*" Pressbauer screamed. Simon, still holding the head, began to whimper and weep. "You have ruined A-11-8216! Desecrated the experiment! And contaminated this laboratory! If you hadn't the stomach for it, you should have told me! Leave this place AT ONCE!"

Simon, crying like a little baby, tried to hand Pressbauer the filthy head, but Pressbauer balked and just shouted a disgruntled cry. Simon placed the head on the countertop. He tried to wipe up the counter with his sleeve but Pressbauer stopped him.

"Never mind that! Just get out!"

Simon shuffled over to the corner of the room, took off his messy smock and hung it on a hook. He put on his trench-coat, picked up his books and binders, and slowly, dejectedly made his way up the staircase, giving one last look behind him to see the Doctor, unmoved since the accident, offering him a fierce and disapproving stare as Simon made his way out of the lab.

Once upstairs he headed straight for the door. The maid watched him pass without saying a word, only offering that same visage of disdain she offered him at his entrance that she apparently keeps on hand at all times.

Outside, Simon looked up at the Moon while closing behind him the gate of the good Doctor's yard. Perhaps he would find his skills are needed in the up and coming industry of space travel. Or perhaps he would spend his life as a lot of college graduates do, as a short-order cook. No. Nothing to do with food. Or death. Or anything with chemicals and smells and freezers.

Simon Bartholomew Wexton walked slowly home that night, wondering what to do with the rest of his life.

EVERETT SLOCUM'S ITCHY HEMORRHOIDS

(and what we intend to do about it)

It's like this . . . Everett Slocum was a pain-in-the-butt—not just to himself, but everyone. He couldn't stop telling everybody about his problem. He told his family first, then his doctor, then everybody at the office, then everybody at the P.T.A. meeting, then bowling night, then bridge night, then everyone at the beach during his vacation. He just plain wouldn't shut up about it. He was obviously getting on our nerves. We had to do something.

There's the simple, basic approach: "Everett, shut up!" That didn't work. Then we littered his office cubicle with boxes of hemorrhoid cream. He would tell us his progress reports on his daily application. Finally somebody found from somewhere a bidet that we placed next to his desk. We could hear him actually use the thing when we were on the other side of the wall. Now it was just an empty shell, it wasn't even hooked up to any plumbing or anything. It was intended as a not-so-subtle gag gift. And yet he used it at the office whenever he decided to apply his cream during one of his breaks. And he would grunt and howl and moan—and that would carry over the partition. Nobody wanted to go back in the corner where he was. Nobody wanted to touch whatever he touched. If he used the water-cooler, people stayed away from it. If he used the coffeepot, people went out to Starbucks.

We talked to the boss about it. The boss said it was creepy, but he didn't think there was anything in the employee rule book or in the state laws that really was against anything he was doing. We supplied Everett with a fresh box of handi-wipes every week, mostly for our own peace of mind. We assumed (hoped) he was using them, and as far as we could tell, he was—but for what?

He did say he was going to the doctor; after all, he told us enough about his anal trials and tribulations that it would have to occur to him (and anyone he lived with) that this problem had to have professional hands-on (so-to-speak) care. And incidentally, who was he living with? We were never really sure. Was he married? Was he living with his Mom or other family members? Was he alone with a goldfish tank? His personal environment was sketchy at best. We never really found out because he never stopped talking long enough about his ass.

So it came down to: fix his butt, get him to shut up, or lynch him. Those were our choices. We heard something about lynching being illegal, so that left us with really two choices. We called a proctologist. Everett said he had a doctor look into the problem (so-to-speak), but he was going to a GP, a basic family doctor. We thought a specialist might be able to deal better with his situation. The Proctologist could offer us nothing except to tell us to send Everett in to him for an examination. Everett said he already had a doctor and didn't need to go to another. Considering how much belly-aching he did about it, we began to suspect it was just an excuse so that he could continue to complain, because it gave him attention, and he really didn't know what else to talk about. We began to suspect he really hadn't gone to a doctor for just that reason.

One person in the office suggested it all may be psychosomatic, and that it really is an appeal for sympathy—and that, maybe if he had something else going on with his life besides goldfish (by now we were pretty convinced he was a solitary, goldfish man) he'd stop talking about his rear end. It was suggested some female concern might help. Some of the women were goaded into talking to him about his life on breaks or off-hand moments.

Because they were annoyed by his subject matter, they agreed, but got nowhere. Then it was suggested one of the single ladies take him out on date—maybe that was what he needed. The ladies (single and married) all nixed that idea. Then it was suggested that maybe he was gay; maybe one of the men— All the men in the office nixed the next idea.

To be quite honest, Everett Slocum was naturally repulsive. Oh, he wasn't so disgustingly homely, just average. And it wasn't that he walked around in rumpled, smelly clothing (although no fashion-plate, he). It really was just that his life was totally engulfed by his anal fixation. And that was a turn-off to everyone.

Well, if you couldn't get him to a proctologist, what other recourse was there? Finally one of the guys in the office hit on a solution. We would go the other route. We would wrap all his chairs and things with broken sticks and barbed wire. Give him something to really complain about. It might drive him out of his mind and out of the office.

Overnight, the guys got together (yeah, some of the women thought it was a bad idea, and all of them refused to participate—but with the guys? now that's different) took apart his desk chair and the one guest chair he had; plus the donut cushion and this barstool thing he sometimes used (usually just to place junk on), and grabbed that disgusting bidet we gave him. On all were placed broken sticks, broken coke bottles, and bits of barbed wire. They wrapped that sharp refuse up in heavy plastic wrap where the cushions should be, and replaced the covers. As for the bidet—we just got rid of it. Snicker, snicker—giggle, giggle. We waited for tomorrow. It was like a bunch of schoolboys placing a frog inside someone's school-desk.

First thing Everett noticed when he arrived the next morning was that his ridiculous unattached to anything bidet was gone. We told him that the fire marshall had been in the night before to give the building a late night check (believe it or not, he bought this line) and determined everything was in order; however, there is a city ordinance that makes it illegal to have an unattached bidet in an office—so out it went. He was, of course, disheartened that his precious bidet was taken away, but didn't question it any further. Apparently just the notion that such an authority figure as a fire marshall stopped by to take a look at his cubicle was enough to convince him that the story was real and that there really was such a city ordinance. Such was Everett Slocum's respect (and fear of) authority figures, it would seem.

Then he sat down. It was all anybody could do to restrain themselves from laughing. Yes, those prudish women who thought this was a nasty trick to play on the poor guy did a certain amount of tsk-tsking and eye rolling; but actually, even they had to force themselves to hold back at least a little bit of a grin.

Such caterwauling! You'd think Everett was a giant tomcat sitting on the fence yowling away in the middle of the night. He hopped from one chair to the next. Each move making him invent a newer kind of howl.

"What's up, there, Everett?" one by one we, straight-faced as we could be, came around to his desk to find out.

"I can't sit down! I just can't sit down!" Everett claimed in a near panic.

"Come over to my desk, maybe my chair is softer," some of the others offered.

"It's no good! I can't sit down! I just can't sit down—anywhere!" he complained.

"Gee, Everett—looks like your problem has gotten worse. Maybe you should see a specialist," the others said to him. "Maybe you should see one right away."

And with that, Everett got on the phone to a proctologist immediately. And as they wouldn't set up an appointment with him until the following week—Everett made us call for an ambulance to the emergency room. Surprisingly, the ambulance people agreed. I guess an ass emergency looks just as good to them on their duty logs as any other emergency. And so they came, and got Everett (who had stuffed a pillow down the back of his pants by this time) and off they went. Yes, those women who disliked the idea in the first place did a bit more tsk-tsking—but what of it?

Problem solved, you think? Well . . . not exactly. Everett actually did have a bad case of hemorrhoids—something that eventually did require a bit of surgery. We actually never doubted that, we just couldn't put up with his whining. But once he had his problem taken care of, he found himself without anything to talk about. Now when he comes into the office, he talks of nothing except how great his ass feels. He'll even ask you how your ass feels in comparison. Now we can't get him to shut up about that. It's embarrassing the women and irritating the men.

Instead of concentrating on Everett's backside, we should have concentrated on the real problem—his mouth. There's already talk about practicing some amateur dentistry. But that's another story, and I'll tell that when some of the tsk-tskers are out of the room.

COFFINS FOR RENT

"Mister Fegley, I'm referred to around here."

"Mister Figleaf?"

"Fegley," he emphasized, somewhat irritated by this misinterpretation. He pulled on the lapels of his very black suitcoat and quickly regained his composure. "And how may I help you? What kind of casket are you looking for?"

"Oh, anything's good enough for the old lady," said the customer. Trailer trash, Fegley thought to himself but did not respond that way.

"She was your . . . mother?" Fegley inquired.

"Aunt," came the answer. "I had several in the family," said the portly man squeezing something that looked like an old, greasy cloth hat in his hands. "This was our least favorite," he offered.

"Ah," Fegley responded knowingly. "We have just the bargains you are looking for . . . right over here . . ." Fegley paraded his suit, with himself in it, over to another room of the building. There, lined up liked cars on display at an auto dealership, were coffins. "These are our rentals," Fegley stated proudly, assuming this was something one is to be proud of.

"You don't say," said the man with the greasy, unworn hat. "And how does this work, exactly?"

"Your funeral is at three o'clock with visitation from one, burial at five," Fegley explained. "That means we have your dear, departed aunt in the box by eleven, she arrives at the funeral home by noon. It's yours until six p.m. when we stop by the cemetery and pick it up."

"And what happens to my aunt?" The man had not shaved before coming here, Fegley observed, he will want the cheapest box we've got.

"She is placed in a serviceable before burial," Fegley answered.

"A what?"

"A serviceable. It's a standard pine box we use for our Jane Does. The coffin is brought back here and used again."

"Uhhhh. So how much does it cost to rent one of these?"

"Five hundred dollars at the going rate."

"That good?"

"Well . . . when you consider the standard coffin ranges from $2000 to nearly $10,000 with all the options . . ."

"Options? On a coffin?"

"There are options."

"What kind of options?"

Fegley hated when they asked questions like this. They both knew this guy wasn't going to sink 10 G's into a coffin. What does it matter what the extras are? Why is this clown bothering to ask? But Fegley didn't say that. Instead, he said, "For example, extra comfortable lining."

"Why would she need that? She's dead, isn't she?"

By now Fegley was getting the urge to hit this poor dumb bastard, but he didn't. Instead, he said, "Some people feel better about things having provided a much more luxurious environment for the deceased's eventual resting place."

"Well . . . I like the sound of that five hundred dollars." No kidding, Fegley said to himself. "That include the . . . 'serviceable' or whatever it's called?" the man added.

"Of course," Fegley reassured him.

"Oh well then, fine! Let's go with that."

"Is there any particular style or color you had in mind?" Fegley continued in his best officiating manner. "Here's one ladies tend to like . . . it has a pinkish hue to its exterior . . ."

"We're not buying something for a baby. Pink for girls, blue for boys. She already knew what sex she was, and has no further use for such things."

"I see. Well, here's a tan number that is very popular, or do you think she would like something in a darker hue? Perhaps something a little more ornate?"

"She doesn't care. She's already dead. As for me, the pine box will do."

"But for presentation purposes . . . there is to be a funeral, am I correct?"

"Yeah. You mean a pine box wouldn't serve the purpose?"

"It would be considered most indecorous. And think of the deceased. Would you want it known when it is your time that you were displayed in a rough-hewn box?"

"I wouldn't care as I would be dead. And certainly she doesn't care now either. No one'll come to the funeral. Nobody liked the old bat, including me."

"Weren't there any arrangements in her will?"

"Naw. Didn't believe in wills. Just popped off and left us stuck with her and all her old crap. You wouldn't have any extra room in the grave to take some of her shit with her, would you?"

"You'd have to deal with the cemetery on that matter. We only supply the caskets and prepare the body."

"Oh. Too bad. Thought I could kill two birds with one stone."

"Yes . . . quite," Fegley responded. "Shall we say the tan one, then?"

"Sure, why not?"

"If you will step into the office, we can sign the papers. When would you be needing your rental? This Saturday, I'm assuming?"

"Yeah. Nobody wanted to take off from work for this. Actually, I didn't. I don't know if anybody else'll be there."

The two men sat in a rather plush looking little office with three-ring binder catalogs filled with examples of models and pictures of happy customers. Fegley sat behind the desk. He pulled an official looking contract out of a drawer and offered his pen to the man in the dirty shirt.

"You take care of everything?" said the man, looking for a final assurance.

"Indeed," answered Fegley. "Sign here."

The man began signing. "What do you do with the coffin once the stiff is removed?"

"We wash them," answered Fegley.

"So it's kinda like popping breads out of a bread-pan."

"Quite," Fegley said, trying not to show his annoyance. "And here," he pointed to the contract, "the name of the cemetery, and here the name of the hospital or service from which to collect the dearly departed." The man continued signing. "From this point on, we will be in charge of everything. Have you made any arrangements for flowers?"

"Nah. The old dame don't need flowers. Is that extra?"

"We can do a simple basic. It would be included in the price."

"The $500?"

"No, the overall price of the entire arrangement which is $750. Only the box—uh, the casket—is $500." The man sat silent for a moment. "I assure you, you will not find a better arrangement for the price in a world where funerals run into thousands of dollars."

"Yeah. 'S'okay, I guess." Fegley fairly winced at the response. "Is there any special music you would like to have played?"

"Nah. I don't know if she liked music. Anything'll do. I'm not paying some guy to come in and play on an organ or anything, am I?"

"With the basic, we simply pipe in something over the speakers."

"Oh, good. Then it doesn't matter. Wait . . . I think she was fond of polka music. Put on a polka, will you?"

"We have our own library we can lift something from—perhaps something a little more appropriate. We will also put up a notice in the paper for you."

"All right, you're the expert."

"Do you have a minister or someone who can give your aunt a eulogy?"

"A what?"

"A speech," Fegley said with a sigh.

"Nah. Just shove her in the box and play your tunes."

"I'll arrange something."

With that the man rose from his chair and made his way to the front door. "Well, I guess that's it. See you Saturday."

"Saturday," Fegley reiterated and watched the man depart down the street. He returned to his office, and stepped into a little rest-room off to the side. He put in some eye-drops and mixed a glass of bicarbonate before returning to his desk.

An assistant came in, a young, barely-weaned boy out of high school in a suit that didn't fit him and placed an inquiry note before Fegley. "I have a woman out here who is inquiring about our rentals."

Fegley rolled his eyes. "It's been non-stop since we ran that ad. I dare say, it seems good for business but at that discount rate, I don't see how we are making any money."

"You haven't heard yet from the state whether or not renting coffins is legal, have you?"

"No. And I don't think we will. Such a practice is common elsewhere. And last night Senator Cornfield was in arranging something for his son-in-law. I had no idea there were so many disposable people out there just waiting for the right price!" Fegley again sighed. He had sighed so much in the past few days, it was becoming a habit—sort of a trademark. "All right, send her in."

The assistant left. Fegley steeled himself to put on his best manner and his most professional smile. In walked a woman who looked like she was auditioning for the role of Eliza Doolittle in *My Fair Lady.*

"You the guys with the coffin deal?"

"Yes," Fegley answered.

"Can you get me a cheap box for my miserable brother?"

Fegley's professional smile froze solid. It took all his strength to rise and say, "What kind of casket are you looking for?"

THE MONSTER BED

And so . . . Creeping into the room . . . I peered . . . The giant bed waited . . . Four-poster, canopy and curtains, old lady lace . . . A sudden gust of wind blew out my candle . . . Slammed the door behind me . . . This old drafty place! This room was always musty. You could sponge it down and sterilize it . . . it always seemed musty. For that matter, the whole house seemed musty.

This was my bed for the night. I didn't volunteer for it. I was "awarded" it. For being a good boy, they said. Phooey! A lot of hooey! They wanted to see me suffer—the relatives. "Give him Gramma's bed! He'll love it! It's Christmas!" Yeah, sure. As long as they don't have to sleep in it.

I approached it cautiously, standing in the dark in my night shirt. Too late to turn back now. The comforter was pulled back making the mattress look like a great yawning mouth. And it smelled like Gramma. Any Gramma. Gramma's been dead for how long? And her smell stays. Don't they ever open a window here?

Outside the wind howled. Too cold tonight to let the windows open now. I didn't know what to do with my dead candle. I finally put it and its little carrier on top of the big ugly bedside table with the brown crinkling varnish that made it look like an aging fat man with a big hat. He looked grumpy but not dangerous. Not like the evil bed.

I stood for what seemed an hour. Do I actually enter the thing and let it eat me? Or do I stand here all night in the draft? Or maybe I should crawl into that big upholstered chair in the corner near the unlit fireplace and place one of the blankets over me. The chair didn't look too inviting either. It was big with a high back and high shoulders—or whatever those things are. It had some kind of nappy surface that no doubt hid fleas or something in its depths. If you sat in it (I did once), it would make a groaning sound like it had arthritis and you were just too heavy to burden itself with—and I had yet to reach a hundred pounds in weight! Actually, the chair was just like Grampa. And nobody wanted to sit in his lap.

So which do I pick, Gramma or Grampa? I was actually tired, so Gramma seemed like the better option. A bed was actually an inviting idea. I don't know why this bed wouldn't be inviting . . . if only it weren't for the fact that I knew, inherently, that it was evil.

I stepped next to it, kicked off my slippers, but made sure they were pointed toward the door. Just in case I had to make a run for it, I didn't want to fumble with my slippers—nor did I want to run out into the hall and get my feet cold. Then, I made the attempt to climb on top of the mattress (I did this after emitting a little prayer). And "making the attempt" to get into it is the right phrase—it was like climbing onto a giant draft horse: a sort of Clydesdale made of wood and straw and goose feathers.

It was chilly. Well . . . the room was drafty and probably nobody slept in it since Gramma died. So you might very well have been inserting yourself into the baleen of a bowhead whale. I laid on my back and tried pulling the tonnage of comforter and quilt up to my neck. Even though I didn't want to bury myself that deep into it, Mom or some annoying aunt may want to stop in and check on me to see how I'm doing. Female relatives always figure your wellbeing is their responsibility, and become irritatingly fussy about such things. If they saw me just sort of laying on top, they'd immediately make some sort of stink about it, and I didn't want that to happen. Besides, I didn't want anybody branding me a coward for not wanting to crawl in. Adults don't get it. They don't understand where evil truly lies.

I did keep my arms out from under the covers, however. I wanted to be able to grab those covers and fling them off at a moment's notice while catapulting myself off the mattress—just in case.

I waited. What was I waiting for? Anything. Maybe I would be lucky and those mysterious powers in the house would have mercy, and I would actually fall asleep until morning without incident. Or maybe the bed actually would act up—and I wanted to be ready to run. Nothing happened. I waited more. Still nothing.

Outside there was a hooting. An owl. I didn't know owls were around here. Downstairs I could still hear the grown-ups giggling over another bottle of wine. Grown-ups need wine to make them giggle. Kids do that all by themselves.

And still I waited. I began to think about the day. The presents, the Christmas cheer. Why wasn't I happy? Well, I was—except for this damn bed. Another hoot from outside. The house was quiet. I must have dosed off. The grown-ups all had left, or had gone to their own rooms for the night. I was alone. And at the mercy of the bed.

I tried counting sheep. Has that ever worked for anybody? Then I tried counting baseball players. That didn't work either. Then I began to notice I was making some sort of snorting sound—it was like it was coming from somebody else, only it was me. I was apparently very drowsy at the time the snorting sound made its presence known when I also began to notice that the bed covers were creeping up on me. My arms were now underneath the covers. When did that happen? Why did that happen?

I tried to turn on my side and couldn't move. I found myself sinking slowly into the tick. The sides of the mattress were moving up around me, higher and higher. The bed started to groan—much like the upholstered chair in the corner. Only this was a much deeper, more satisfied groan, like that which comes from the belly of a whale when it is devouring a mouthful of krill.

I began to panic. The bed was swallowing me alive! I tried to kick and flail about, but I was pinned down by the great weight of the covers. I wanted to scream, but my own snorting got in the way, and all I could let out was some sort of ridiculous gurgle that only a mouse on the bedpost might hear. And I sank deeper and deeper into the groaning mattress. I shook violently with all my might. The curtains around the fourposts quivered and even made a jingling noise—some old necklace draped over one of the posts, no doubt left there by Gramma to signal her victory over little boys she wanted her bed to swallow. Gramma always was a mean old bird in that way.

I found myself finally screaming an "Uhhhhhhh!" like a drunken sailor wretching over the pier as he steps from the nearest tavern he spent the night in. I doubt if anyone other than me heard that noise. All around me, over me, suffocating me, was mattress and cover—cover and mattress. I was about to die.

And suddenly I woke up. The, "Uhhhhhh!" I emitted startled me into wakefulness. The sun was peeking through those dreadfully dark and heavy curtains that hung over the windows. It was already morning. I was lying on top of the bed. I must have tasted awful, because the bed, it would seem, vomited me out of its huge maw.

There was a polite little knock on the door. That could only be Mom.

"Are you awake?" came the voice. Yup, it was Mom. "We're making waffles this morning!"

I decided I wouldn't tell her about my awful experience the night before. I sat up and pushed back the covers. I was alive. Something had saved me. Maybe Gramma had a kind heart after all. I was ready to get up. Only . . . I was still so tired . . . so tired from a long night of worry. I was just about to bounce out of bed when . . . I suddenly got really drowsy again.

Birdsong. I remember birdsong. In December? There were birds outside my window singing. Winter birds. Not that awful owl. Songbirds. I couldn't stay awake. I fell back on my pillow and didn't get up for another two hours—safe and sound, no further incidents. Just an extra couple of hours of sleep.

What the hell—it's Christmas.

THREE ANECDOTES:

DON'T FART TOO MUCH
DON'T LET THE MAN FINISH
TOO MUCH FUN

DON'T FART TOO MUCH

"Really."

"Really?"

"Really," the Doctor said. "If you find yourself having gastric troubles, try to relieve them with some form of bicarbonate or other such things. Try not to fart too much."

"Oh," said the steely-eyed patient. "And what if I can't help myself."

"You'll find yourself being impolite," the Doctor responded. "Shunned from society," he continued. "And likely to explode."

"Explode?"

"Explode," the Doctor emphasized. "You have a peculiar condition wherein, if you allow your intestines to generate enough gas, you will inflate them beyond repair. This particular condition is likely to become so volatile of a gaseous mix, that at the first wink of the anus, you will, no doubt, detonate the mixture inside; thus creating enough explosive force to blow your colon out your backside in a violent conflagration. I need not tell you what a difficult and expensive undertaking it would be to surgically put you back together—not to mention the danger to your health. Once it starts, further more, there's no telling where it will end. You could go off like a Roman candle or a Chinese firecracker string on New Year's. When the solution is simple enough. You can deflate these potentially dangerous signals at the first sign of bloating with a little bicarbonate."

"My goodness, Doctor! This sounds serious!"

"Not if properly handled."

"How long will this condition last for me?"

"I've put you on antibiotics. It should lessen in a few weeks. In the meantime, stay away from curry, or Mexican food, or beans of any kind."

The man took the prescription, put his shirt on, and left the examination room with a worried look on his face.

"Remember," the Doctor added as the man was heading toward the front desk, "Don't fart too much."

"A lesson I shall always remember," said the man—and walked on.

DON'T LET THE MAN FINISH

"Indeed," Celine stated, sipping her tea.

"Indeed," said Esmeralda nibbling on a bit of croissant. "But what can you do with them when they get like that?"

"You have to deal with it as best you can," Celine continued with an air of finesse. "They are what they are and there's no changing that."

"Exactly," stated Esmeralda taking a flake of croissant with her fingers and delicately slipping it into her mouth. "There's nothing to stop them. They only understand what they want."

"Exactly," returned Celine, "which is why one has to measure one's response. You know that once they have that you are unlikely to receive a call again."

"Isn't that just like them," Esmeralda conceded, "One would think you were just a bauble to be used at their discretion. Why, a woman would not retain any self-respectability under such circumstances."

"Indeed, one would not," added Celine. "And do they bother to call you afterwards?"

"NOOOOO!!" they said in unison.

"And yet . . . it is difficult to be entirely removed from that field of experience," Esmeralda sighed.

"Of course," Celine rejoined thoughtfully.

"If it were possible to live in a world where they did not exist, one may not miss such creatures, or the benefits that their presence may create. And I, for one, would miss that."

"I, too," Celine agreed. "As they say, you can't live with them and you can't live without them."

"But for all that, we do live in a world beside them; and one has to get along somehow," Esmeralda chimed in.

"Unquestionably," Celine traced her finger along the saucer in her hand.

"So then, how does one compromise between these two schools of thought?" Esmeralda questioned. "How does one have the best of both worlds?"

"Well . . . there is a way . . ." Celine said, mysteriously.

"How?" Esmeralda was intrigued.

"You can get them to your porch without allowing the goats to become what they truly are inside."

"And that is? . . ." Esmeralda displayed every indication she was hooked.

"I have a secret one may utilize to one's benefit," Celine intoned secretively.

"A secret?"

"A secret?"

"Really?"

"Really."

"Do say."

Celine leaned in conspiratorially, "There is a way to keep them at your beck and call."

"How?" Esmeralda leaned in herself, croissant forgotten, and on pins and needles.

"If you want them to obey you, respond to you as you like . . ."

"Yes? . . ." the suspense was killing Esmeralda.

"Do what I do," Celine took another sip of tea. Esmeralda was nearly bursting with impatience. Celine weighed her words carefully, and delivered them—slowly, "Never let the man finish."

Esmeralda sat back in her chair as if pushed, jaw dropping. "Really?"

Celine gave a knowing look and a nod before sipping more tea. "Don't let the man finish. Ever." She punctuated. "Really. It drives them absolutely crazy. They'll keep coming back for more."

"Indeed."

"Indeed."

"And has this always worked for you?" Esmeralda asked, intrigued.

"Always," Celine emphasized. "It will work for you too. Just as I said. Exactly," she implored firmly.

"Exactly!" Esmeralda cried.

Esmeralda lighted up, and munched a bit more of croissant thoughtfully, dreaming of situations beyond her former reach. Celine finished her tea. Each looked about and at each other and smirked and even let out a bit of a giggle.

"Hmm-hmm," Celine intoned.

"Hmm-hmm," Esmeralda responded. "Indeed," she said.

"Indeed," Celine said.

TOO MUCH FUN

There he lies, passed out on the dance floor. Would somebody get a doctor? A doctor was found—luckily everybody comes here to whoop it up. What does he look like, Doc?

Bad, very bad.

The doctor looked and looked. He poked and prodded. He sniffed and listened.

Dead. The man was dead.

What did he die of, Doc?

Well, considering how he was pitching and yawing like a boat in a storm, considering how he was weaving and heaving, considering how he was swelling and yelling—I would have to say, without much equivocation, that he died of too much fun.

Too Much Fun?!!

Can such a thing be possible? Can one die of too much fun?

Oh yes, yes, indeed, yes! Just look at the poor chap, all bloated and waxy, all gray and fey, all hither and thither, wither and weather, hinter and yon. The heart, the brain, the lungs, the legs, the liver—something gave out on him. You don't just end up like that.

Blimey—for those people who say, "blimey"—can anyone die of too much fun?

Absolutely.

Let that be a lesson to you then. Have fun, but watch yourself. You don't want to end up like him. Be kind, be vigilant. Be vigorous, be sedate. Take time to consider options. Allow yourself a moment to hesitate. Or you too will end up on the floor in the middle of a crowded place, making a posthumous spectacle of yourself, by dying—of Too Much Fun.

ALL YOUR HEART'S DESIRE

"What if you wished for it, and everything you wanted could be yours?" he asked. "What if all wishes came true. Would you want them to?"

"Why not?" the other fellow questioned softly, not knowing where this was going.

"Just think . . . wish for a lot of money, you'd have to pay a lot of taxes."

"Couldn't you wish to be exempt from the IRS?"

"You could, but how practical would that be? Wouldn't eventually somebody find out about it and start up some kind of protest against you?"

"You could wish to quash the protest."

"And have unlimited credit? Wouldn't that eventually cause problems for the bank?"

"It wouldn't have to be unlimited."

"Oh, just enough to be comfortable, not greedy?"

"That's right."

"And what would your comfort level be?"

"So that I never have to worry about money again."

"Regardless of inflation and other worldly occurrences?"

"That's right."

"And what would you do with your money?"

"Do? Live! Isn't that enough?"

"Don't you think you might become bored?"

"Why should I?"

"I don't know. What kind of person are you—would you become—if you had everything you wanted?"

"I'm not sure."

"No one does—until it happens to him. So you wish for all this money and all your bill problems to go away . . . and you wish to be tax free and problem free of worldly concerns. Will all that make you happy? Would you be able to stave off inner conflicts with family and friends who come to you to solve their problems? Would you be able to stave off inner conflicts with yourself when all this prosperity becomes too much of a bother? Would you get depressed, contemplate suicide? Or would you become a menace, taking life and property, and other people's lives and other people's property so cavalierly that you become a reckless gambler, whore-monger, murderer?"

"It wouldn't mean I was exempt from the law."

"But you have all the money in the world to buy off police and politicians. You can pray on people via their basest instincts. Even if you aren't greedy (somehow with all this money at your disposal) other people around may become so. Soon nobody loves you for yourself, you become a personal ATM machine people come to for their own needs—and you are surrounded by yes men and sycophants everywhere you look."

"I could do good with my money. I could be a philanthropist and give to charity."

"How much money would you give away? And wouldn't you be buried in people looking for handouts?"

"Not necessarily. Not if it is managed right. There are billionaires who do this sort of thing."

"And you'd be one of them?"

"I'd just have to stipulate in my wishes for proper management of funds."

"How many conditions are you imposing on these wishes of yours? And how many wishes are you expecting to receive? And are you sure you have covered all bases so that you would not be undone by your own methods? What if you were given just one wish? Do you think you could frame it so that all these conditions apply?"

"Well . . . okay. I'd have to think carefully, and make sure I framed the wish properly. But let's say I didn't wish for money. Let's say I wished for something else?"

"Such as . . . ?"

"Fame? Power? Lots of women? A cure for cancer!"

"And you somehow think none of that has a down-side? You don't know what unseen consequences hide behind even the most noble wish could bring—such as curing cancer. That's the strange thing about wishes—once they are in place the world goes about its business in its usual way, and there isn't any accurate measure by which to judge what the consequences of any sudden windfall may be. Until, of course, it happens."

The two men drank their coffee in silence for a while, thinking over their discussion. The second man then poured out a dram of sugar on the café table and arranged it into a neat little round pile. And then he fell to challenge his friend again from across the table. "So, there you have a button. All you have to do is press it once, and all your wishes come true," he said pointing to the pile of sugar. "With one press, you will achieve all your heart's desire. No consequences. None that you can see. Do you do it?"

"No consequences?"

"None you can see."

"That's different. If you said no consequences, period, that would be a different story."

"Would it? You press this button to be happy forever, as far as you can define happiness now, and except for your wish, the rest of the world goes about as it always does. You'd think there would never be any consequences to your actions?"

"I could wish to change the world."

"And take away free will?"

"Everyone would still have free will. They would just make the right decisions that benefit everybody."

"Such as yours to make you rich."

"I thought we were now talking happiness."

"Ah. So everyone will be happy from now on. Regardless. So then, no change."

"There could still be change, but everyone would be happy about it."

"You don't see that as static? Let's say to get there, everybody gets all their wishes to come true—you see no conflicts in that?"

"Well . . . they would balance out."

"Would they? And who's to decide what all these right wishes and right decisions would be?"

"They would just balance out . . . somehow."

"Put it in God's hands, so to speak."

"I guess."

"But why hasn't he done that already, if that's what he wants."

"I don't know."

"So potentially your wish might be going against God's will."

"Did I say that?"

"Everyone is to be free, everyone gets all their wishes fulfilled, everyone is to be happy forever—correct? That's some wish. Do you even believe in God?"

"Well . . . yes and no. I mean . . . I don't believe what the church usually says he is."

"But? . . ."

"But I believe there is some . . . power or force out there watching over us."

"And yet he's too lazy or incompetent to grant everybody peace and prosperity. You have to step in with your mighty wishes to fix all that. And you say you aren't going against God somehow."

"I didn't mean that. I just meant . . . well, I don't know what I mean."

"Ah. So you admit wishing for things via a magic button has some complications to it."

"Yeah. Moreso than I thought at first."

"And you wonder why we aren't granted magic wishes."

"Well . . . I can see where it may not be a boon to everybody."

"It may simply create new problems while it is solving some old ones."

"I guess."

They finished their coffee and asked for the check. The man who was the recipient of this philosophical inquiry, spent time contemplating what had been said. The man who spent his time extrapolating arguments spent his time philosophizing. They paid their tab and left a tip, and exited the coffee shop into the brisk winter air that permeated the city. They nodded a polite adieu. The Philosopher went his way. The Contemplator went his.

The Contemplator strolled along the sidewalk stepping over ice chunks, crunching through patches of snow, watching the frost-covered cars roll down the street. Children leapt about in the field of white that was their playground behind the fence that kept them in bounds of school. People went by on the street preoccupied with their own affairs scarcely noticing each other. The sun tried to peek through the clouds, but it was just too much effort to do so that day.

He went home and sat and sat. He made himself some tea, read for awhile, heated up a supper from whatever remains he found in his refrigerator, and went to bed early without the usual noise that came from the television recounting the often unsavory events of the day.

He lived alone, the Contemplator did, in an apartment on the second floor of the three story, and quaint, but none too impressive apartment building. While not far from the noises of the city's downtown, his neighborhood had the old world feel of what was once long ago an exclusive neighborhood, and now had been dominated by college students. There were bookstores and coffee shops galore in a place like this with bargain-basement budget cinemas nearby showing films from Germany and Indonesia that would fail in any other part of the city. It was a place to be smug and superior if one couldn't actually be wise or thoughtful. And while no one was really upper class who lived here, one certainly could behave as if one was—as long as one stayed within the bounds of the neighborhood and the nearby University.

The Contemplator took in a folk-singer over lunch on the stage of a nearby salad bar, and waited until four o'clock when he would again meet the Philosopher for coffee.

"I had some thoughts on your book," said the Philosopher when he finally met the Contemplator over scones. "This book you're writing," the Philosopher began, "in some way has to do with the conception of time—correct?"

"Yes."

"And you've stressed the importance of memory in dealing with the past and in imagination—projection, if you will—in dealing with the future. Is that not also true?"

"For the most part."

"But the fact is, we always live in the immediate now. We are sitting here, talking NOW. In another few minutes, this discussion will be replaced by another NOW, in which we get up and go our separate ways, which at the moment is the future, and this will at that point be the past."

"I'm following."

"So that the past is always in memory, and the future is always in imagination. And we are always placed in the immediate NOW from which we can't really escape. Time is linear—it always moves, and it always moves forward."

"Yes."

"So in an argumentative sense, neither the past or future is actually real. Neither exists: one, because it hasn't happened yet (and may not); and the other has already happened and is gone, it cannot be altered. Our only connection to the past is memory, and our only indication of the future is imagination."

"So the argument goes."

"Yet both can effect the NOW. The future, because we can grasp very strongly to the plans we intend to commit; the past, because it is our experience and greatly shapes how we behave in the NOW. For instance, if your past was as a rock musician rather than a college professor on sabbatical, your NOW, would be different. You probably wouldn't be sitting here talking to me at the moment."

"Probably."

"As for your future, it would probably be even less likely that you'd be interested in writing a book. Particularly the book you are planning to write."

"I would agree with that."

"So then . . . does the past—or the future—hold undo influence on the NOW."

"Undo influence? Possibly. I guess it depends on the individual."

"And the experience. Right. If you were a Jew who had been imprisoned in a Nazi concentration camp as a child, and somehow managed to survive—though you were an old man now, that experience of the past would no doubt have colored your NOWS, your back then futures, with a certain flavor, attitude, approach to things, or thinking. Right?"

"I assume."

"Or say the opposite. Say you grew up as a talented child in the Hollywood studio system and became rich and famous and had everything you wanted, so that you were always happy."

"Actually, I believe few childhood stars actually were all that happy—"

"Granted many were not, but some certainly were. Or a child brought up in a monarchy as a prince or princess and raised with enormous privilege. Again the argument can be made some were happy in those circumstances and some weren't—but the point is, some have had a life of suffering, others have had an easy time of it. Whatever your background is, it would color your NOW, and your projections of the future."

"Agreed."

"Now flip that and aim at the future. Suppose you were this young man and dreamed of becoming this famous rock musician, even worked and struggled for it over an extended period of time. This was your plan, your projection into the future."

"Okay."

"And let's say you made it, but let's also say it wasn't what you dreamed it would be and you became one of those famous burnout cases who drives himself to death with drug overdoses."

"Cheery thought."

"Or perhaps you never made it, because you didn't have the talent or drive or luck or whatever, and are always driven by what you hoped for but never achieved. Or maybe you aspired to be President of the United States, or whatever, an Olympic Champion, say."

"Go on."

"Here's what I'm getting at . . . In either case, the person with unflinching, indelible past, or the overreaching projection of the future—your NOW is colored by that. Both effect the NOW. Yet the NOW is all you will ever be, because you can't escape it."

"Well, you can't escape the past or future either—until you're dead."

"Correct. But you will always be in the NOW. The NOW is the most important thing."

"Are you trying to emulate the Hippies of the 1960s by saying only "now" counts? Or trying out some pseudo Buddhist manifestation of centralized personal peace to remove all desire?"

"Not exactly. Besides Buddhism isn't about removing desire, just understanding it. No. My point is this . . . do you believe that either the past or future, or rather one's interpretation of it, can have a powerful, even crippling effect on one's personality—and on one's NOW."

"Of course. That's why I'm writing the book."

"What I submit to you is that it is not the past—memory—or the future—projection—that has that effect, but the VALUE of it. So it is VALUE, not time we are talking about."

"Value."

"Exactly. Every day we go through routines and live our lives. We, for example, frequently meet here for coffee. Other people, us included, live their days through habit and comfort and routine, most of which don't make much of an impression on us—except for a certain comfort level that habit establishes for us. I can't remember what I had for breakfast yesterday. I only know that I probably had something because I usually have something to start the day. However, I do remember my first lecture at the college. I do remember working on my thesis. I do remember the first time I got lucky with a certain young lady I was enamored of in the backseat of my father's automobile. These are things that moulded my character. They are of the past and are gone, but they have VALUE. And because they do, there is something about them I carry with me that effects my NOW, and projects into my future."

"I see."

"So your argument is not necessarily TIME in the sense of past and present. Your argument is the VALUE of experience, and the projection of that experience."

"Oh."

"Whether I succeed or fail in the future depends a lot on my personal fortitude (which is always in the NOW) and on the VALUE of the experience I carry with me through memory of my past."

"I guess I can't argue with that. But why did you bring it up?"

"Well what governs all of these experiences? Past, future, now?" The Philosopher waited an appropriate time, perhaps for dramatic purposes, for the answer to come. The Contemplator did not provide him with the answer, other than a simple shrug.

"Your heart," the Philosopher stated. It surprised the Contemplator somewhat as he had known of the Philosopher as a rather cerebral gentleman, and not one prone to sentiment. For him to suggest feelings are the principle mover and shaker in the scheme of things was something of a stretch for the Contemplator to recognize.

"It goes back to our conversation yesterday," the Philosopher said, "What if you could wish for anything in the world, and had access to some power that could make it all come true. What if you could get all your heart's desire? What would it be? Some live their lives as if whatever that was, was still coming. Others live as if it has passed them by and never will be.

Both live in the NOW effected by the VALUE they place on their past and futures."

"I see."

Another afternoon coffee had come and gone. The Contemplator and the Philosopher said a convivial adieu and went their separate ways. They would meet again in the near future to talk about other things over biscotti and latte. That was their habit. But, the Contemplator wondered, what was in their hearts—both of theirs? Specifically, what was in his own? What was it that he wanted? What was his heart's desire, and if he could attain it, easily and magically, would it make him happy? Would he even recognize it?

Perhaps, he began to think, one should not write about happiness until one discovers it. Was he happy? He didn't even know.

He walked along the icy sidewalk passed the school and into his quietly stuffy but thoughtfully youthful neighborhood, and watched as the irrepressible crows scoffed at the chilly weather and went about looking for scraps of food. And the sun seemed on a course of constantly barging in through the clouds to brighten up the day, but somehow never managed to do that. He wondered why he had been alone so much for so long, and if teaching at the university was all there was to his life. He wondered why he was writing a book.

But this was his NOW. And he felt he was stuck with it.

THE INCREDIBLE MR. FITZWATER & HIS
HORRENDOUS HURDY-GURDY MACHINE

Everybody thought Mister Fitzwater was peculiar. He had no wife, he had
no children. He had two dogs: LeRoy and Hal. LeRoy was a something
or other, and Hal was a something else. Mister Fitzwater lived at the end
of town. He had a small house that people were afraid to visit, because it
had a yard full of even more peculiar junk. Mister Fitzwater saw himself as
a sculptor and went to the junkyards frequently to pick up all manner of
junk. He would bring the junk home in his weather-beaten pick-up and
dump all that junk in his rather spacious yards that surrounded his grungy
little house and even grungier garage/workshop. He could never park his
truck in the garage—there was no room for it.

Anyway, the junk got dumped in his yard, and with it he made even
more ugly junk he fancied as art. Mister Fitzwater had no visible means
of support—he had no job. He inherited the house from his parents who
had one child—him—and immediately quit after that. Mister Fitzwater
was a bit chubby, and had been so all his life. He was bald on top with
an unkempt straggle of gray around his ears and the back of his neck. He
had an unusually high voice, not helped by a touch of asthma—again a
lifelong condition. And he seemed to spend much of his time laughing

his life away. He was, in a word, jolly; and because of that, and despite his many odd habits (like walking around the yard with a candle in his hand at three in the morning to see if the wild rabbits were comfortable), people liked him. Kids liked him. Dogs liked him. Kids and dogs tend to like the same things, including smelling poop. I know, because I was involved in a poop smelling contest with some of the other kids when I was that age.

Small town life is different than big town life. You need someone like Mister Fitzwater to give you things to talk about. Mister Fitzwater was a show and a half. He always dressed up like a clown for the Fourth of July parade. He also dressed up like a clown for Thanksgiving. The fact that clowns have nothing to do with Thanksgiving did not deter him.

He bought a calliope from some circus going out of business and put it in his backyard. During warm summer days, at the instigation of kids and dogs, he would warm it up (it seems one has to cook a calliope like heating a pot of soup on the stove) and begin to play it. *Boop-boop-boop-boop-boop!!* It scared the birds out of the trees. Crows would sit on his worn and peeling fence and caw back their disapproval whenever he was done.

The neighbors—that is, the grown-ups—hated that thing. But then grown-ups have been taught to hate fun anyway, and spent their time in barber shops and beauty parlors ridiculing Mister Fitzwater. Unfortunately for us, and luckily for the neighbors, the calliope was old and was practically falling apart when he got it. A couple of summers out in the rain (not to mention standing through the winters) and it rusted to pieces and fell apart—only to become parts of more of Fitzwater sculptures.

Somehow or other Mister Fitzwater was able to talk a gallery owner (or oddball collector) into thinking his art worth something, and he began to sell a piece here and there, which no doubt helped with the property taxes, so he didn't have to live on inheritance alone.

He would go to the butcher shop and buy meat for dogs. Then he would hand out pig's ears to us kids and tell us to go find a dog ourselves that may want it. I kept one pig's ear for five years in a closet somewhere. I'd forgot all about it until we developed an ant problem in the very same closet.

Since Mister Fitzwater liked music, it was not above him to make his own instruments—usually out of junk. He invented some sort of blowing mechanism that utilized an ordinary electric fan that blew wind across the top of some ceramic jugs. What came out was more eerie than musical, but you had to admire the inventiveness; however impractical. He also found an old rusty bicycle with mismatched wheels, and an array of bicycle horns, bells, and jingling trinkets—all of which he mounted on the vehicle. He would ride this lop-sided bike down the center of the street, honking and jingling and tinkling away, with the dogs riding in a coaster-wagon strapped to the back. Since some of the horns had cracked rubber bladders, they tended to wheeze or make farting noises instead of honking. This made us kids gleefully happy.

He tried to capture lightning once and put it in a jar. He stayed out all night in a storm wearing a complete suit of tinfoil, holding onto a kite with a key at the end just like Ben Franklin. None of us kids were allowed out to watch, but we did hear after a particularly loud thunderclap a scream, a squeal, a cry, and a hooting like: *hoo-hoo-hoo-hoo-hoo!!* We don't know if that meant success or failure; and as far as we know, Mister Fitzwater never tried it again—or what the purpose was for to begin with. We just know that if he succeeded, he also survived, for we saw him the next day. His hair (what was left of it) looked extra crispy and static-y, and he had a rash like a sunburn, oddly shaped about him. The only thing he ever told us kids was: "God works in mysterious ways."

Mister Fitzwater wore mismatched clothes and funny hats. I think he did that just to infuriate his neighbors and make them think he was nuts. Well . . . he was . . . kind of. He was fond of pinwheels and his yard was full of them—many of them home-made constructed from umbrellas, chamois, pastry-bags—you name it. He strung up his bicycle and his pick-up with them as well.

But the best thing I remember him for was his hurdy-gurdy machine. He found an old hurdy-gurdy from somewhere, broken, of course, and not satisfied just to repair it, he built it bigger and better than it ever was, and found someway to amplify it by putting it in some kind of wagon and letting the wheels pump in air. It seems he had to do something to replace the rusted-apart calliope. It made a horrendous racket, and was just the thing to put a smile on his face, and smiles on the kids and dogs in town.

He would just show up, unannounced, in his clown-suit, his dogs about him, pulling this monstrosity he made, covered in pinwheels, with his bicycle. And it would be harrumphing and honking and hollering like a dragon with asthma all the way. Even us kids believed it made a horrendous noise. Our parents were outraged, but the local Sheriff refused to do anything about it. In his view, Fitzwater wasn't harming anybody and a motorcycle makes as much noise.

He, Fitzy as he often liked to be called, would pull to the side when enough kids and dogs had congregated, and started doing magic tricks. He pulled flowers out of the hurdy-gurdy. He pulled flowers out of his suit and hat. It was magic. No matter that the flowers smelled like plastic. We didn't know how it was done. Then he'd get us to sing a song with him. And after that, he'd ask: "You want to go to the Moon?!"

Of course we hollered, "Yes!" What did we know about the Moon? We followed him to the nearest park, the dragon-bellowing hurdy-gurdy spinning wheels in the wind and popping plastic flowers and confetti from air-gun tubes all the way. He made us close our eyes and cover our faces with our hands—and spin and spin and spin until we fell down. And just like that we were on the Moon! A dozen kids with a dozen dogs and maybe a squirrel and a rabbit or two. He told us to fly, fly, fly! We were no longer bound by Earth's gravity.

We visited the Prince and Princess of the Moon in their Moony castle, with the stars and the cratered mountains all around. Who knew the Moon had a prince and princess? And we walked through Moony rock-gardens and drank from Moony springs, sang Moony folk-songs that the little ruddy Moonfolks sing. And then we encountered Moon Giants in all their fearsome aspect, but who turned out to be rather gentle lambs when you sang the Moony songs to them.

Finally we were threatened by the Black Moon Dragon that belched fire and smoke and sounded like a hurdy-gurdy; and we flew back to the Moon castle before saying goodbye to the handsome prince and pretty princess, who gave us each a little shiny glass button full of Moonglow and a handful of Moondust—both full of magic! And when we woke up we were back in the park—all kids and dogs—each one of us with a glassy magic button in one hand and some confetti looking moondust in the other. Mister Fitzwater said we should immediately sprinkle ourselves with the moondust to keep us from flying back unwittingly to the Moon; and hang on to the Moon stone for good luck always. Some of us even sprinkled the dogs with dust. We didn't want to see them flying back accidentally through the sky.

And then we made our way back home, the hurdy-gurdy howling all the way.

Mister Fitzwater lived in a world of fantasy, and us kids always joined him whenever possible. But reality and fantasy are two different things, and it wasn't too long after the summer of the hurdy-gurdy exploits that Mister Fitzwater was stricken with cancer. This was one adventure he could not extract himself from.

His house was sold and his junk—junked, to make way for a Tastee-Freeze at the end of town where all the teenagers hung out and spent their money. But somebody got the idea of building a memorial to Mister Fitzwater out of what remained of his junk, in the very park where we all flew to the Moon. There sits now a curious mixture of sculptures and pinwheels attached together, surrounding a hurdy-gurdy type of box that has no power of its own, but allows the wind to blow through it and make a slight wheezy hum whenever conditions are right. And framed around it is a bas-relief of Mister Fitzwater, surrounded by colorful glass Moonstones.

Mister Fitzwater is now the Clown Musician Magician Extraordinaire of the Royal line of the Prince and Princess of the Moon.

IN OUR HOUSE

"Would you like a cup of tea?" Mrs. Sprightly said.

"How could I refuse?" I answered with a smile and in my most polite manner. How could you not be gracious to gracious people?

"There's always room for tea!" Mr. Sprightly said with a grin in his most ebullient and robust manner. Mr. Sprightly could have passed for a Teddy Roosevelt lookalike back in the day when such a thing might have mattered; but that was decades in the past and wasn't important now—and besides, Mr. Sprightly had too deep a voice to carry the illusion on.

I went into their home that was well furnished and spoke loudly of bourgeoisie. A home that had enough money to boast for itself, without declaring, "We are (or soon aim to be) stinking rich!" I was there on a neighborly visit. Something about a committee to achieve funding for statues in the park. Certainly the Sprightlys, as suits their station, are concerned about public art.

Mrs. Sprightly welcomed me inside and brought out a magnificent tea service. Was this just for me? Wasn't I trying to impress her, rather than the other way around? She placed it on the coffee table, Mr. Sprightly helping her (after all, it was a huge tray with huge tea-making implements on it) showing what a good husband he was.

"It only takes a minute to reach the correct temperature," Mrs. Sprightly told me. "In our house, we like to have our tea at the precise temperature for adding sugar."

"Not too hot, not too tepid," Mr. Sprightly added. "Tea should stand up to three blows—no more!"

"You do take sugar, Mr. Zepperell?" Mrs. Sprightly continued.

"Oh yes," I answered.

"That's fine," she seemed pleased. "Tea should have a precise amount of sweetener—no more, no less. And cream—always cream. Never milk!"

"Oh never!" Mr. Sprightly intervened, "No never!"

"You do take cream in your tea as well, do you not, Mr. Zepperell?"

"Actually, I can take it or leave it," I answered, and both seemed to react as if I squirted lemon juice in their faces.

"Well," Mrs. Sprightly straightened herself, "In our house we take cream."

"Cream is fine," I added. "I'll have cream." Mrs. Sprightly seemed not only pleased with that remark, but relieved. I wondered what she'd have done if I had said, "Skip it."

"The tea should be ready now," she said, "It only takes a minute." It was as if reminding me what the rules of tea are. She began to pour from that opulent porcelain teapot edged in gold into an equally opulent cup.

"Guests first!" Mr. Sprightly boomed from his chair opposite me. This was the rule also.

Mrs. Sprightly poured it to exactly one-half inch below the rim.

"Do you take more than one lump, Mr. Zepperell?" she inquired in that musical voice of hers that can suddenly screech if something is out of order.

"One is fine," I answered.

"In our house, we take one lump per cup," she continued.

"Not too sweet, not too bland," I said with a smile, again trying to be polite by reinforcing their pattern. This was not received well—rather, they both tried to ignore it as if I had not spoken.

"How much cream?" she asked, still polite, but a touch colder than just a minute ago. Did they assume I was making fun of them?

"I don't care," I answered.

"In our house, we use a thimble full of cream per cup. It gives the right balance between tea, sugar, and cream."

"How do you know what a thimble full of cream is?"

"We measured it," Mr. Sprightly interjected. "Mrs. Sprightly got out a thimble from her sewing basket and she practiced until she could precisely gage how much cream is a thimble full. To this day no one is as exact with cream as Mrs. Sprightly. She'll not even allow me to pour cream on my own anymore." That seemed to be a statement of pride coming from Mr. Sprightly. Was this an achievement to be admired?

"That will be fine," I told Mrs. Sprightly, and she seemed delighted to be pouring her judgment of a thimble full of cream into the cup. She then placed a spoon in it, a rather ornate piece of silverware I should state, and handed the cup to me. Then she proceeded to pour a cup for her husband and eventually the same for herself—all exactly the same. I began stirring my tea.

"In our house," this time it was Mr. Sprightly's turn to make some declaration, "we only stir the tea five times. That is all it takes to sufficiently mix the contents and give it enough of a cool. The rest is accomplished by three soft blows over the top." He then showed me exactly how it was done. Mrs. Sprightly sat in her chair, beaming approval as if her favorite dog had just shown her guests its latest trick. She then complemented Mr. Sprightly's gestures by doing exactly the same thing.

Mr. Sprightly, having performed his tea ritual, took his first sip, smacked his lips and said, "Ahh! That's tea!" Now I would have thought that was simply a peculiarity of Mr. Sprightly as a reaction to the moment; but then, Mrs. Sprightly did the same thing, finishing with a, "Ahh! That's tea!"

They both stared at me, waiting for something to happen. Uncomfortable, I stirred my tea five times, gave the cup its required three blows, took a sip, smacked my lips, and then, my voice faltering somewhat, I said weakly, ". . . ah . . . that's . . . tea? . . ."

They both seemed pleased at the results, noting that the stranger will no doubt get the hang of it someday. I set my tea and saucer aside and began, "Now the committee for Public Improvement stated that you were a frequent donor and that you were very interested in community projects and improvements to the city."

"Indeed we are!" Mr. Sprightly said.

"Would you care for a biscuit?" Mrs. Sprightly interrupted.

"No thank you," I answered. Mrs. Sprightly looked hurt, but said nothing. I continued. "Now the committee feels a statue in Regency Park honoring our veterans is long over due. A proper memorial, as it were. As you know, there have been many people from this area that have fought in past wars over the decade, and a place designated as a testimonial to their service seems something we lack as their efforts have obviously played an important part in our lives."

Mrs. Sprightly handed Mr. Sprightly a tray of 'biscuits' while I spoke. Which he accepted while politely listening. The Sprightlys were no more English than I or anybody else in town, but apparently Mrs. Sprightly liked to refer to her tea cakes and cookies as 'biscuits.' Perhaps they seemed more proper that way. But I continued, "Now nothing has been definite yet, and no specific plans for a memorial have been introduced; but the committee feels a sounding board should be created to develop such plans. And once the plans are introduced, we can address the matter of funding, as you might assume there will be no money in the community budget for such a thing. It will have to be raised independently of tax dollars."

"Why might we assume that?" Mr. Sprightly asked, at least showing some interest in what I was saying.

"When it comes to things like memorials, taxpayers seldom want to put in for that, being not a necessary expense. Memorials are almost always raised with private funds."

"In our house, we at least have one biscuit with our tea," Mrs. Sprightly said, completely ignoring the conversation as it was going. She had now lost her smile and was simply staring at me. I shrugged and grabbed one off the plate and stuck it on my saucer.

I continued, "I was wondering if you wanted to offer up your time to participate in the sounding board . . . or in any other way possible."

"Oh . . . it's possible, I suppose . . ." Mr. Sprightly began.

"In our house we tend to discuss such matters after dinner. Would you like to stay?" Mrs. Sprightly suggested.

"Well, I do have other calls to ma—"

"By all means stay!" Mr. Sprightly added. "We always have dinner at half-past five, and it's close enough now that a good meal might give us time to dwell on the subject." The Sprightlys were really big donors to the community chest in such matters. It seemed wrong not to let this fish off the hook. I stayed. Mrs. Sprightly, delighted, dashed off to the kitchen while Mr. Sprightly invited me to smoke from one of his many pipes while taking in the view from his front porch. It was a view of the street, but it was a view. I tried to steer the conversation towards the committee and things concerning the parks, but Mr. Sprightly would have none of it. We just sat their smoking our pipes and enjoying the view, with Mr. Sprightly occasionally remarking, "Look, Redwing Blackbird. Damned fine bird if you ask me."

"Yes, I suppose it is."

When dinner was ready, Mrs. Sprightly appeared on the porch with a little bell in her fingertips. She couldn't just say dinner was ready, she had to ring the bell. *Tinkle-tinkle-tinkle!* "Dinner, Gents!" she said gaily.

"We've hired a cook, you know," Mr. Sprightly said, rising, "but Mrs. Sprightly does much of the cooking herself. The other gal does mostly prep work and serves. I hope you like lamb."

"I love lamb," I answered. And followed Mr. Sprightly inside as he took the pipe from me. We sat at the dining table—I in the presumed guest chair. Mrs. Sprightly rang her little bell.

"You may serve, Silvia," she said to a frumpy looking matron whom I took for granted was the server/cook employee, who then wheeled things in on a cart. "In our house," Mrs. Sprightly began, "we say grace."

"Sure," I answered. And folded my hands. The Sprightlys did not fold their hands but bowed their heads.

"Grace," said Mr. Sprightly. "Grace," said Mrs. Sprightly. "Grace," said Silvia, standing by the cart. I had never heard Grace done in such a way—with everyone simply saying the word, 'grace.' I noticed the others were staring at me, so I said, "Grace." And Silvia started to serve. We started with soup.

"Do you wish crackers, Mr. Zepperell?" Mrs. Sprightly asked.

"Sure," I answered.

"How many?" Before I could answer, she said, "In our house we have three if soup is a main course, and one if it is a side dish."

"One will be fine," I said taking my cue.

Silvia handed me a tray on which there was one cracker. I cracked it in my fist and poured its crumbs into the soup. Both Sprightlys stared at me with big eyes but said nothing. I noticed that they kept their cracker on the edge of the soup plate and nibbled off a small bite from its edge along with a spoonful of soup as they go. They continued to say nothing, but I got the feeling that in their house they did not crunch crackers.

They also blew each spoonful once. Once and no more. I did the same. Then the lamb.

Did they normally eat like this, or did they prepare this meal in anticipation of me coming along? I must say the dinner was very good. If they normally eat like this, they normally eat very well. It was quite a layout. But I found myself watching them as to how they proceeded and imitated them as they did so. After all, it was 'their' house. I also found them watching me as if waiting for an opening to say something—regarding my behavior, that is—but didn't.

Instead we talked of roses and flower gardens—their ambition to install a hothouse on their property in the near future. And we talked of antelopes and gazelles, and their importance on the plains. And we talked of unicorns. I don't remember how we got there, but it must've been an outgrowth of our conversation on antelopes and gazelles. And then dessert came.

"Would you like coffee? In our house we take coffee after the meal and with dessert," Mrs. Sprightly insisted.

"I'll have some," I added, noting how the trend was moving. Silvia brought in a baked Alaska, and poured coffee from another glorious porcelain pot.

"Shall we take brandy on the porch?" Mr. Sprightly said. I agreed, thinking now was the time to get serious about what I had come for—the community project. "In our house, we always take brandy on the porch after a meal. Silvia does the dishes." Mr. Sprightly got out the decanter and the glasses and off we went to the front porch to sit and watch the street as the sun went down.

"Now, regarding the memorial . . ." I began, thinking it was my cue. Instead, Mr. Sprightly stood at the porch rail, patted his stomach vigorously, and let out a loud and ghastly belch that echoed down the street. Much to my surprise, Mrs. Sprightly did the same.

"In our house," Mr. Sprightly told me, "we feel it's good to let the accumulated wind out of one's system after a heavy meal." The two stared at me without saying anything.

I got up and put my hands to the rail, swallowed some air, and let out a disappointing (by Sprightly standards) but nonetheless audible belch. Mr. Sprightly clapped me on the back. "You'll feel better in the morning!" he said, approvingly. Then let out the loudest noise from his backside I had ever heard. "We let out wind both ways!" he encouraged.

I heard a similar, if more delicate, trumpet call from Mrs. Sprightly, following. And although I did not feel like it, I did my best to duplicate the effort.

"Now, what were you saying?" Mr. Sprightly asked. By this time I was distracted and couldn't remember my starting point.

"The . . . memorial . . ." I began and tried to get back on track.

"You know what goes well after a good meal?" he asked. I had no idea. "A sauna! Healthiest thing in the world for you! Did you bring a towel?"

I was completely caught off guard. I answered, "No."

"Well, I think we can supply the lad with something, don't you, dear?"

"I'll get one for him," and Mrs. Sprightly dashed off.

In minutes I found myself undressing and climbing into a sauna they had in the backyard, along with Mr. Sprightly. In minutes I was sweating profusely. "Now about the memorial . . ." I began once again. Then in walked Mrs. Sprightly wrapped in a towel and proceeded to splash some water on the rocks.

"In our house, we sauna together," Mr. Sprightly said, then slapped me with a handful of branches. He handed me them immediately after and said, "Go ahead, give Mrs. Sprightly a few good whacks." So I did.

"One of the things we are going to build next is a cold bath for you to jump into. Does the body good! Unfortunately, we'll simply have to hose you off with the garden hose. Works just as well." Mr. Sprightly grabbed me and pulled me from the hotroom. He had me stand behind a screen, drop my towel, and spray me with the chilly contents of the garden hose. I choked and screamed, and Mr. Sprightly laughed, then handed me my towel.

"There's a shower directly inside with your clothes. You'll feel good as new! I'll be in in a little while. I have to hose off Mrs. Sprightly."

So I went inside and showered. I sat in the living room as Silvia went around turning on lamps. Silvia looked at me as if I were a piece of rotting fish, but left the room. A little while later, Mr. Sprightly came in and looked me over.

"Good as new," he said, and began patting his head. "In our house we pat our heads after a sauna and a shower to stimulate circulation." So I patted my head. Moments later Mrs. Sprightly came in, now dressed and patting her head. So the three of us stood in a circle in the living room patting our heads.

Then, Mr. Sprightly broke the spell. "Care for a nightcap?"

"In our house—" Mrs. Sprightly began, but I cut her off.

"Sure," I said. I wasn't going to protest about a nightcap. She frowned. The most impolite thing I saw her do the whole evening.

"Port or Kahlua?" Mr. Sprightly said. "In our house, we usually have a glass of port before retiring. But lately I've taken to Kahlua. I don't know why!"

"It's the rebel in you," Mrs. Sprightly indicated. It was not a joke. It was also not a condemnation—although there was a whiff of disapproval imbedded in it.

"I'll take the Kahlua," I answered. Mrs. Sprightly looked as if she would frown but caught herself in time. Mr. Sprightly poured two tiny glasses of Kahlua, and one of Port, which he gave to his wife.

"What'll we drink to?" Mr. Sprightly asked. Before I could answer, he said, "The memorial!"

And so we drank. "Speaking of which . . ." I began.

"Well! It's passed our bedtime—and yours too, no doubt!" Mr. Sprightly said, pushing me towards the door. "In our house, we do not keep late hours, nor do our guests!" Mrs. Sprightly had long lost her smile and was staying in place watching me being exited from the house.

"If we could just spend a minute—" I tried.

"It's been a very pleasant evening. Thank you for coming. Do come again when you're invited!" Mr. Sprightly was saying as he led me over the threshold. "I've enjoyed your company." Mrs. Sprightly stood there and said only, "Yes, do come again someday," without a smile on her face.

"I hope you can see your way," Mr. Sprightly said as the porchlight was flicked on and the door was closing behind me. It suddenly swung open briefly again.

"Oh, about the memorial," Mr. Sprightly said. "Count us in! Just let us know what it is and send us the bill. We'll pay for it!"

"Mr. Sprightly," I started, "That's very generous, but the expense could run very—"

"Good night," he said and closed the door. I stood there for a few moments, wondering what just happened. And then the porchlight went out. In their house, a guest doesn't stand very long on dark porch. A guest goes home.

So I did.

ANGRY WIENER DOGS

It was a night of evil omens. Moonlight pierced craggy fingers through the clouds. Red stars were the only ones that shown through the breaks in the upper atmosphere giving us the eye. I was on my way back home from a night at the observatory where we had spent the better part of a week looking at unseemly lights in the sky. I was given the remainder of the night off and as I drove down Highway 101 at 3am, I spotted the first in what was to be a series of meteorites smashing their way through the atmosphere.

Now, I am not a superstitious man. I am not given to flights of the imagination. I am a scientist and deal with facts and reason. And yet I felt an onslaught of an unmistakable presence—one of darkness and loathing, one of foreboding and evil—on that night on the highway as the first meteorite crashed. For lo and behold, it was not a meteorite at all—but *a thing from another world!*

I had already gone off the main highway and on the county road I usually take to and from work. I got the first message of portent as I swung my trusty Edsel around after seeing the smoke plume on the hilly horizon, and headed down a dirt road in the direction of the impact site. However, the road curved at the closest access point, and from there in it was a walk in the fields, over a hill, and into the woods until one came up on the side of an adjoining hill where the projectile hit. I parked the car along the road's shoulder (what there was of it) and began to walk. There was just enough light to see by, but by the time I got to the hill top and looked down into the valley, the cloud cover again was too dense, and I knew I would simply get lost in the woods below if it continued to remain that dark. As it takes awhile for a meteorite to cool, especially one of any notable size, I decided that there was no hurry and would come back the next day to see what had happened and what fell.

I made my way back to my trusty Edsel and drove home, half-expecting a violent thunderstorm by the look of the clouds; but it never did rain that night, and I went home and put myself to bed to wake up to the noon civil defense whistle—which is kind of routine for me anyway.

The next day I had my usual noontime breakfast and heard nothing on the radio regarding anything unusual coming out of the sky. Could I be the only one who saw what I saw during the night? I called the observatory and asked. Nobody there saw a meteor in descent but they did notice some time in the night a small fire burning in the distance—a fire that eventually extinguished itself—and didn't think much beyond that.

So, it was time to get back into the Edsel and go take a look for myself.

When I got out there, all I saw was a large burn mark where something had crashed; but there was very little in the form of a crater. It was more like something skidded and smashed into some trees, and set part of the woods on fire. I drove to the nearest gas station and phoned in to my cronies at the observatory. Sure enough, it brought them all out there, rising from their daybeds to take a look at a nearby meteorite hole. One of the guys—Lloyd—brought along a Geiger-counter . . . something he tends to do anyway, even when he's at the beach . . . and found that the crater (dent, really) was able to make it tick. Not a lot, mind you, but enough to make us all go: *Hmmmm.*

We went back to the observatory and Felcher, the group photographer, stepped into his dark room and started developing his pictures. We stared at them the early part of the evening while they were still drying, instead of working like we were supposed to be doing. One of the odd things we noticed in several of the photos were a series of small dog prints in the ashes and mud surrounding the site. Had something in the crash attracted some of the dogs in the area? If so, what?

And here was another mystery that we couldn't figure out . . . *where was the meteorite?* Normally in such a crash, there is an iron rock at the center of the crater that was the leftover material from outer space. And it usually makes one of two things: a deep well-like hole in the center of the crater; or, a little mountain peak with the iron ore inside created from the uprising of material after the initial slam. Well, that's in a normal crater. This 'crater' was made at a slant, which could've meant the meteorite plowed itself in at a severe angle—maybe even rolling itself out to tumble down the hill into the woods. No such thing here. No hot iron rock anywhere to be found.

Okay . . . so then it wasn't a meteorite . . . a plane crash? No wreckage. No reported aircraft in distress that night. So what the hell were we looking at? The beginnings of a new volcano? I distinctly saw something fall from the sky. Volcanoes don't work that way. So we scratched our heads and went back to work, spending a few moments on coffee breaks to talk about the strange visitation from above the night before.

And then we all forgot about it.

It was the weekend and I was off duty and could relax. It was night and I was at home, reading a newspaper (with nothing about the meteorite in it), and had the tv going, but wasn't paying any attention to it. My pipe went out and I was just about to tap it into the ashtray when I heard a scratching at my door. It was very faint at first and I could barely hear it—so faint in fact that I thought I was imagining things. But it continued. And got louder. I set aside my paper and got up to switch off the tv. There it was—scratching. Then I thought I heard a kind of whining—like a dog trying to get passed the barrier in front of it and unable to do so, and hoping for a human to come by for an assist.

I went to the front door and opened it. Nothing but the empty street was there in front of me. I stepped outside to look around, but nothing unusual was to be seen. The street lamps were on. A car drove by. Some guy at the corner had left his lawn sprinkler on. Nothing unusual. I went back inside and sat down. I refilled my pipe and heard the scratching again. This time I made a quick exit towards the door. Nothing. Again the scene hadn't changed from a moment ago. I decided my mind was playing tricks on me and thought I'd make an early night of it. Maybe I was just over tired.

I poured myself a small brandy, brushed my teeth, and put myself to bed, spending a few minutes with Mickey Spillane before dosing off.

In the morning I got up to bring in the Sunday paper. The kid has a tendency to throw it in the bushes, so I make a point of not going outside in bare feet. First thing I noticed was a bad smell. Next thing I noticed was that the smell was coming off my bedroom slipper. And the next thing I noticed after that was I had stepped in dog poop. Right on my front step. Now I became suspicious. What did dog prints at the meteor site, scratching at the door, and dog poop on the step have in common?

There was more to it than that. On the way to work the next morning I heard a seemingly endless number of dogs barking. Why? Just something I never noticed before? There were more dogs in my neighborhood and I somehow just never paid it that much attention in the past?

I asked the guys at work if they had heard a lot of dogs that morning. I assumed they would think I was delusional and was asking a silly question. Instead they took me seriously. While some didn't notice any difference, others said, "You know, now that you mention it, it did seem as if there were a lot of dogs barking this morning where I live." Then still others would chime in with confirmations. While it was a curiosity, we tended to pass it off after break and went about our business and didn't think any more about it the rest of the night. I was reminded again after a night's work when I arrived home at dawn and heard lots of barking dogs. But I was too tired to give it much thought and promptly put myself to bed.

Then I woke up around noon, like I usually do. I spent some time downtown after my breakfast looking at some of the shops. I had some family birthdays coming up, and although I am not much of a shopper, on this day, I decided to be one. Once again I seemed to hear a lot of barking in various directions, but didn't see where the sources of the noise were coming from. There were a few people walking their dogs up and down the street, but they didn't seem to be the animals doing the barking. I did notice one curious aspect of it, in that everyone who could be seen walking a dog was walking a dachshund. I didn't think any more of it than that.

The later part of the afternoon I spent working on the house. The rain gutters were weakening and I needed to bolster them in some way. So I was up on a ladder for awhile inspecting and tinkering with the gutters and their weakened attachments to the roof. On my way down from the ladder on one of these occasions, I nearly stepped on a small dog that had found its way into my yard. It immediately began snapping and barking angrily at my foot as soon as I tried to step off the ladder.

"Sorry, fella," I said to the dog, "I didn't even know you were there." Well, dogs really don't understand English, just voice intonation. But whatever I said, and however soothingly I may have said it, it did not seem to satisfy the little brute. It raised itself on its hind legs and leaned forward as if to climb up the ladder after me. And barked and barked and barked, fury gleaming in its eyes.

"Easy, boy!" I said. "Where did you come from, anyway? Who do you belong to?" I could see it had no collar. But it kept barking, and even though small in size, tended to frighten me at least a little. "Shoo! Get away!" I finally scolded. It didn't seem as if it wanted to let me off the ladder. It even tried a bite at my pants leg. "Hey! Get lost, you little brat!" I yelled. The more I talked to it, certainly the more I yelled, the more intensely it barked back.

Then suddenly it was gone. I don't know what made it stop. It was certainly nothing I said or did. Poof! Just took off, its fury spent. I came down the ladder cautiously, expecting the little varmint to jump out of the bushes and bite my leg at any moment. But, nothing. Gone.

When I went to work that night, I told the guys at the observatory what had happened. Several of the guys laughed, as I expected they might. Then Jim, the chief engineer, said, "You know, that's funny, before I came to work there was a little dog who parked himself in the middle of my driveway. Kept on barking. Wouldn't let me back the car out."

"What kind of a dog was it?" I asked.

"Oh, you know, one of those little wiener dog types."

"That's the same kind of dog that came after me!" I added. Although we all kind of made a *Hmmm* noise and reminded ourselves of our conversation yesterday about all the dog barking, it was passed off as nothing more than an odd coincidence, and we went about the night's work.

About four o'clock in the morning, we could hear the strangest chorus of dog howlings coming from the valley—coming right through the opening where the telescope peers out at the night. Hal, the meteorologist on staff, was the first to notice it. He got everybody into the main scope room where we could hear it coming through the opening. We all let out another *Hmmm* but passed it off again as mere coincidence.

On the way home, I nearly ran over a dog that refused to move out of the road. I stopped to see if I hit it, but I couldn't get out of the car. The dog ran right up to the car door and put its front paws on it, and began barking at me through the window space. It even tried leaping up and snapping at my face until I rolled the window up. It was a dachshund. It was still dark enough that I couldn't tell what sort of markings it had, so I couldn't tell if it was the exact same one that came after me earlier. I kind of doubted that anyway, since the locations were miles apart. All I knew is that it was some kind of wiener dog with an irate disposition. I stepped on the gas without making any attempt this time to calm the animal down. I could see it in the rearview mirror holding its ground, glaring back at me with those angry eyes.

That night, or morning rather, as I lay in bed, I dreamt about angry dachshunds running after me.

Soon after my breakfast, as I was reading the morning paper, I found an article about how several pet stores had been broken into, and bags of dog food had been forcibly opened. Teeth marks were present. My doorbell rang and as I answered it, I found my neighbor, Mrs. McCracken, standing there with a glazed look on her face. She was carrying a leash and at the end of it was a little dachshund. I'd known Mrs. McCracken for awhile, and though she lived right across the street, I never knew her to be a pet owner—let alone have a dachshund.

"Yes?" I answered her when I opened the door.

"Keep an eye on my house," she said, almost as if she had been programmed to say it as if she were a robot. "I'm taking Sparky for a walk."

"Okay," I answered. "Are you all right, Mrs. McCracken?"

"Yes," she said with the same blank stare and dead-ended monotone she spoke with before. The dog, meanwhile, just stared at me from his seated position at her feet and growled at me, but did nothing else. No, it was not the same dog that accosted me on the ladder or I found in the middle of the road. Just thought I'd mention that.

Why Mrs. McCracken felt compelled to have me "watch her house for her while she was gone" just to walk the dog, I have no idea. She didn't stick around long enough for me to find out. She just turned in a mechanical way, and seeming to follow the lead of the little dog at her side, and walked down the street—the dog giving me what seemed a look of rebuff over its shoulder as it turned the corner of my front gate. It should be noted here that I never saw Mrs. McCracken return, nor did I see anyone occupy her house after that. As a matter of fact, I never saw Mrs. McCracker or her little dog again.

That afternoon as I was finishing my coffee during what was my lunch, just before going to work; and as I was looking out the window, I saw three dachshunds sitting on the sidewalk in front of my house, staring at the front door. Then they up and left. I made my way cautiously to my car, but nothing unusual happened. I turned on the radio as I drove, and just like the newspaper, no further word on the meteorite that crashed a few days ago.

When I got to work, bad news greeted me. It seems Roger, our radio guy, crashed his car on the way home from work, and was killed. We were all very glum that night around the observatory and went about our jobs without much enthusiasm. Roger was a nice kid, just out of graduate school. A young wife. A baby on the way. The details came in by phone from his brother who called us around midnight. It seems around the crash site were all sorts of footprints made by a small dog—or more likely, many small dogs. And Roger's body was marred by teeth marks—also made by small dogs.

This was the last *Hmmm* the boys and I put together in the observatory. What do all these incidents have in common over the last few days? Are they related? And more importantly, do they have something to do with that meteorite from almost a week ago?

Hal, the chief resident astronomer, tried to dismiss this all as poppycock, but admitted it was all too weird. After all, what would a meteorite have to do with the behavior of small dogs—and one dog type in particular? Still, coincidences were adding up, and too many coincidences mean something is afoot.

Again, that night we heard the howling in the distance; but this time, with Roger's death on our minds, the howling took on a more ominous meaning.

Then it happened. Appearances in the morning paper about people being attacked by small dogs began to encroach, first the back page, then the front. The evening news had one or two reports on unusual sightings of too many dogs gathered of their own apparent will in places, like parking lots, where they shouldn't be. The reports stated of harassment of customers and then the dogs' sudden departure before authorities arrived. One hotel manager was severely bitten when he tried to shoo-away a dog from the front door that wasn't letting guests inside.

And in all cases it was the same type—wiener dogs. Where were they all coming from? Dog pounds were checked, but they were empty of the breed. It would seem these dogs knew how to escape from any form of capture. Breeders were contacted. Yes, some of their animals had escaped the compound—even attacking their owners. But it still didn't account for the number of animals sighted. And all of them, based on the reports, were of a mean disposition.

Out of curiosity, I drove back to the site of the meteorite on my weekend off. I walked and walked, circling the area. The ditch created by the blast was already overgrowing with weeds. Then as I made my way back to my Edsel, I felt as if I was being watched. And I was. I was within a hundred yards of my car when I saw all these little faces staring at me from under bushes and between branches at the edge of the woods. All at once they charged—dozens, maybe hundreds. I didn't stop to look. I ran with all my might to get back to my car. My hat blew off, and my glasses fell. I didn't bother to go back for them.

I got in the car just in time as they slammed themselves against the car door that I slammed once I made it inside. They were on the hood and on the roof and on the trunk in no time. Yapping, barking, showing their teeth. All of them with those evil red eyes filled with anger. I found my extra glasses and started the car. Twice. Three times. It wouldn't start at first. I was in a cold sweat as the dogs banged their snouts against the windshield. When the car started, I stepped on the gas a little too hard. I heard the rear wheels spin and thought I had gotten myself stuck; but it thankfully pulled itself out. I spun the car around, sending dachshunds flying and sped down the road, little dogs bounding after me with that bumping, lumping run of theirs.

I immediately went to the observatory and told everybody on the weekend crew about it. I was in an agitated state, and they offered me some gin to calm me down. I said I believed the hill where the meteorite hit to be their "hangout" for lack of a better word. I still saw it as a local phenomenon. But then news came over the radio that President Eisenhower had been bitten by a dachshund while making a public appearance in Seattle. All of a sudden our little local incident was seen as taking on national significance.

I wondered what we should do. Hal came in by that time and I repeated the story to him. Whereas I was still overexcited about my escape, Hal seemed to take it more coolly; but still took it serious enough (since Roger's recent death) that he decided to call the County Sheriff. Hearing the news about Eisenhower, as well as more reports of incidents coming into his office, he too took my report seriously and promised to send some of his boys out to the hills to see what may be going on there.

That night, the howling and barking around the observatory was more intense than ever. It not only sounded closer, it was continuous throughout the darkness, and not just intermittent like it had been before. Then, just as some of the guys were stepping outside for a cigarette break, they found dozens of dachshunds waiting for them as they left the building. There was quite a commotion as they scrambled to get back inside. And Felcher, poor fellow, being the last in line, was taken by the many jaws that snatched at him. He fell behind as the rest of us tried to reach out to him. But he couldn't make it. We had to slam the door and leave him to his fate outside. We stood helplessly silent from our perch on the balcony as the little dogs bit and scratched and tore at him until there was no life left in the poor guy. Then they just left him to bleed to death and stared up at us with snarls in all of their throats waiting to get to us.

We were prisoners in our own bubble. Clearly whatever was causing this phenomenon was no set of idle coincidences. Something was causing all these dogs to appear and attack. Hal made a second call to the Sheriff, but heard on the phone the screams as the Sheriff and his men were under attack themselves.

Was this only happening in California? There was the Eisenhower report. Were wiener dogs all over the country attacking? Should the National Guard be called out? Hal tried to get the line to the National Guard, but the line was always busy. We just had to wait it through the night until rescue came. So we took turns standing guard on the balcony. And there they all were below us, still with that angry snarl in their throats whenever we moved.

Sunrise and they were still there. Now we could actually count them. Almost a hundred, waiting for us to step out of the building. And we waited. And the phone lines were always busy. And then they went dead. Reports were coming in on the radio. Angry wiener dogs were attacking citizens everywhere. There were also reports of human beings, dachshund owners, with blank expressions and glassy eyes following their charges on leashes, walking their little wiener creatures endlessly down roadways following some yet-to-be explained purpose. Zombie-like humans with dachshunds on leashes were pulled together in groups that were meeting in various state parks. Anyone coming near them to find out what was going on was immediately seized on and bitten by the little monsters.

Eisenhower got an infection and took sick. There were reports of angry little dogs just outside the radio station itself. Then the radio station went dead. We were advised that if anything happened, we should turn to the civil defense station. All they kept saying was: stay in your homes and lock your doors. The problem was everywhere and the military was called out.

That was the last we knew.

*   *   *

So I decided to write all this down in my observation log as we await rescue. It's been another day and night, and we have heard nothing new. The dogs remain, still snarling, still angry. Felcher lies out there, dead in a pool of blood. They have not tried to eat him, so it's not as if they have all decided to eat their masters. It's more like they have decided that they are our masters and want control of the planet. And they may have chosen to kill us all to get it. We don't know why.

So we sit here awaiting rescue. And clinging to hope. We still don't know if the meteorite had anything to do with this, or was that an idle fancy; but my own personal opinion is: yes—I just don't know what the connection is.

All I can say is, don't cross the path of an angry wiener dog. Run. Stay inside. Lock your doors and windows. And pray. Pray.

TOURISTS

Mr. Spader, or Grampa, as he was known, sent the Sborinka out into the blue sky for Davie to catch. It's a lot like taking a dog for a walk, he thought to himself. Just send out the Sborinka and the dumb kid will retrieve it. He didn't think much of his grandson. He didn't think much of children at all, as a matter of fact. They were a nuisance: loud, boisterous, full of energy, stupidity, and disrespect. But it was a nice summer day and the kid liked to romp around in Grant Park next to the lake. It was the biggest piece of green Chicago had to offer and it didn't smell like the rest of the city—as long as the breeze was coming off the lake.

"I got it, Grampa, I got it!" the little boy shrieked, the glittering, glowing blob in his hands hummed its own joy at having been received.

"That's good, Frederick," Spader encouraged. "Now send it back." Frederick. He hated the name his daughter gave the kid. Sounded like a funeral director. And why not Freddy? Why always insist on Frederick?

Zzzhhoooommm!! The Sborinka took off. The nice thing about this gadget, unlike tossing a ball back and forth, is that no matter where Grampa was, the thing would fly to him. Frederick could toss it as hard as he liked, and throw it anywhere he liked (a good thing considering Frederick's lousy aim) and it would still land gently in Grampa's lap—even if he had fallen asleep on a bench. And Grampa would hardly have to use any energy to toss it back, just kind of flip it in the air, and it would whiz back to Frederick no matter where he was, even if he was standing on his head. Damned clever those Japanese. Actually the Sborinka was invented in Stockholm, but the Japanese immediately took the market over.

Brrrp-brrrp-brrrp! The Sborinka announced its presence as it approached Grampa, who in fact did decide to sit down on a bench. It landed in his hands, blinking lights and all, and purred like a kitten. "Here, catch!" Spader yelled without any enthusiasm and flipped the device over his shoulder. The mechanical blob, nonplussed, levitated for a moment to get its bearings and then immediately whooshed in the general direction of Frederick. The boy jumped and chased as it swirled passed him. The Sborinka seemed to pick up Frederick's giggles of glee and spun around his head to tease the boy into delight. Grampa had set the toy on 'advanced' just to watch the kid try and tackle it, and thereby give him an extra minute of rest, before the thing would come back his way.

As he was watching Frederick collide with his own feet and fall on his face—something Grampa found particularly funny and which was a welcome diversion—a bus pulled up in the parking area behind him. It was one of those big things with a glass roof coated gray to keep the sun from frying the passengers inside. Out stepped a whole bunch of crazy looking characters (as Spader referred to them). And they were in all manner of colors: blues, greens, pinks, yellows. Every size and shape imaginable.

The Tour Guide stepped out. He was a young, sandy-haired fellow in a pale blue uniform with a visor cap on his head. He also had a loudspeaker clipped to his waistbelt and a tiny microphone planted on his collar.

"Oh, fuck!" Grampa grumbled to himself.

"I almost got it, Grampa!" Frederick hollered. Distracted, Grampa looked back over to where his grandson was leaping after the Sborinka. Apparently the fall didn't hurt him. Spader was glad he set the machine on advanced. It'll keep the kid busy for awhile.

The Tour Guide, meanwhile, was gathering everybody into a circle. "Gleep glop glerk gleck glokka glok glerra glarra glepl!" he was telling them. "Glokka gleek glekka glopl glepl glep!"

"Oh shit, here they come," Grampa grumbled to himself.

The Tour Guide brought the group along the walk heading right where Spader was sitting. He was pointing at the buildings, at the lake, at the sculptures and the fountain, even the birds. For this group, all of it was fascinating. They were taking out little devices they were holding in their—whatever they used for hands—and pointing them at things. Apparently those things were cameras of some sort. Spader didn't pay attention to the tech stuff brought in from the outer planet worlds.

"I got it!" Frederick hollered.

"That's fine," Spader barely had breath to show any life in him. "Send it back."

"Here it comes!" Frederick threw the device with all his might, and the Sborinka zoomed and fluttered and floated until it landed on Spader's lap. The tour group seemed in awe and immediately began snapping their little pocket pictures at him as they were nearing.

"Oh fuck off," Grampa grumbled and threw the Sborinka back at Frederick as he saw them approach. "It's a kid's toy, for Chrissakes!" They took more pictures of Grampa playing Sborinka catch with his grandson. How very Earthlike! How very quaint!

One of the eight-footers, the one with the tan hide, the big spots and the long tail came by to take a close-up of Spader. "Yok yoke yok yik yak!" it said to him as it snapped his picture. Spader made a growling noise but he doubted if the alien understood that interpretation. The creature gave a wave, something it no doubt learned from the Rosetta Stone discs it received before coming here, and walked away, happy with its picture. Spader found himself waving back, but the creature was immune to his irony.

"Come on, Frederick! Let's go!"

"Aww, Gee! We only got here a minute ago!"

"We've been here for a half-hour. Besides, it's getting crowded!"

"Just a little while longer?!"

He hated when the kid whined. "Okay! But not too long!"

Meanwhile the tour was making the rounds and after Grampa mustered a few more Sborinka throws, the tour was making their way back to the bus. One of the fuzzy blue things stopped by to take a picture of Frederick.

"Hey, you! Stay away from the kid, all right?!"

The blue fuzzy thing didn't understand and snapped a picture of Frederick anyway, then came over to Spader and took his image as well. It made something like a farting noise, which could only be assumed was 'thank you' in its language and ran back to join the group.

"Blick bleck bliggle bloggle blick!" the Tour Guide was saying, and the group started boarding the bus.

"Tourists!" Grampa grumbled.

"Just one more throw, Grampa, honest! Just one more throw!"

I wonder if they kill their kids in outer space, Spader wondered as he watched the bus drive off.

KILLER KUNTS

Jack the Ripper had nothing on him. He liked nothing better than to pick up a prostitute, make use of her services, then kill her and take her money. The pimps never got wise. He eluded everybody: police, thugs, you name it. He was bad-ass to the bone. And he always had his trusty knife ready to slice and dice a healthy piece of prime booty. Call him Mother Fucker, call him Son-of-a-Bitch, call him Asshole-of-the-World. He prided himself on what he did. A sick-fuck, yeah, that's what they call him, a sick-fuck.

He saw his work in the paper: another hooker gets it here, another one is found in a ditch there. A body found in an apartment? Hey, the apt was rented to nobody. A hotel-room blood bath? Who was it who registered? Where are the finger-prints? I recognize the girl, officer, but not the john she came in with. How is it nobody seems to know who he is?

He was on the prowl. Ready for another take. See the pretty blonde over there? Trash, pure trash. Something should be done about her. Wipe them all off the face of the Earth.

Already he felt himself getting hard just thinking about her. Pick her up. Take her somewhere. The park, maybe. Yeah. Look at that sweet ass. She's gotta be fun to cut up.

Pull over, hey honey, got some time? She turns around. She's fabulous. A real knock-out. Short leather skirt and boots. Black gauntlets laced with rhinestones. Looking for some action? She declares. How about down the road at the park?

She gets in. She smells of lilac. She checks her cellphone to let her pimp know she's got one on the line. Fine. He can handle cellphones, and pimps. But he much prefers to handle the girl. They drive to the park. They find a small dark place to hide. He gives her money. She lifts her skirt. She pulls down his pants. She straddles him.

And *CHRIST!!!* . . .

He shrivels up and dies.

She steps out of the car. No pimp, but three of her girlfriends show up—each one a bomb. Mankillers with wild hair. The four of them look him over. A shriveled up, dried up husk.

"That's the end of your rampage, hon," the blonde says to the dead body in the car. "You've just met up with the Killer Kunts."

The four walk away into the night, looking for some other asshole. Mutants—all four of them—who use beauty as a lure and a vagina as a weapon. They kill with coitus, and save their targets to all those creeps who do women harm.

There's another guy beating up a nurse making her way home from the hospital. He's a stalker first, an attacker second. He follows her all the way to her home, then slips in between the houses and attacks. She screams, she tries to beat him off, he gags her and rips her uniform. He's ready to perform his humiliating deed.

Only the Killer Kunts are there, lurking in the shadows.

"Grizelda," the blonde says to the brunette, "this one's yours."

"You got it, Ally," Grizelda says back, and leaps down from her spot on the balcony over-looking the attack.

"Hey, hot-shot!" Grizelda says to the surprised attacker. "How about some of this, if you want real action!"

The man turns and watches the brunette strip off her street-wise uniform. The nurse, finding an opening, pries herself away and escapes into the house. Grizelda lunges for the creep and ensnares him in her arms. There he is with his stupid pecker hanging out and a naked woman in front of him. She grabs him and makes sure he's upright and ready. She straddles him and sends his member deep into her.

The man's eyes light up with fire, as he finds he is being crushed and bleeding. He screams in pain and crumples like a piece of paper—dead.

"Pick on somebody your own size!" Grizelda tells the corpse. The other girls join her.

"Get dressed, we've got more to do!" Ally says.

They climb into their car. Check the GPS and the satellite that tracks potential crime sites. They start up the black Mercedes and cruise.

A bar. A bunch of drunks. Two guys taking advantage of women. The Kunts pull up. Ally driving. "Lulu and Janine, these are yours," she states. The red-head and the Asian girl step out of the back seat and head to where the punks are causing trouble. Stiletto heals and swishing tails attracting attention.

"What seems to be the trouble, boys?" Janine, the red-head declares.

"You're wasting your time on those cows," adds Lulu. "You want some real action? Step inside and offer a lady a drink!"

The punks let out a whoop and follow the girls back in. The abused women are let go.

"They can catch up to us later," Ally says to Grizelda as she speeds the car away.

Back at the Kunt Kave, Ally gets on the phone to the Police Commissioner. "I count 6 tonight we've taken care of."

"Good work, girls," the Commissioner's voice breathes out. "We've got their addresses on the monitor. Those punks' bodies won't be found for some time until we can invent a good cover."

"And you were opposed to working with Mutants!" Ally adds as Grizelda pulls a cool one out of the refrigerator.

"I was. We just can never go public with this stuff, you realize. I'd have to deny knowing anything about you."

"We realize," Ally adds, taking her shoes off, "But Detroit is a whole lot cleaner since we started and a whole lot easier to police now isn't it?"

"Your latest check is already in the mail," the phone clicked off. The Commissioner went back to his fund-raising dinner.

"What'd he say?" Grizelda asked.

"The check is in the mail," Ally sighed.

"It'd better be, this place costs money," Grizelda flopped herself on the couch.

Just then Janine and Lulu entered the huge, pink upholstered cave to join the others.

"Mission accomplished," Janine said.

"I need a bath," topped Lulu. ·

"So . . . what took you so long?" questioned Ally.

WENDELL WESLEY HOWARD'S
WONDERFULLY WACKY WISDOM WIDGET

"It makes you wise," Wendell Wesley Howard told his guest, Mister Phillip.

"How?" Mister Phillip responded.

"Step up to the circle and see!" Wendell Wesley Howard was very proud of his invention. It promised instant wisdom. And these days, who couldn't afford a little instant wisdom? Howard had been working on his machine in his basement for months. Now it was time to show it off.

Mister Phillip, was a banker. Not of the investment kind, just a banker who hordes money for other people to use on occasion. Mister Phillip was a casual friend of Wendell Howard's. They met some years back in a bowling league before both dropped out. Howard would still run into Phillip from time to time and keep him advised on his latest invention. Such devices as Wendell Howard could conceive never really worked out: like his electric toilet paper dispenser, and his automatic pancake flipper. So Phillip was always a bit wary. But Phillip did consider himself a friend, and when asked to try out the Wisdom Widget (as Howard called it) Phillip felt compelled to at least give it a whirl. If it turned out to be another dud, well, what's the harm? And who knows, he may be onto something. If he was, he promised Howard that he would pass along the idea to some of his colleagues who were investment bankers, and maybe Howard could secure a patent and acquire the loan to start a big business. At any rate, Phillip would see what all the fuss was about.

So there the two men stood in Howard's basement directly in front of the Wisdom Widget. It was a big clanky device, standing about six and a half feet tall, made up of tubes and gears and braces. It looked like a combination exercise machine and garment bag coat hanger.

"You mean to tell me such a contraption as this makes people wise?"

"Try it," was all Howard said.

"And how will an assemblage of random spare parts do that for anybody? And just exactly how do you expect to make money on imparting a machine's 'wisdom'."

"Everyone needs wisdom. Imagine all the scrapes you could've gotten out of as a teenager if you'd have had some wisdom! Imagine the pitfalls of marriage and how they could be avoided if you just had wisdom! Imagine how much money you would save if you only had wisdom guiding you!"

"And this machine of yours can do that?"

"I guarantee it."

"Well then . . . let's see if I have the 'wisdom' not to invest in such a product."

"Just stand here where the circle is marked on the floor."

"All right. Now what?"

"Just ask the machine any question you've got bothering you. Any question at all."

"Wendell . . . I hate to rain on your parade, but this sounds just like Magic 8-Ball or some penny arcade device. A mechanical Tarot deck. A metallic fortune cookie."

"This is different. Go ahead. Try it."

"Very well, what question should I ask?"

"Anything. Anything at all."

As Phillip was about to speak after a moment of searching his thoughts, Howard stopped him.

"Put a coin in the slot first."

"Oh." Phillip began searching his pockets for some change. "Quarters will do?"

"Certainly."

"See, it already seems like an arcade game."

"And even if it was, think there's no money in arcades?"

"Good point." Phillip dug out a quarter and put it in a slot near his shoulder. Immediately the clanking bit of junk hummed to life. Small little button lights brightened and the thing shuddered a bit with the electricity that went through its bones. Then it hummed placidly awaiting a command.

"Go ahead, ask it," Howard urged.

Phillip cleared his throat and scratched his head. "Should I take Wilma—that's my wife, Wilma—on a cruise this year?"

The machine vibrated and made some sort of mechanical 'thinking' noise. Then a metal arm of a sorts with an inflated glove at its end (looking like some primitive baseball mitt) swung itself over to Phillip and gave him a smack on the side of the head.

"Shut up!" the machine told him. And then shut down.

Phillip was stunned and perplexed. After a minute to recover from the blow, Phillip looked first at the machine while holding the side of his face and then at Howard. "What the Hell was that?"

"Your answer," Howard replied confidently.

"Is this some kind of a joke?"

"No. It gave you the answer you were looking for."

"Shut up? That's the answer to my question?"

"So it would seem."

"And it smacks me on the side of the head?!"

"That's to bring the message home."

"And this imparts wisdom?!"

"Did you feel it answered your question?"

"NO!!" Phillip was incredulous. "What kind of ridiculous idea is this?!"

"Sometimes the effects of wisdom aren't immediately apparent. You may have to sleep on it to see if the machine is accurate."

"Accurate—nothing! It told me to shut up and belted me on the head!"

"I would call that tough love, Charlie."

"Ridiculous! A machine administering tough love!"

"Go ahead, try another question. Give it a workout."

"What and get another clout? Who's getting the workout me or it?"

"You've only asked one question. Give it another try."

"Oh . . . all right. But if I get anymore smacks, I'm through with this!"

"Put another coin in."

Annoyed, Mister Phillip made a second brave attempt to talk to the machine. He sacrificed another quarter to the experiment by dropping it in the slot. The machine clanked and hummed back to life. Phillip cleared his throat and gave a pause in thought.

"Will I have a successful year in business next year?"

The machine vibrated again, and once again the arm with the big glove swung out. "Shut up!" it told Phillip before giving him a second haymaker and switching off.

Phillip stumbled about clutching his jaw. "I'm bleeding!" Phillip said with total incredulity, seeing a drop of blood left on his fingers from his lip. "This is insanity, Wendell! I'm getting out of here!"

"But did it answer your question?" Howard tried to prevent him from leaving.

"Out of my way! I've become accustomed to some of your looney experiments before, but this time you've gone too far!"

"But did it answer your question?!"

"NO!!" Phillips pushed his way, stumbling and sort of bleeding his way out of Howard's basement.

"Think on the answer," Howard called after him, "It may have been right after all."

"Nonsense!" Phillip left the building.

"Wisdom never comes easily!" Howard shouted, hearing the door slam in return.

It was unlikely that Howard was going to receive money for his invention via the Phillip route. So he sighed and put it outside. He didn't give up entirely. He noticed some of the local kids poking their noses around the thing as it sat by the side of the house.

"Got a quarter?" he told one surprised teenager. "Put it in the slot and stand on the marked circle." The boy did so and waited. "Now ask it a question," Howard encouraged.

The boy shrugged and asked, "Will I get an A on my history test?" Immediately the boy got a smack on the head. Being a skinny lad, it knocked him down.

"Is this thing a joke?" the boy asked, incredulously.

"It's wisdom," Howard answered.

The boy ran off and nothing more happened for a couple of days. Then Howard found a gang of teenagers near his door, not intending themselves to be obnoxious or threatening, but they came to try out the machine. They all had quarters in their hands. The same teenage boy that had stood there the other day was back.

"Hi, Mister Howard!" the boy said. "Can we try out your machine?"

"Of course you can," Howard was pleased. "Were you satisfied with the answer you got the other day?"

"Yes! And it was right! I immediately went home to study for my test! And I got an A!"

"Good for you! Go on, boys, give it a try!"

One by one they began to ask the machine their questions. And their questions were about all kinds of things that teenage boys ask about: their driver's licenses, their classmates, girls, the track team, girls, a summer job, girls, what about college, girls, cars, and girls. And one by one they landed on their backsides having been smacked about by the Wisdom Widget.

The boys left happy. So Howard put the machine out on the front lawn with a big sign over it that read: "WISDOM 25c. Ask anything 24 hours a day."

To Howard's underestimation and surprise, people began showing up and asking questions of the Widget. It didn't matter how many times they were socked. They came back for more advice. Some of the teenage boys felt it was kind of a game. For those boys who underestimated the machine's trappings they would ask it a fake question and try to duck the Widget's punch. They were often surprised by a boot that came flying up from around them to kick them in the rear—or a boxing glove with a sucker punch that hit them in the stomach. The Widget didn't like challenges and false questions and would have none of that.

One day Howard was unloading the coin box that the Widget held. Howard was starting to make a killing on his invention just by keeping it on the front lawn. That day, Mister Phillip returned, this time with some of his banker buddies, all sticking out like sore thumbs on the street in their suits and ties.

"Wendell! A word with you!" Phillip began. "I apologize for my rudeness the other day. I'd like you to meet some colleagues of mine: Mr. Brewster, Mr. Cunningham, and Mr. Spindler."

"Hello," Howard nodded towards them all. He couldn't shake hands, the cashbox was rather heavy. Something that Phillip and the bankers didn't fail to notice.

"Business is good, I see," Phillip stated, almost salivating.

"My widget has become popular."

"Yes, we've heard. My son seems to think this is helping him pick a school upon graduation."

"That's nice."

"And that's the magic of this thing. You know those questions I asked? Well . . . I was thinking it over. You know about taking a cruise with my wife? Well, did I really want to do that? The answer was no. I even asked her about it. You know I'd been promising her one for ages. Well, she told me she would rather visit her sister in Omaha. Imagine that—a sister in Omaha as a vacation! Well, I had no intention of doing that. So we decided on *separate* vacations! I'm going fishing in Nova Scotia! We couldn't be happier! Your machine was right!"

"That's wisdom," Howard answered placidly.

"And as for business next year—well! That's what I wanted to talk to you about. Ever since you've given your . . . *widget* . . . as you call it, a trial on your front lawn . . . your home has been quite popular. And you've made yourself a tidy sum in just a few short weeks. Have you ever thought of mass producing it?"

"I'd given it some thought," Howard told him.

"Good, good! You know, my partners and I . . ."

"Partners?"

"Partners, and I are willing to invest a neat little sum to get such a program up and running and give it a healthy try-out on the market. Would you be interested?"

Howard looked suspiciously at Phillip for a moment, then asked, "Charlie, do you really believe my machine imparts wisdom; or do you just see it as a novelty that can supply a good cash flow?"

Phillip smiled, "Do *you* believe it imparts wisdom?"

Howard returned the smile, "In a way . . . yes. It brought you back, didn't it?"

Phillip added, "And as you told me, what difference does it make if it really answers your questions or not, or if it's just another machine in an arcade? As long as it continues to fill that cashbox you've got in your hand, what more can you ask of it?"

"Indeed," Howard added. He gave a look around at the gentlemen before him, reattached the coinbox, and then, stepping into the circle, put his own coin in the machine.

"Should I take these men up on their offer?" Howard asked his own Wisdom Widget. Immediately the gloved arm came around and smacked him with the accompanying, "Shut up!"

They drew up the rudiments of a contract right then and there. And Wendell Wesley Howard . . . and company . . . were on their way to becoming very rich.

What Wendell Howard knew all along and what his machine simply imposed was that sometimes the path to wisdom is a smack upside the head, and the ability to shut the hell up.

MARGRET VERA MIDDLETON'S VERY MAGICAL VAGINA

They only recently discovered about Margret Vera Middleton's magical vagina. Even Margret Middleton didn't know she had one. Women quite frequently don't know what's going on with their body parts; it seems to be a mystery even to them. That's why a whole industry of medical science has risen up around such mysteries to meet the challenge.

Margret was just going in for a check up, complaining about women's usual complaints, when the mystery was unveiled. The Doctor came out to the waiting room and said to Mister Middleton, "Are you sure your wife hasn't been complaining until before this?"

"Why? What's the trouble, Doctor?"

"I think you should see this." The Doctor brought Mister Middleton back into the examination room. There was the Nurse with a gravely motherly look on her face. There was Margret on the table, her legs up in stirrups. A sheet drawn up over her legs.

"What's going on?" Mister Middleton asked, a puzzled look on his face.

"I thought it seemed odd," Margret stated.

"What's wrong? Are you feeling alright?" Mister Middleton asked.

"Oh, I'm alright, I guess," Margret answered.

"I gave her a relaxant so that she wouldn't get upset," the Doctor told him.

"Upset from what?" Middleton now looked very worried.

"It's hard to explain," the Doctor said. "Perhaps you should have a look for yourself."

With that he flung the sheet back that was covering his wife's lower extremities. A light suddenly blazed out at him from under the sheet. Middleton was aghast. And both Doctor and Nurse, having seen it before, were still amazed.

"M-M-Margret!" Middleton stuttered, "You have a light inside you!"

"I know," Margret answered. "Do you think it's from something I ate?"

"There is nothing I know of that creates this effect," the Doctor returned. "And look," he continued, and held up a piece of paper to the beam of light that was pouring from her like a fountain. The paper immediately caught fire. The Doctor threw the scrap away.

"What does it mean, Doctor?" Middleton asked.

"Without more tests, I'm not sure. I'd like to keep her overnight to have her evaluated. Perhaps have a specialist come in."

"Are you sure you're not feeling any pain?" Middleton asked.

"No," Margret answered, "but I am getting a bit hungry."

"That's the medication," the Doctor answered, "It'll wear off in a minute." He covered her back up. "Just relax now," the Doctor reassured her.

"What do you think we should do?" Middleton asked.

"Until we have more conclusive evidence on just exactly what her condition is, I can't really say. We'll have her transported to the hospital wing right away for evaluation. I'll need you to sign some papers."

"Of course," Middleton said, "Whatever she needs."

"Don't worry about a thing, Mrs. Middleton," the Doctor patted her on the shoulder. "We're going to get you a room in the other wing and have you stay over night. We'd like to do some tests. I'll just borrow your husband for a few moments to sign you in."

"Makes no nevermind to me," Margret answered, who by now was assuredly feeling no pain.

Mr. Middleton dutifully signed all sorts of papers admitting his wife to the hospital. And then stayed with her through the evening to make sure she was comfortable. Margret, on the other hand, didn't seem to be bothered by much of anything, and looked as if she enjoyed her little vacation from home, even if a hospital room was not the ideal place to be. Luckily she had the room to herself for the night, and by the time visitors were required to leave, she had grown quite sleepy and scarcely noticed the departure of Mr. Middleton.

That night Mr. Middleton phoned her mother, his mother, her friends, his friends, and anybody else he could think of. He tried to be discreet about his wife's condition, not trying to say too much that might embarrass her, him, or anybody else. And he lied awake most of the night worrying.

The next morning, he took the day off and showed up to watch his wife eat breakfast. Again she seemed in a cheery mood, and gave no evidence that she had any ill condition whatsoever.

And then the stampede of nurses, doctors, and specialists came in and pushed Mr. Middleton out of the room. He waited outside in the hall and heard a series of *Oohs* and *Ahhs* as if these men of medical science were at a fireworks display. They left, writing notes and scratching their heads.

Then the Doctor, her primary doctor, returned and asked him in. The Doctor's faithful Nurse was by his side. "I want you to witness something extraordinary," the Doctor told Middleton and pulled back the sheet from Mrs. Middleton. There it was the bright light that was shining as they saw yesterday. "Look how it stays in a steady stream right up to the wall," the Doctor pointed out, as if it were important. "Now watch," the Doctor seemed to have yet another surprise in store. "Margret?" he began, "I want you to soften it." The light dimmed. He put his hand in the beam and encouraged Middleton to do the same. "Now Margret, strengthen it." Mrs. Middleton seemed to be offering no physical effort on her part. From what Middleton could tell, she merely changed her thought pattern.

The Doctor pulled out another piece of paper and put it in the light beam. The paper immediately caught fire. "You see there," he said, "She can control its intensity."

"How did you do that?" Middleton asked amazed.

"I don't know," Margret answered. "I just do what he says."

"Now think blue," the Doctor encouraged. Immediately the light turned blue. The Doctor once again encouraged Middleton to put his hand in the beam.

"It feels cool!" Middleton was more amazed than ever.

"It is cool," the Doctor stated. He showed Middleton a thermometer the nurse had handed him, and then placed it in the light beam. When he took it out, he showed it to the anxious husband trying desperately to understand what this all meant. The thermometer showed the temperature had dropped by ten degrees.

"The light changed the air temperature?" The Doctor nodded. "What does this mean?"

The Doctor sighed, "I don't know. We need more time."

"How much time do you need?"

"Well, another day, at least. She's not feeling any pain, and there is no indication she's not in prime health—other than she's emitting a beam of light."

"Well that's enough for me!" the frustrated husband indicated. "I would think a woman who spouts rays of light from her privates is somehow out of balance!"

"I would think so too, I just don't know what to make of it. Please, Mister Middleton, this is something new for all of us. I want to help. I just don't know how yet. Not until we know what we're dealing with."

Mister Middleton was sent home still wondering what this was all about. Meanwhile, Missus Middleton seemed to take it all in stride, and even with a light and breezy air. She kissed him good night. Had a late night snack of Jell-O that the hospital provided, and slept until the next morning. Mister Middleton went home to drink and woke up with a fuzzy head from a little too much Bourbon.

The following day, Middleton returned to find his wife had been taken to a separate wing and a separate floor. He was led around by an orderly, and when he got to the designated room he found a Marine guarding the door. The orderly told the Marine, "It's the husband," and the Marine stepped aside to let them pass.

In the room were doctors, nurses, and various people with smocks and significant looking uniforms, and an Army General.

"Hi, honey!" Mrs. Middleton waved from her bed, it having been raised so she could sit up.

"What's going on?" Middleton said weakly to anybody and everybody.

The Army General stepped forward, "Mr. Middleton, your wife seems to have stumbled on to something that may involve national security. Because you are her husband we've allowed you to participate in the examination process; but keep in mind you are doing so at the invitation of the United States Government, and everything you see and hear must be kept strictly confidential at all times, is that clear?"

"Confidential?"

"He means we're all supposed to keep our mouths shut about this," Margret stated from her bed.

"I know what it means. But why?"

The Doctor approached him, "Mister Middleton . . . your wife has developed an extraordinary ability. It seems she has been able to breach dimensions."

"What the hell are you talking about?" Middleton looked to his wife for explanation. His wife just shrugged.

"May I?" the Doctor asked the General. The General nodded.

"Why are you asking him?" Middleton quizzed.

"Margret? If I may?" the Doctor said.

Margret Vera eased herself back on the bed as the bed was lowered. Once again the sheet was removed from her and her legs were raised at the knees. Once again a light was shining into the room from her. The Nurse had the lights in the room switched off.

A rainbow of colors was showing up on the walls—all from Margret. And there was something else. Music was playing. Soft music. Like harps and angelic voices, only not quite. It was hard to make out.

"What the hell is this?!" Middleton asked.

"Prepare yourself, Mister Middleton," the Doctor said, "for the ride of your life."

The Doctor positioned Middleton right in full aim of the light coming from his wife. The light engulfed him, the music grew louder, a feeling of electrical vibration carried through him. Suddenly, Middleton was gone. The room had one less person in it, and the absent person was the husband.

Middleton for his part, found himself inside a luminous cave with phosphorescent rocks of all colors—glowing, changing shades. The music was permeating everything. In the distance he could see a magic garden with giant tulips and huge lollipops growing out of the ground.

"Where the hell am I?" he muttered to himself.

"Hi, honey," came a voice echoing down the cave as if it had come across the other side of a canyon. It was Margret.

"Margret?!" Middleton called.

"Yup! It's me, alright!" the voice returned, cheerful as ever.

"Where are you?!"

"I'm right here! I'm everywhere!" the voice continued, and it certainly sounded as if her voice were coming from everywhere. "You're inside me!"

"I'm WHAT?!"

"I said you're inside me!"

"How is that possible?!"

"We don't know!"

"You mean to tell me I've somehow shrunk and am now walking around inside your—"

"Uh-huh!"

"That's impossible!"

"Well that's what I would've said, but everybody in the room has taken a trip in there, so it must be true."

"How do I get out?"

"Oh, don't worry about that! I can expel you easy. I just have to think it."

"Are you aware there's a garden and a glowing cave inside of you?"

"So they tell me! You should've taken a camera along so that you could bring back some pictures!"

"I didn't think of that. I mean I didn't know. I mean—*HUH?!!*"

"Well, you know, I can't see inside that thing myself."

"I suppose not," Middleton mumbled watching a little man in a green suit come by to water the flowers with a big purple watering can.

"What?!" Margret responded to his mumble. Middleton still had his eyes on the little man in the green suit.

"Hi diddledy dee!" said the little man, tipping his hat.

"You've got a leprechaun in you," Middleton stared incredulously.

"*What?!!*" she answered.

"I said, DID YOU KNOW YOU'VE GOT A LEPRECHAUN DOWN HERE?!!"

"Yeah! They told me he was there!"

Little pink bunnies began to peak out from behind the leaves of the flowers. They all started giggling like little human children.

"Holy shit," Middleton said to himself. "What is all this?!"

"What?! You're going to have to speak up, honey, I really can't hear you very well!"

"I SAID, WHAT IS ALL THIS?!!" Middleton listened to his own echo die away.

"They don't know," his wife returned, "but they seemed to think I'm somehow a bridge between dimensions!"

"How did that happen?!"

"You'll have to ask the Doctor!"

"Well, where is he? Put him on the line!"

"I'm not AT&T, honey! He can't hear you anymore than you can hear him. It's only my thoughts you're hearing!"

"Oh. Can I get out of here now?"

"Certainly."

The leprechaun gave him a wave as Mr. Middleton suddenly found himself back in the midst of the others in the hospital room. The Doctor quickly covered his wife and the Nurse turned the lights back on.

"What was that?!" Middleton, surprised to see himself back, asked to the group.

"It's no hallucination," the Doctor stated. "You were definitely gone. All of us have had a turn and we've all disappeared from the room whenever we stared intensely into your wife's light."

The General spoke up, "We don't know what we've got here, and what it all means. We do believe Mrs. Middleton has somehow created a channel to some other dimensional force. It may be a fluke, then again, it may be something that can be regenerated at will not only by her but by others if we understand the how and why."

"And the Army wants to know?"

"The Army wants to know," the General nodded. "Have no worries, Mr. Middleton," the General tried his reassuring best, "From now on the United States Government will handle all of Mrs. Middleton's expenses. You and your wife are from this moment on, our new Manhattan Project."

"Manhat—Oh, no! Oh, no! My wife is not going to be some kind of guinea pig!"

"I'm afraid I have to agree with the General," the Doctor chimed in, "We don't know what we're dealing with and only something as big as the federal government can get to the bottom of this."

"I assure you," the General continued, "We will take the best of care of both you and your wife. You'll both be on the government payroll. You'll quit your job and come live with us. All your needs will be taken care of."

"We'll be prisoners!"

"Let's not look at it that way," the General continued, "You are free to travel about as you please. But you will be sworn to absolute secrecy. And we have a document here you'll both need to sign in order to assure that. Your wife is very valuable to us, you know. Why would we let anything go wrong?"

"But it could, couldn't it?"

The General shrugged.

"There's a goddamn leprechaun in there!" he pointed to his wife. "What does that mean?"

"It means, whatever is going on with her—it's magic!" the Doctor encouraged.

"Magic?! Coming from a medical doctor?! There's pink bunnies bouncing around among lollipops!"

"Well wouldn't that indicate it's magic?" Margret added.

"It may have something to do with her childhood or psychological make up," the Doctor added, "which influences what we see. But if she thinks it's magic, and until we have a better explanation—why not think of it as such?"

"I need to sit down," Middleton said.

"Of course," the Doctor answered. And a chair was brought for him.

"Magic fairylands, music, Army generals, doctors believing in magic dust, Manhattan projects—all in one soup. This is all too much to handle."

"I can prescribe a sedative, Mr. Middleton, if you think you need one."

"It's an adventure, honey! Wouldn't you like to find out where this goes?" Margret said, brightly.

"You approve of all this?"

"I have to admit, it's all very weird, but it looks like something special has been handed to us. Why not take it and run with it?"

Middleton had had enough. He was given his own room and put to bed. The next morning the situation had remained every bit as weird as the moment before the sedative. And he didn't know what to make of it.

Wearily, he signed whatever papers he was handed and the couple was whisked away to a luxurious resort somewhere in New Mexico.

"Imagine," Margret told him looking out the window. She was up and around and feeling fine. Every day she had to put in a couple of hours of examination while hordes of scientists with lots of equipment were sucked inside her to study the premises and then expelled out again with puzzled faces and no new clues. Then she was free to do as she pleased the rest of the day. Mr. Middleton watched television.

"Imagine what?" he said, smoking a cigarette. He had never smoked before.

"I'm the start of a new campaign, a new secret weapon—if they can ever figure out what to do with me. Just like in the cold war. I'm the start of a new world order. Kind of exciting, isn't it?"

"And how's the leprechaun taking it all" Middleton responded, blowing out smoke.

"You always look at the down side," she scolded. "You're the glass half-empty type. I'm the glass half-full."

Middleton just blew more smoke into the room, and reached for a glass of Scotch.

CANADIAN CANOODLING

The is the story of Julie Bruly from Saskatoon, and Dewey Twohy from Moosonee but originally born in Cameroon when his parents had gone there after a June cruise. Julie and Dewey first met in a brewery where they began to canoodle in the afternoon—hiding in a room full of brooms. Seeing what comes of canoodling looming on the horizon, they soon made a plan to take a schooner on a honeymoon. But being frugal, they moved to MooseJaw after a stay in Goose Bay where they were caught canoodling in a supermarket.

So at noon the bride and groom-to-be made marriage vows their key to an open bloom of future views by spreading news their nuptial fuse would happen at the zoo. From there they packed up kit'n'kaboodle, even took along the poodle, and in a balloon sailed to Dune Lake, but were caught in the wake of a sudden typhoon that blew them to Rangoon where they landed in a lagoon. They ate macaroons as the monsoon came doon until they found a saloon that promised them strudel for a yodel. Dewey used to croon in a tune for a bottle and thought he could do so for a yodel. From a hotel, he was able to wire back to Saskatoon and Moosonee where oodles of boodle awaited his toodle. His Google concluded, while Julie had doodled, and got them suited for Newark. At Newark they faired to Canada air, and Ottawa landed them home.

But Ohhhh, they tried again, and goooo, they did again, landing in Nova Scotia to go trowling for fish in the sea. And there on the schooner with beer in the cooler they froodled their days away. Until up a storm came, and Dewey in pain from fish he had eaten at noon, got up way too soon and starting to swoon, cracked his noodle upon the boat's boom. Zoom went the schooner and everything sooner or later had entered the sea. And Julie and Dewey were rescued on Tuesday. By then they were soggy but free.

So back home to MooseJaw and so ends the first law of Canucks who proodle in public at ease. So please be careful when having a snootful of somebody's sample spoodle. Keep your cool, stay in school, don't act like a fool when love's voodoo is making you coodle. Let Canadian ways impose a few stays. Stay sweet but discreet when you're out on the street. Keep cautious when inclined to canoodle.

SPACE BITCHES

"Look out! The Space Bitches are coming!" Lieutenant Gastronal was peering out the cabin window watching for any sign of incursion. "What do we do, Commander Courage?!"

The Commander stepped forward to stand beside Lieutenant Gastronal's position at the window. "Radar scope!" the Commander bellowed.

Ensign Slavish perked up from his console panel, "Nothing, Commander."

"Space Bitches are notorious for not being seen on radar," Lieutenant Gastronal reminded him.

"Anything else on screen?" the Commander called.

"Negative, Commander," Ensign Slavish returned.

"Pilot, ready engines," the Commander ordered.

"Readying engines, aye," Pilot Scrotum responded. The ship immediately began to hum and vibrate with the engines coming to life.

"Bring weapons to bear," said Courage.

"Weapons, aye," Lieutenant Thyroid, the weapons officer answered.

The Commander peered out the window again. There in the distance, just beyond the horizon of the planet below were four little dots. And he could tell that those dots were moving quickly, and steadily growing in size as he watched. No doubt about it, they were under attack.

"Move to course one-nine-zero," Courage ordered.

"One-nine-zero, aye," Pilot Scrotum responded. The ship began to whirr and pitch as the pilot took it into a different orbit.

"They're following!" Lieutenant Gastronal called.

"Steady, Lieutenant. Mind your console."

"Yes, Commander."

"Weapons, can you get a bead on them?"

"They're awfully small, Commander."

"Prepare to fire. If we can't get them out there, break out hand weapons should they infiltrate."

"Aye, Sir."

Again Commander Courage peered out at the black and sparkling sky. The four dots were becoming bigger and bigger. Now they were taking on the shape of mosquitoes or gadflys. Large flying insects that seem impervious to the hazards of space.

"Radar?"

"Still nothing, Commander."

"Weapons, can you see them?"

"Not on scope, Sir. Going to visual."

"Fire when ready."

"Got them on visual. They're spread out, sir. It'll be a tough shot."

"Go for the leader. Just take one."

"Annnnd . . . firing."

The ship shuddered with the release of the death ray blast. Outside, a sparkle near one of the insects.

"They're too maneuverable, Commander. I don't know if I can hit them."

"Try again, they're almost here."

"Firing." Another shudder. Outside, another splash of light. And another miss.

Thunk! "They're on the hull!" Commander Courage yelled, "Break out hand weapons. Prepare for a breach."

The weapons officer immediately ran to a cabinet where the personal weapons were kept. And, unlocking it, pulled out the arms and began passing them out. Commander Courage meanwhile listened intently as pairs of feet could be heard walking about on the exterior of the ship.

All was silence for a moment. Then a siren as the outside hatch was suddenly forced open.

"Security breach!" Lieutenant Gastronal stated. Then he yelled with a startled jump as looking out the window, he saw a face looking back in at him. She was blonde, with fabulous makeup and a startling outfit to match—all coated in what seemed to be a layer of transparent plastic. A Space Bitch.

"Easy Lieutenant. We're about to be boarded." With that recognition by the Commander, the outside hatch closed. And with a hiss the inside hatch opened up. There they were—all four of them. Stilletto heals, silver leotards, golden gloves, fabulous hair, jewels with insignias around their throats, ray-guns in their hands. Each had two pairs of wings like dragonflies that folded elegantly behind their backs. They were all shiny from the coating of clear plastic that covered them from head to foot, so that they could fly in near space without freezing or burning up—some of the jewelry cleverly disguising the miniature air compressor they used to breathe in outer space. The leader was a brunette with a tiara on her head. Guns were pointed at the crew. The crew pointing guns back.

"Who runs this ship?" the brunette demanded.

"I do," the Commander responded, "Commander Courage, United Planets, of the Search Ship Stratagon. And you are invading my ship."

"Am I?" the brunette stated, and moved seductively into the cabin, her minions taking positions behind her.

"Who am I addressing?" the Commander asked.

"Who do you think?" the brunette answered. "I'm Queen Caterwaul, Space Bitch. And you're not authorized to be here."

"We've been authorized by the United Planets to—"

"The Space Bitches do not recognize the United Planets!" she answered loudly.

"You have never been to the bargaining table. But the Celestial Council has brought in your planetary government, and the people of Progesterone have expressed interest in our being here—"

"The Space Bitches do not recognize the government of Progesterone!" Queen Caterwaul interrupted. "They are fools, idiots!"

"They are the majority of your planet," the Commander reminded.

"They are weak and stupid! Even if they are the majority. The Space Bitches rule here."

"So you say, but my orders are otherwise. I am here to set up a parley with Progesterone's duly elected leaders and members of the United Planets for inclusion in the society."

"I am the leader of Progesterone."

"You were invited but declined the invitation. As a matter of fact, we never heard from you. And, you, and your fellow bitches, represent a minority of Progesterone's ruling elite."

"Hah! Formalities, committees, negotiations! Why would we want to join with your stupid society?"

"For trade, mutual protection, mutual good will."

"Space Bitches protect themselves—and their planet. And what need we of trade and good will? We're Bitches!"

"But the rest of your planet is not. And trade and good will may come in handy some time."

"So you say. You may not be here to attack us, but you are to exploit us."

"Not if you are at the bargaining table and negotiating the deals by which this alliance is created. We, and all the other planets, would have to obey the tenets that are written into the code."

"So you say. I've heard of this game before. Sign a treaty, get yourself screwed."

"It is not that way with us. We have centuries of history to prove it."

"And centuries more before that to prove otherwise."

"Perhaps, but we must learn to trust each other some time. We will inevitably run into each other again and again. Why not on friendly terms?"

The Queen paused a moment, then said, "Ladies, put your arms down." Lieutenant Gastronal (and the others) heaved a sigh of relief (while, incidentally, continuing to ogle the blonde that first peered in his window.

"Weapons aside," Commander Courage ordered. The ray-guns were held at bay.

"I'll listen to whatever you have to say—but I'm not promising anything."

"Granted," Commander Courage responded.

"I'll overlook the missile-rays fired at us this time," the Queen stated leaning in for a closer look at the Commander.

"We acted in self-defense as under attack. Standard procedure," he answered. "If you had hailed us, and asked permission to board—"

"Never mind," the Queen said, dismissively. "We'll leave you. I'll expect to see you at my capital."

"No sense leaving us. You are welcome to stay. We shall take you there. Pilot Scrotum! Set a course for P.Emmess below. Your Highness, we will land in 15 minutes."

"All right, I guess I can allow you to be gracious for a little while. It wouldn't hurt. Ladies, stand at ease. I'm going to talk to the Commander in his private quarters."

"Right this way," Commander Courage offered.

The two disappeared behind the quarter door: Ship's Captain and Queen Bitch in what promised to be a rather personal parley. The rest of the crew waited as the ship dove into Progesterone's atmosphere. Men staring at women, women staring at men. Perhaps this would be the meeting—long overdue—between the way of the space probe and the way of the temperamental space babes. Only the bitches knew for sure.

WEIRD CHILDREN

Der stranger komm dat day. Dat day ve go to picnic. But picnic called off because rain happens. Der stranger komm to haus an' ask directions, Ya? Vhy icumen hier? He komm to village and Liesl, she ist polite to him. She give him direction. She give him milk, Ya? He like Liesl. Ve do not like the way he look at Liesl. Liesl ist der eldest among us. Liesl ist zenn-und-sechs.

Dis happen before. Der married couple. Dey komm. Dey stay. Dey vant to talk to children zo dey talk to us. Dey talk about adopting children. But ve haff no vish to be adopted. Ve do not have a Faater unt Muuter. Faater unt Muuter die a yarr ago. Heinrich vass playing in the yard, Ya? Unt Heinrich break Mama's dish in vindow vhen he trohw da ball. Da vindow break. Da dish break. Mama all upset. She tell Papa. Papa komm out in yard and scold Heinrich. Heinrich bad boy, Papa say. Heinrich punished by being put in room over night mit out supper. Heinrich run away.

Faater unt Muuter look for Heinrich. Heinrich found dead in river. Ve very angry vit Faater unt Muuter. Heinrich one of sechs of us, now ve only funf. Liesl love Heinrich very much. She very broken-hearted. Heinrich da yuungest. Mama put Liesl in charge of Heinrich because Mama tired.

Too many kinder, she say, in too few yarren. So Liesl adopt Heinrich like her own baby. Now Heinrich gone.

Liesl begin disobeying Mama. Mama angry. Papa get angry. He punish all of us. Ve angry too. Liesl tell us about automobile. Automobile need wires to make things vork. Cut wires, things no vork. Faater unt Muuter go to town. Buy groceries. Drink beer. See a show. Don't remember. See a show, dey say. Maybe do other tings. Mama unt Papa don't come back. Accident on road. Ve no longer have Faater unt Muuter. Now Liesl take care of us all.

Official komm by, vant to break us up. Say ve need grown-ups. Liesl say she manage. Official say Liesl also kint. Official go away. Ve no see official no more. Old Frau show later. Old Frau say she take Liesl unt alles to berg vhere ve find new Faater unt Muuter. This time Fritzy get angry. This time Old Frau disappear. This time Fritzy say he make her disappear.

Other grown-ups komm after. Say break up family. No guut viss out Faater unt Muuter.

Ve take care of cows. Ve take care of cabbages unt carrots. Say ve are strange kinder since Faater unt Muuter left—since ve all komm down vit illness yarren ago. It made us bald, changed our kopffen shapes, dey say. Liesl alveys sad about losing hair. Being das madchen, it bother her most.

But ve are fine. Ve don't like strangers no more. Strangers alveys try to break us up. Villagers don't like us. Say ve are der Divil's yuungen. Villagers stay away now from farm. Until stranger komm und ask directions. He komm. Liesl give him directions. She give him milk. She give him food. But he stare at us. He stare at Liesl. He say she pretty, but no see her vittout scarf on, vittout haif.

He tink he can do tings to her vit no Mama no Papa near. Liesl stop him with fork. Ve kommen to her call. He stare at us. He look at funf balden kopffen. He stare at Fritzy who hate all who komm to call now. He stare at Liesl who say take him. Ve take him. Stranger scream. He try to run. He no place to hide—ve stop him from direction he say he go.

Stranger put in cellar. Liesl unt Fritzy take care of him. Ve hear screams all night. Ve never see stranger again. He no need directions. Villagers stay away. Ve tend cows. Ve tend chickens. Ve tend cabbages und carrots unt peas. Ve no longer need Faater unt Muuter. Ve have Liesl unt Fritzy. Ve take care of us.

Ve vait for officials. Ve know they komm. But ve not go. Ve home. Dis ist home. Ve are free. So Liesl say.

THE MAN WHO WALKED THE EARTH

Nebraska has flat spaces. Nebraska has rolling spaces. If you are lucky, you can find trees—usually next to wherever there might be a river in the land-locked environment. If you're not lucky, you'll find corn. Corn wasn't what was here originally. Originally, it was just grass. Lots of grass. So thick it was matted down to several feet below the surface. They called the white people who settled here, sod-busters. The only way they could stick it out was by ripping up centuries of sod and knocking a hole in the soil to plant crops. Those crops eventually became just corn. Meanwhile those old pioneers built everything out of sod. Sod was the one commodity they had to give away. There was nothing else of value here.

That was then. Somehow, those pioneers stuck around long enough to build modern cities and highways out here in all that sod. Generations grew up around what was a lot of prehistoric sod. Now we plant layers upon layers of corn, so that pioneers 30,000 years from now will stop by and dig up all those corn roots, and plant something else.

If you go really far back, Nebraska was a sea. Way before the corn. Way before the sod. Bones can be found in this soil of gigantic creatures that used to swim here before they died. Before the grass covered their bones.

And now we have highways and trees. And little towns like the one I live in. I don't farm. I won't have anything to do with corn. Or sod. I just live at the end of the stretch of street we call "Main Street" before it turns back into a highway. This is a town that people pass through, or pass by, but seldom notice. I live in a house that may at one time have been a farmhouse, but no longer is. It's just and old house sitting on the edge of the main street/highway, just before people speed up to 60 mph.

We have a big yard and a long driveway we finally had the money to pave last year. We were the last in the neighborhood to do that. I have a son who runs up and down the driveway with his tricycle. He's learned to stay off the street, you never know who will come racing by, and stick to the sidewalk. Yes, we have a sidewalk. Part of civic improvement from ten years ago.

I teach English at the local middle school. We have a grade school and a middle school. No high school. For that, you have to go into the next county, which is actually about three miles from here. Our town holds less than a thousand people, but we are easy distance from bigger towns and even bigger cities. We're not so isolated as it may seem. Just quaint. We are quaint.

It was in summer, and I was hosing down the rose bushes I keep in the front to make it appear as if our house had class. Actually, our yard already had several trees, a godsend in August. So there was nothing to feel inferior about. But at some point I felt we needed rose bushes out front, so there they've been ever since. The boy was going up and down the sidewalk on his tricycle, and the traffic was few and far between. Unusual for a Saturday.

That's when he came.

He was tall and gangly. A giant. A basketball player perhaps. And black as the tar on the road. We don't see many black people in Nebraska. He was alone. He wore a loose-fitting garb that hinted of African fashion. He had a slight pack slung over his shoulders. And he had well worn, leather-skin shoes, more like boots. He came walking all by himself down the main road. There weren't very many people about, it was a small town after all.

But what few were there stopped and stared. They weren't being rude, just curious. Even my son stopped his tricycle at the end of the driveway as the man came.

He saw my son and gave a big toothy smile as he approached. My son, curious, almost fearful at first, suddenly warmed up and offered him a smile in return. He had never seen a black man in person before. Then my boy waved at him. The tall, opaque stranger waved back and said, "Hello, boy! Hello, boy!"

"Why are you walking?" the brave lad asked the stranger, who came to a stop on his journey out of town.

I stepped over to intervene, "Tommy, it's not nice to ask people such questions!"

"I don't mind," the tall man said, beaming. He turned to my son and bending down like a giraffe might, said to him, "I walk because I choose to."

"Don't you have a car?" the boy returned.

"Don't need one," the man replied, "I have feet!"

The man spoke with a definite African accent. And now my own curiosity would not stay put. "Where're you headed?" I asked.

"Nowhere. Everywhere!" he answered, his responses full of joy.

"You're not from around here, are you," I stated the obvious. "Where are you from?"

"A long way away," he said with that charming African lilt.

"Care for some water?" I asked, wanting to know more about this guy.

"Thank you, I do carry some of my own. But if you don't mind, I'd accept a refill from your garden hose."

"Oh, I can get you something better—"

"No no no no no no! Please! This will be fine!"

So I held out the hose for him and opened up the valve. He pulled out a small container from a belt that was around him which had one or two others just like it hooked to him, and filled it up. Then before I could douse the hose, he stooped down to take a sip as the stream splashed on the grass before him. Then he pulled his head back and straightened up to his full six-and-a-half to seven feet height.

"Ahhh!" he said, "Water! So good no matter where on the planet you are!"

That encouraged me to take a swig of water from the hose myself (which I hadn't done since I was a kid), and Tommy, being a kid, did the same.

"Where are you bound?" I asked, knowing I had already done so with this question.

"Wherever my feet take me," he answered. "I am walking the world."

"No kidding," I don't know if I actually understood him properly. He seemed to want to explain.

"I started on one continent, and I go to another, and then another. And before you know it, I am right back in the same place from where I left!"

"Can't you go back home?" Tommy puzzled.

"Of course. But never back. I only travel forward."

"Why?" the boy continued.

"Because the world is round. So when you walk far enough, you end up where you began."

"What will you do when you get there?" Tommy kept questioning.

"Walk back," the tall man stated.

"You mean go around the world again?" Tommy's questions were getting whiny which the man did not seem bothered by.

"Yes. Only in the other direction. But forward. Always forward!"

"Why?" Tommy couldn't resist.

"Because I enjoy living!" The tall man turned to me with his big smile and gave a slight bow. "Thank you for your precious water!"

"Don't mention it," I said.

"Goodbye, boy!" he waved to Tommy. I gave him a quick wave too and watched him depart along the sidewalk until there was no sidewalk, and then carry himself along the roadside.

"He's a funny man," said Tommy, who decided to resume his tricycle trip.

"Yeah," I added, "Funny."

And down the highway where houses turned into rows of corn, the tall black figure made his way over the rolling hills and walked on.

THE SAGE & THE PURPOSE OF LIFE

I had spent years searching for the man with the answers. I had read books, sat through seminars, consulted priests, was ready to give up any number of times. But then something inside me said: go to Nepal. So I went. Flight to London. Flight to Istanbul. Flight to Calcutta. Flight to Kathmandu. From there, a train, then a jeep, then a donkey ride. Finally the foot of the mountain.

A day's climb, just to reach the monastery. There the monks were kind enough to greet all outsiders. I stayed in humble lodgings. Humble food. Humble people. The weather itself is humbling. One does not find the purpose of life with a big ego. Anything worth this struggle is also worth the effort—so the saying goes.

I stayed a week to acclimatize myself. They insisted. Thin air. Thin thinking. You don't focus properly when your brain is deprived of oxygen. I had to adjust to the food as well. How far can you get on rice and tofu? It wasn't meant to send a warrior into battle.

I talked with the people there. I was surprised. The monks were struggling with the same questions I had rolling around in my head. Only they were professionals at it. They dedicated their lives to that pursuit. I was an amateur. A hobbyist. I was doing this all on a whim. But they respected me for it. It was an itch to scratch. It just one day suddenly bugged me and I absolutely had to find the answer to it. What *WAS* the purpose of life?

I worked as a computer programmer. Got tired of that, especially when the field filled up. Became a short-order cook. Got tired of that. Contemplated going to sea. That ended up to be a screwy idea, so I worked in a warehouse. Okay, so I've been bobbing around looking for my purpose—the real purpose in life. Obviously, I'm not finding it. Had to go to Nepal. Saved up my money. Gave up all my other hobbies and alternate quests. Only these guys didn't have the answer either. They told me I could find a hut of my own another 1000 feet up the mountain where I could meditate all day. Okay, so I gotta do what I gotta do.

Sat there a week. Nothing. Climate sickness. That's what I got. God didn't talk to me (if that's what was supposed to happen here) and I didn't get any insights. I was impatient. I really wanted to talk to somebody with the answers. Have them all spelled out for me so I wouldn't have to think.

Well . . . there's a guy up there. There's always a guy. He's the Great Sage. He's been sitting on top of the mountain for decades. He's wise (so they say) and he may speak to you (so they tell me). Well . . . I had heard of him before. And he really was the guy I wanted to talk to. And why I came all the way here. But you don't act like a pushy American around these people. Not if you really want answers. And then there is the question—if he's so wise, why has he been sitting on top of a mountain for decades? Wouldn't you do something better with all that wisdom—like start your own tv network, or something?

Anyway, I had to see him. I came back down from my hut after a thoroughly boring and discouraging week. They kept me on for a few days while I readjusted myself, and got used to someone else's cooking besides my own (it was all just boiled rice and tofu, no matter who prepared it, so what's the difference?). Then one of their people, a guide who is used to hauling it up the mountainside with yet another dumb-ass city slicker behind him wanting to talk to the Great Sage up on his precipice overlooking most of the rest of Nepal, led the way.

I got winded several times—damn, these mountains are high! My guide waited patiently for me to catch up. He took me all the way, and then left me. And there He was: the Great Sage.

He was an old man, as was expected. Long growth of silver white hair and beard. He wore a simple, tattered monks robe. He sat in lotus position at the edge of the cliff staring out over the valley. 'Staring' perhaps, with eyes closed. I slowly approached the man, encouraged by my guide who waved me on (before he high-tailed it out of there). He even told me before he left, "Go ahead, ask your questions. He doesn't mind."

So I crept up to the old man, and bowed (why I don't know, he couldn't see me) and hunkered down next to him. "I've come a long way," I began. No answer. "They tell me I can get my answers from you." Still no reply. "I need to know—desperately. It's been driving me crazy for so long that I can't think straight without it. Is it okay if I ask you?" Not a stirring, not a sound. Was he even alive?

"Oh Great Sage," I began, talking myself into going through with it since I had come all that way and practically emptied my bank account to be here, "I need to know . . . *what is the purpose of life?*"

For a long, seemingly endless moment, there was nothing. Just silence. Then slowly, that great hoary head turned to me. The eyes opened to barely more than slits, but they opened. And with the slightest of breaths taken, he said to me, "To learn not to fuck up."

And then his eyes closed again and turned his head back to 'staring' out over the valley.